Prais

MW01135173

"Fun cozy mysteries that will keep you laughing and on your toes all the way to the nail-biting end."
Dorothy St. James, author of *The White House Gardener Mysteries*

"Murder and mayhem are on the table in this excellent second book in the Cue Ball Mysteries. I loved all the colorful new characters that were introduced in *Double Shot.*"
Cozy Mystery Book Reviews: Keep Calm and Read a Cozy Mystery

"Jessie is a fantastic character, I loved the inside look at her writing life, and I found myself laughing out loud at some of her antics."
Melissa's Mochas, Mysteries and More

"Cindy Blackburn is right on cue with her page-turning debut *Playing With Poison.*"
Tonya Kappes, bestselling author

"Like Jessie Hewitt, her intriguing pool shark/romance author heroine, *Playing With Poison* author Cindy Blackburn knows how to start with a fast break and run the table, leaving readers applauding her skill."
Linda Lovely, author of *The Marley Clark Mystery* series

"Jessie Hewitt seems prepared to handle anything life throws her way."
Joyce Lavene, author of *The Missing Pieces Mysteries*

Also by Cindy Blackburn

Playing With Poison
Three Odd Balls

Double Shot

by
Cindy Blackburn

A Cue Ball Mystery

ASIN(Kindle): B009P3KYV8
ISBN-13: 978-1480157224
ISBN-10: 1480157228

For Teddy

Acknowledgements

I could not have written Double Shot without gobs of help from gobs of people. Thanks to everyone who offered me their support, encouragement, and time. I am bound to forget someone, but here goes: Jean Everett, Anne Saunders, Sharon Politi, Jane Bishop, Joanna Innes, Bob Spearman, Kathy Powell, Megan Beardsley, Betsy Blackburn, Martha Twombly, Karen Phillips, Shari Stauch, Teddy Stockwell, Sean Scapellatto, Carol Peters and my friends at the LRWA. Special super-duper mega thanks to my husband John Blackburn, my technical guru extraordinaire and my hero.

Chapter 1

"Candy Poppe has a poodle named Puddles, and I'm suffering from plot plight," I informed Wilson the minute he walked through the door.

He set a bag of groceries on the counter. "Excuse me?"

"Candy, Wilson. My downstairs neighbor? Pretty, perky, petite. Prone to miniskirts and stilettos?"

"I know who Candy is, Jessie. She got a poodle?"

"A puppy from the pound. He's not a purebred."

Wilson blinked twice. "Have you met Puddles?"

"He came up to play today," I said, and we both instinctively glanced at Snowflake, who was perched on her favorite windowsill.

"What did you think of Puddles?" Wilson asked my cat.

She yawned abundantly while I answered, "Puddles pranced around, and Snowflake supervised from where she's sitting right now. All went well until Puddles piddled."

"She disapproved?"

"She was most displeased." I waved at the expanse of wood floors in my condo. "Although wiping it up was pretty painless."

Wilson shook his head. "If I hear one more P-word—"

"You'll pull out your pistol?" I smiled at my profound powers of alliteration, but my beau the cop was unimpressed.

"Maybe we should move on to plot plight," he suggested.

I agreed that was probably a good idea and pulled a bottle of champagne from the fridge.

If you ask me, everything works better with champagne. And trust me, the rather unlikely saga of *An Everlasting Encounter*, my latest literary venture, would definitely be easier to fathom with bit of bubbly. I popped the cork while Wilson got dinner underway.

"Think Cinderella, but with a wicked sister-in-law," I began. I handed him a glass and found my favorite barstool.

"Sarina Blyss has run away from home. She had to leave because her brother Norwood inherited the family estate after their father died. That shouldn't have been a problem, but then Norwood married Agnes. And the altogether evil Agnes quickly turned poor Sarina into a virtual slave."

Wilson tossed a handful of garlic into a sauce pot. "Did you take those meatballs out of the freezer like I asked?"

Of course. If Wilson Rye wants to fill my freezer with all kinds of homemade Italian delicacies, the least I can do is follow a few simple instructions. I pointed him toward the fridge, and he dumped the thawed meatballs into a hot frying pan.

Snowflake hopped into my lap, and together we watched him do his magic. Spaghetti and meatballs here we come.

"So now it's three years later," I continued.

"Later than what?"

"Three years after Norwood married the bitch. Now, I don't actually call Agnes a bitch in the book, but my readers will get the idea."

"Agnes who?"

"Wilson!" I put down my glass and waved a hand to get his attention. "Agnes Blyss! The altogether evil sister-in-law. Sarina got tired of scrubbing her floors and left home with a small satchel of all her worldly belongings, including her most cherished possession, the golden necklace her mother bestowed upon her the night she died."

"Bestowed upon her?"

I nodded solemnly. "Sarina was a mere child when her mother passed away, and then her father died when she was sixteen. The poor thing is an orphan."

Wilson rolled his eyes, and I suggested he drink some champagne.

"Sarina had an important decision to make the day she left home," I said. "When she got to the crossroads at the end of the lane, she had to choose between walking to Priesters, the charming village she used to visit with her father, or heading in the opposite direction toward the big town of St. Celeste. She knew St. Celeste was twenty miles away, but she had never been there."

"So let me guess. She chose the charming village."

"No!" I jumped a bit. "That surprised me, too. Sarina decided on St. Celeste. She pulled her necklace out of the satchel and clasped it around her neck for good luck. Then she embarked on her journey to St. Celeste, where she knew not a soul, mind you. But after a couple of hours she grew weary and stopped to rest beside the lavender fields."

"And let me guess again. That's when she got herself kidnapped by the sinister Lord Snip, or Snap, or Snoop, or whatever." Wilson twirled his wooden spoon in the air for emphasis. "And now she's trapped in this guy's castle, waiting to be rescued by some stupid hunk with a huge—"

"No, Wilson," I interrupted. "That's what happened in *Temptation at Twilight*. But we are now discussing *An Everlasting Encounter*. It's a completely different story." I tossed my head in a haughty manner reminiscent of one of my heroines. "Adelé Nightingale never repeats a story."

"Whatever you say, Adelé." He chuckled over my pen name, but I ignored him and moved on.

"Just as Sarina stood up from the lavender field, determined to finish her arduous journey, a handsome stranger driving a white carriage came along and offered her a ride. And of course, the stranger became smitten with Sarina along the way."

"Of course." Wilson shook salt into a pot of boiling water and poured in the spaghetti.

"But unbeknownst to Sarina, the handsome stranger is none other than Trey Barineau, the Duke of Luxley! Can you believe it?"

"Not really."

"The trouble is, Sarina had somehow torn her frock during this whole encounter, and so Trey dropped her off at the dress-maker's shop in St. Celeste. And then the proprietress Winnie Dickerson shooed him away before he could properly introduce himself or even learn the lovely damsel's name."

"Why didn't the evil baron-guy just kidnap her, Jessie? Isn't that what always happens in your books?"

"Nooo. That is not what always happens in my books. And Trey Barineau is the hero, for Lord's sake. He would never kidnap anyone." I sighed dramatically. "And therein lies the dilemma."

"Huh?"

"Would you please stay with me here? Sarina has found employment with Mrs. Dickerson. Because, despite her delicate hands and fingers, she is quite talented with a needle and thread. And now this lowly seamstress must somehow come back into contact with the Duke of Luxley. Meanwhile, Trey is up in Luxley Manor, simply beside himself with lustful longings for the lovely and lithe Sarina, whose identity he knows not!"

Wilson squinted up at the heavens. Or at least at the skylight.

"So?" I asked. "How will their chance encounter in the lavender field become everlasting?"

"Who's that?"

"Oh, for Lord's sake! Trey and Sarina! Any ideas?" I appealed to my beau for inspiration.

My mother refers to Wilson Rye as my beau, and for lack of a better alternative, so do I. Beau may sound a bit southern and old-fashioned, but I was born and raised in South Carolina, and have lived in Clarence, North Carolina for decades, so I am a southerner. And although I won't claim to be old-fashioned, I am getting old.

Which is why I refuse to call him my boyfriend. I'm fifty-two and he's forty-seven. Boyfriend seems too juvenile. Lover could work, but since the L-word had yet to be spoken between us, that seemed a bit premature.

My beau was staring at me. And from the look on his face, I assumed he had nary a solution to offer Trey or Sarina.

I reached over and turned off the stove. "Okay, what's wrong?" I asked. "You've had more on your mind than dinner ever since you called this afternoon."

He frowned and slowly spooned the meatballs onto a plate lined with paper towels. "I was going to ask you to do me a favor," he mumbled eventually. "But never mind. It's too dangerous."

Too dangerous? Well, now he had to tell me.

I hopped up to set the table and began with the most obvious question. "Does it have something to do with your job?"

"It's kind of complicated," he told the meatballs as he transferred them, one by one, into the sauce pot.

"Why am I not surprised?" I looked up from folding the napkins. "Is this about what happened at the Wade On Inn? Didn't I read something in the paper?"

No answer while he pretended his spaghetti sauce required his urgent attention.

"If you refuse to tell me what's going on, why bring it up at all?" I asked with a pointed glare.

"I keep you in the dark for your own safety, Jessie."

"Yeah, right." I dropped the silverware and returned to the stove. "Perhaps things did get a little tricky during the Stanley Sweetzer episode," I said once he would finally look at me. "But that's no excuse for you to be so cagey about your work, Wilson."

"A little tricky? You almost got yourself killed, darlin.'"

I folded my arms and glared. "As I recall, the lead investigator of the Clarence Homicide Squad accused me of murdering Candy Poppe's fiancé. Forgive me if I got a little carried away trying to prove my innocence."

"I only accused you that one time."

"Gee thanks."

Wilson took a deep breath. "Okay, here goes. Two murders at the Wade On Inn. Last week. Both victims were regulars at the pool table." He stopped and waited for my reaction.

I pursed my lips and decided to stir the pasta.

"You ever play out there, Jessie?"

"Umm, I might have."

He took the spoon away from me. "That," he said, "is exactly what I was afraid of."

"Come on, Wilson. It was a long time ago."

"What do you know about the game at the Wade On Inn?"

"I know it's the hottest table in town. They shoot nine ball out there, if I'm not mistaken."

He squinted at me, suspicion veritably oozing from his pores. "When were you last there?"

"Oh, for Lord's sake! I haven't set foot inside the Wade On Inn or any place like it for close to thirty years.

"However," I added when he seemed a bit too relieved. "If Adelé Nightingale's books ever go out of style, I do believe I could pop on down there and get enough action to pay my mortgage, no?"

Wilson turned to Snowflake. "That," he said, "is exactly what I was afraid of."

Chapter 2

"Aggravated assaults, drunk and disorderlies, prostitution." Lost in a litany of the various and sundry crimes associated with the Wade On Inn, my beau the cop stirred the sauce more and more rapidly with each new offense.

"Okay, okay," I interrupted a description of a recent drug bust. "We both know the place is the diviest of dives. But what about these murders?"

"The first victim, Angela Hernandez, was killed Saturday night." Stir, stir. "She worked for the owner Elsa Quinn, did her bookkeeping, and stayed late most nights to close out the cash register."

"She was killed after closing?"

"Yep. Someone waited for her in the parking lot, shot her, and dumped her into Shinkle Creek. Handy, huh?"

I groaned. The Wade On Inn is located on the outskirts of town and on the banks of Shinkle Creek. The name doesn't really do it justice, though. Shinkle Creek is more like a raging river, waterfalls and all.

"She was killed two days before her body was discovered downstream," he added.

I tapped his hand to slow down the stirring. "And the second murder?"

"Same thing, a few days later. The guy was shot in the parking lot and dumped in the water."

"What about fingerprints or DNA evidence?" I thought I sounded oh so knowledgeable, but Wilson reminded me it had rained a lot that week.

"Anything in the parking lot washed away, and Shinkle Creek took care of whatever we might have found on the bodies. All we do know is that both victims were killed by the same gun."

"You found the gun?"

"Not yet and not likely. The murder weapon's probably at the bottom of the river. But we have the bullets.

I grimaced. "So who was the second victim?"

He went back to stirring the sauce. I took his chin in my hand and forced him to face me. "Who else got killed?"

"His name was Fritz Lupo."

I dropped his chin, but unfortunately Wilson continued staring at me. "He made his living hustling at the pool table out there, Jessie. And he was teaching Angela Hernandez how to hustle. I think he killed her."

He frowned and pointed to the pasta.

I grabbed two pot holders and drained the pot. "But if Fritz—I mean, if this Lupo-guy—was teaching Angela how to hustle, why would he turn around and kill her? And then who killed him?"

"I don't know. But I'm ninety percent sure something went wrong at that pool table. A bet didn't get paid, someone cheated. It's a rough game out there, as you know."

"Oh, I get it. Fritz Lupo was a pool shark, and Angela Hernandez was a wannabe, so of course they had to come to a violent end." I shook the water from the colander with far more vigor than necessary. "Pool players aren't all criminals, Captain Rye. I thought I already proved that."

"There's only been one other murder out there in the past twenty years, Jessie. Lupo was involved in that one, too."

"What!?" I spun around from the sink, and Wilson nodded.

"Manslaughter, actually. Thirteen years ago he and some other guy had themselves a shoot out. The bullet that was meant for Lupo hit the bartender instead."

I closed my eyes and prayed for strength.

"Did your daddy ever mention Lupo?"

I poured the spaghetti into the sauce and concentrated on stirring our supper. "It's kind of complicated," I said eventually.

"And? Did he know Lupo?"

I kept stirring and thought about my father. My beau the cop might not approve of what he did for a living, but Daddy was darn good at his job. In his heyday Leon Cue-it Hewitt was the best one pocket player south of the Mason-Dixon Line.

"Lupo?" Wilson repeated.

"Okay, yes." I stopped stirring and braced myself for Wilson to overreact. "Daddy knew him, and umm, I might have played Fritz once or twice myself."

"What!?" he overreacted. "I thought you told me you haven't hustled for years."

"I haven't. But I can still remember people, can't I? If memory serves, Fritz was known as the Fox—sharp eyes, red hair."

"Memory serves," Wilson grumbled and dished up our spaghetti.

"Now, I never actually saw Fritz at the Wade On Inn," I continued as we sat down to eat. "But Daddy used to bring home lots of the men he worked with. Especially on holidays, to partake of one of my mother's fantastic meals."

"And meet you, presumably?"

"Well, yeah." I devoured a meatball slathered in sauce. "Daddy liked to show me off, but he wasn't about to take me to a pool hall. So he brought the pool hall to me."

Wilson stopped eating. "You're a little scary. You know that?"

I continued my trip down Memory Lane. "Fritz Lupo was one of my father's younger friends."

"He was sixty-seven when he died."

"And Daddy would have been eighty-five this year." I did the math. "So, I was around sixteen or seventeen, and Mr. Lupo was in his early thirties when we played."

Wilson glanced at Snowflake, who had returned to her windowsill. "She's shot pool with Fritz Lupo," he told her.

"Nine ball, eight ball, straight pool, one pocket. Daddy and his friends taught me everything they knew." I pointed to the spaghetti. "You're not eating."

"What was Lupo's best game?"

"Nine ball, definitely. By the 1970's nine ball was every hustler's game of choice." I speared another meatball. "Fritz was good back then. But I wonder if he was still any good?"

Wilson dropped his fork and pushed his plate away. "That's one of the things I'll need you to find out."

I held my meatball aloft and digested that interesting statement.

"Oh?" I said.

"I need to put someone undercover at that pool table, Jessie. Someone who can shoot a decent game and gamble like they know what they're doing."

A slow smile made its way across my face, and I winked at the cat. "A decent game, you say?"

***

But Wilson was still talking. Something about a lack of manpower. I straightened my smile and tried looking sympathetic.

"No one in the whole department can play for squat," he said.

"Except you."

"Maybe, but everyone at the Wade On Inn knows me now. I've been over there all week, flashing my badge and trying to learn something useful." He picked up his fork and began tapping the edge of his bowl.

"What about Russell?" I asked, thinking of Wilson's partner. Like his boss, Lieutenant Densmore is tall, dark, and handsome. But Russell Densmore's twenty years younger, twenty pounds heavier, and black.

Wilson stopped tapping and rolled his eyes.

"Okay, so Russell stinks," I concluded.

"A few of my other officers claimed they could play, but we had tryouts this afternoon. Fogle, Simmons, Leary—all pathetic." He went back to tapping a fork on his spaghetti bowl. "Only one of my people did at all well."

"Oh? Who was that?"

"Tiffany Sass is a pretty good little player," he informed the cutlery.

It was my turn to roll my eyes. "She's not as good as me, Captain Rye. I'd bet my Daddy's cue stick on it."

Wilson grinned. "No one's as good as you, darlin.'"

"Remember that."

He cleared his throat. "I asked Sergeant Sass to pretend to gamble with me, and we play-acted a little. I was the tough guy at the Wade On Inn, and she was the new kid interested in some action."

Okay, so I may have snorted. The young and nubile Tiffany Sass was indeed interested in some action. Just not at a pool table.

"And?" I had to ask.

"And she had no idea how it's done. She got flustered just pretending with me."

"Wilson!" I was beyond exasperated. "The girl—and I do mean girl—got flustered because you were paying attention to her. She has a huge crush on you."

"Can I help it if I inspire respect?"

"Respect, my a—" I noticed the damn grin and stopped. I was not about to lose my dignity over the likes of Tiffany La-Dee-Doo-Da Sass.

I stood up to fetch the Korbel bottle. "So I guess it's up to me," I said as I refilled his glass.

"But it's too dangerous, Jessie. The last time you got involved in a case, you ended up dangling by your toenails off the roof." He pointed at the ceiling. "You remember that?"

"Ancient history." I sat back down and poured my own glass.

"We're talking double homicide this time. At the Wade On Inn of all places."

"I put myself through Duke University hustling at places just like the Wade On Inn," I argued. "I can handle it."

"You're out of practice."

"What? Has the game suddenly gone high tech?"

I might have been a bit sarcastic, but the man did have a point. Hustling at age fifty-two would require a different strategy than what had worked in my twenties.

Maybe my young friend Candy could help? Snowflake could outshoot her at a pool table, but Candy has other talents. Clad in one of her miniskirts, she would provide a great diversion. My neighbor Karen Sembler might help also. What would Karen's role be, I wondered.

The sound of Snowflake purring distracted me, and I glanced over to find her sitting on Wilson's lap. Everyone was staring at me.

"I'd place undercover cops in there to protect you." Wilson stroked Snowflake under her chin.

"Well then, I'll be safe," I said and stifled a frown when even I noticed how naïve that sounded.

"What about your looks?"

"Excuse me?"

"You're too easily recognized, Jessie. You do remember how Jimmy Beak plastered your lovely mug all over the news last month?"

I sat up straight and sputtered out a four-letter word.

Right behind my ex-husband, Channel 15's star reporter is my least favorite person in town. Jimmy Beak makes a habit of annoying Wilson whenever he has a tricky case to solve. And during the pesky week when I had been a murder suspect, he hadn't exactly ingratiated himself to me either.

"Jimmy knows what's going on?" I asked.

"Most of it, but he steers clear of the Wade On Inn. He's scared of the place."

I sighed a sigh of infinite relief.

"Don't get too comfortable," Wilson warned me. "You won't run into Beak, but I bet there's plenty of people who remember his reports about the notorious 'borderline pornographer.'" He pointed at me, and I repeated that four-letter word.

"What can we do?" I asked.

He scowled at the top of my head. "How about your hair?"

"I can go brunette," I suggested. "I warn you though—you won't like it."

He pulled on my one-inch blond locks. "I promise not to laugh."

"Gee thanks."

"What else?" He leaned back and assessed my person as if I were a batch of spaghetti sauce that hadn't turned out quite right.

I pursed my lips and waited until he lost the frown. "I can change the way I dress," I said. "Candy will help me."

Wilson raised an eyebrow. "Miniskirts and stilettos? The idea is to keep you safe out there."

I assured my beau a miniskirt was not in my future. "But I can borrow some of Candy's jewelry," I said. "The gloriously tacky stuff. And I'll wear way more makeup than usual, and maybe a pair of tight jeans."

He raised his other eyebrow, and even I had to chuckle at the uncharacteristic image I was conjuring up.

"What about your car?"

My face dropped. "What about it?"

"You can't be driving into the Wade On Inn's parking lot in a silver Porsche with those vanity "Adelé" plates."

"You are jealous of my car."

"We'll switch vehicles. You can use my truck."

"No way!" I protested. Surely the man didn't expect me to drive around in his beat-up, rusty old pickup truck? Ugly? You have no idea.

"I'm not crazy about being seen in your car either," he said.

"Liar."

"No, really. Everyone's figured out the Add-A-Lay thing, Jessie. You should hear the jokes that go around the station."

"My pen name is brilliant, I'll have you know. It ever so subtly reflects the nature of my stories."

"Subtle?"

"Your friends are just jealous." I stood up and shooed Snowflake from his lap. "I mean, how many other men your age have a lady friend whose mind is constantly in the gutter?"

Wilson told me I'm a little scary and buried his face in my chest. "So you're willing to do this?"

"Of course," I said as he unbuttoned my blouse and pulled me closer. "But I do have one question."

"What's that?"

"Do I get to keep my winnings?"

***

Wilson got around to addressing that last question a bit later. He rolled over from what was fast becoming his side of the bed and fished his wallet out of the back pocket of his jeans.

"I realize this is pathetic," he said. "But the chief would only allot five hundred cash for the whole Wade On Inn operation." He counted out five one-hundred-dollar bills and laid them on my night stand. "Sorry, Jessie, but that's all we have to play with."

Snowflake walked over from the foot of the bed and sniffed the money with what I can only describe as disdain.

"Five hundred should get me going." I tried sounding optimistic. "But I can't walk into the Wade On Inn flashing hundreds right off the bat. I'll start with a few twenties."

"You're the expert. But if you lose that, our little game is up."

"If I lose?"

"Oops."

"Now I will lose some of it," I said. "But only to lure the regulars into complacency." I patted his chest. "I'll be playing to win, and therefore, I will."

"Well then, you can consider whatever you win as your official salary, courtesy of the Clarence Police Department."

I thought about my father and laughed out loud. "Daddy must be rolling in his grave right now."

"Why's that?"

"Because, Captain Rye. Cue-It Hewitt's little girl has managed to get the Clarence Police Department to be her stakehorse. I have the cops—the cops!—bankrolling me."

I laid back and stretched contentedly. "Daddy would say this is one sweet gig."

Chapter 3

Who was that vision of loveliness? Who was she?

Trey Barineau stood at the window of his drawing room, but he barely noticed the hamlet of St. Celeste nestled in the valley below Luxley Manor. For the Duke was thinking only of the lady of the lavender fields, and of that glorious moment two days earlier when he had lifted her into his carriage.

Trey reminded himself he was a gentleman, but he couldn't help but notice how her bodice had gotten torn. Her left shoulder was bared, and as she leaned forward, he had caught the slightest, sweetest glimpse of her bosom.

The Duke broke out into a cold sweat and had to sit down.

As they drove into town, he had endeavored to engage the fair damsel in conversation, but she was far too distressed and clutched the golden necklace she wore, as if for courage. At last she seemed to relax, and as she released her necklace, Trey again noticed her almost-exposed bosom.

He had gotten a bit distracted just then and lost control of the carriage. As they veered off the lane, the startled lady clutched his arm, clinging to him for fear of life and limb. Thank goodness he had managed to right the carriage before they tipped over!

Trey wiped his brow and returned to the window. He again reminded himself he was a gentleman, but still his thoughts wandered to what might have happened if the carriage had but overturned. Surely the lady would have fallen on top of him? And her frock would have ripped open even further?

The Duke of Luxley stared out the window, but his mind was most assuredly somewhere else.

***

The Honorable Trey Barineau might not have understood what had gotten into him, but Adelé Nightingale certainly did. *An Everlasting Encounter* had to have at least one vivid sex scene within the first fifty pages or the thing would never sell. So until I concocted a scheme to get Trey and Sarina back together again, in the flesh, the Duke of Luxley would continue to enjoy a hearty and hale imagination.

But I had been writing all morning, and Snowflake was literally screaming for attention. She paced the windowsill in front of my desk until I closed my computer and glanced up. And that's when I noticed the scene down on Sullivan Street.

"No way," I hissed and leaned forward to get a better view.

Candy Poppe was out walking her poodle in a purple mini-dress. Candy that is, not Puddles. But even that cute little puppy could not distract me from whom my neighbor was talking to.

"No way," I tried again.

Snowflake stopped pacing, and together we stared aghast as Candy spun on her stilettos and pointed up to our window.

Three minutes later someone was knocking at the door.

"We're ignoring that," I said firmly.

"It's me, Jessie," Candy called out.

I eyed the door suspiciously. "Are you alone?"

"Puddles is with me."

I opened the door, and Puddles bounded in.

Mayhem? The puppy ran to and fro, back and forth, and hither and thither, his tiny toenails pitter-pattering and clitter-clattering against the wood floors. In the space of thirty seconds he managed to find every one of Snowflake's toys.

But the cat was not in the mood to play. She sprang to the top of the refrigerator and offered a disapproving yowl.

"Did you see us talking down there?" Candy asked me. She threw a kiss to Snowflake and commenced tossing a jingle-bell ball for Puddles. "You'll never guess in a million years what he wanted."

"Therefore, I won't even try," I said, and before she could enlighten me, I changed the subject. "I need your help tonight, Sweetie."

I kept my plea for assistance brief for a couple of reasons. First of all, Puddles had gone a whole five minutes without piddling, and I didn't want to push my luck. And more importantly, I didn't think it prudent to mention the Wade On Inn at all. Despite the lack of details, or because of it, Candy was willing to help.

I glanced at Puddles, who had taken an inordinate interest in Snowflake's scratching post. "He'll be okay alone for the evening?" I asked doubtfully.

"Gosh, no. But Mr. Harrison just loves him, Jessie. He says he'll babysit anytime I'm away. He says Puddles likes piano music."

Our elderly neighbor Peter Harrison lives on the first floor, across the lobby from Karen. Once upon a time he taught music at Clarence High School. Nowadays he gives piano lessons in his home. "To stay young," as he puts it.

I watched Puddles take yet another frenzied romp around my condo and wondered just how youthful Peter Harrison was feeling these days.

Candy and the puppy decided another trip out to the fire hydrant was in order. And while Snowflake reclaimed her toys and inspected them for damage, I called Karen Sembler. I used the same vague approach that had worked with Candy, and lo and behold, she was also agreeable. We would meet at my place at eight.

***

Sally Caperton proved less compliant, however. My hairdresser stood behind me at her station at Charlotte's Web Hair Emporium and frowned.

"I don't get it," she told my reflection. "I thought we decided the blond suits you, Jessica?"

The blond did suit me, but I was due at the Wade On Inn in six hours, and this was no time to quibble. I lied and said my publisher wanted me brunette for my next book.

Sally pouted and ran her fingers through my hair.

"It's only temporary," I tried. "I'll get the official photograph taken, and then we'll go back to the blond, okay?"

Sally repeated how she hated to do it, but that it was possible. "But," she warned, "your hair has been bleached, so I can't guarantee how the brunette will take. It could end up extremely dark."

Charlotte, the beautician at the other booth, scowled at my reflection as she tossed a cape over her next client. "You better want to be a brunette," she said ominously. "I mean, really, really brunette."

Okay, so the experts were not joking. A mere half hour later I was blinking at the new me in the mirror, marveling at how so little effort on Sally's part could produce such catastrophic results. With my fair complexion, I looked positively ghoulish underneath this deep brunette, nay black, head of hair.

"Perpetual Pleasures Press wants me to look dramatic," I squeaked once I had regained my voice. I appealed to Sally, and Charlotte, and the woman sitting in Charlotte's chair, hoping someone would agree I looked dramatic.

No such luck.

And the more we stared, the darker it seemed to get. Even Charlotte's client, a woman with sheets of foil decorating her head and smelling of peroxide, looked better than I.

"While we're at it, Sally." I remained resolute. "Would you comb it back, away from my face? Maybe use mousse or gel?"

"You're kidding, right?"

"Dramatic," I said firmly, and she reached for the mousse.

Five minutes later we were marveling at how much worse a little mousse could make things.

Sally managed a weak smile, and in a strained voice explained how she would eventually pull me out of this hideous hair hell. She swore that since my hair is so short, it would only take twelve weeks to get me back to blond.

"Three cuts and colors." She held up three fingers and offered a brisk nod. "And we'll have you looking normal again."

I resigned myself to living with abnormal for three months as Sally whisked off my cape.

"I can't quite place it." She rested a hand on my shoulder to keep me seated. "But with your hair like that you remind me of a TV star, Jessica. From an old sitcom, maybe?"

She and Charlotte squinted at me in the mirror. "Someone from the sixties," Charlotte said.

"They run the repeats on cable," the woman in foil chimed in. "What show is that?"

The three of them kept scowling and squinting.

"It'll come to me." Sally twirled the chair around, and I stood up.

I paid my bill, but she wouldn't let me leave until I promised to tell no one—no one!—who had done my hair.

***

Speaking of hideous, I also had Wilson's truck to contend with. And no sooner had I driven home in that stupid thing, than I was facing Ian Crawcheck, my lowdown, no-good, conniving, cheating, and altogether despicable ex-husband. He was sitting on the top step leading into my building, apparently waiting for yours truly.

I stopped short at the bottom step. "What are you doing here?" I asked cordially. "And why were you harassing Candy earlier?"

He squinted for a full five seconds before curling his lip in recognition. "What the hell did you do to your hair?"

"Answer me, Ian. Or I'll call Wilson and have you arrested."

Wilson likely had better things to do, but Ian took the hint. "Like, duh," he said. "I'm here to see you, Jessie. I work in the neighborhood now. When I ran into your trampy little friend this morning, I asked about you."

"Speaking of tramps, how's your wife?"

Ian's face dropped, and he stuttered out something I didn't quite catch.

"She threw you out, didn't she?"

"How do you do that?" he snapped.

I said intuition, but truth be told, in this instance simple logic would have sufficed. Through every fault of his own, my ex had gotten himself into a heap of trouble during the past few months. He broke several laws, and who knows how many professional and ethical standards, and his CPA license had been revoked.

It really didn't take much imagination to surmise how his lowdown, no-good, conniving, cheating, and altogether despicable new wife Amanda felt about the demise of his career and social standing.

"What do you mean, you work in the neighborhood?" I had to ask.

Ian jerked his head toward my building. "Can we go inside?"

"Keep dreaming," I said.

But then I reconsidered the option. I had no desire to invite this man into my home, but I wasn't keen on creating a scene outside either. We could have walked across the street to The Stone Fountain, but the thought of having a drink in my friendly neighborhood bar with Ian Crawcheck was downright nauseating.

"You look like hell," I said as I climbed past him and unlocked the front door.

"Look who's talking." He stood up and followed me inside, and continued to critique my new hairdo as we climbed the three flights of stairs to my condo.

I stopped and turned at my door.

"What?" he snapped. "I'm just telling you the truth, Jessie."

"Upset Snowflake and I will throw you out a window. Do you understand?"

He nodded, mute for a nice change of pace, and I opened the door.

The poor cat was a bit disconcerted, what with my new look and the presence of our ex, of all people. She offered him the look of sheer disdain she had been using with Puddles and found her perch on the windowsill.

"Sit." I pointed Ian to an easy chair, took the chair opposite, and waited while he glanced around. My condo is huge, but with its open floor plan, Ian could see virtually the entire place from his vantage point.

"This is really nice," he concluded.

"What do you want?"

He mumbled something about patience and finally told me the latest. After losing his accounting firm, he had decided to open a small bookkeeping operation. "Playing with other people's money is all I know how to do," he explained. "But I'll be honest with you, Jessie. Business isn't good."

"What a shocker," I said, the sarcasm veritably oozing from my voice. Call me unkind, but I have little sympathy for the man who sold confidential information about my finances at a poker game. And I'm not the only person Ian Crawcheck defrauded. Nobody in town trusted him anymore.

"Things will pick up," he insisted.

"And you just happened to set up this promising new business in my neighborhood?"

He pointed out a window. "I'm at 209 Vine Street—the second floor."

I closed my eyes and prayed for strength. My ex-husband's office was within spitting distance of my condo.

"What do you want from me?" I asked for the umpteenth time.

"I need a place to stay."

I guffawed.

"Just until I get back on my feet," he clarified, and I guffawed again.

Then I asked if he were serious, and then I said no.

"I have nowhere else to go," he pleaded. "I can't afford renting this new office and an apartment right now."

I closed my eyes again, only to notice the enormous headache I was growing.

"Come on, Jessie. You're the only friend I have left in this town."

Demonstrating how highly-evolved I am, I let that delusionary notion slide without comment. "Does this new office have a couch?" I asked.

"Well, yeah."

"So then, you do have a place to stay."

"Give me a break. There's no kitchen, no shower, and the couch is lumpy."

I groaned audibly, and Snowflake hopped into my lap to commiserate. I have no idea what she was thinking, but it had to be something more pleasant than the image haunting my own head. I pictured my ex-husband wandering around my neighborhood, looking and smelling like a vagrant.

Unfortunately, I came up with a solution. Why, oh why, am I such a creative thinker?

"Okay, so here's the plan." I stared at Snowflake but spoke to Ian. "You can come over here once a day to shower and shave. You will arrive at eleven a.m. sharp and be out of here within the hour. You will leave not one trace of your existence. And," I added, ignoring Ian's protests, "you will leave the bathroom cleaner than you found it."

That last stipulation would be hard to accomplish since I keep a spotless home, but that was Ian's problem.

"What about my stuff?" he asked. "My clothes, for instance?"

"Not my concern. Oh, and you can scoop out Snowflake's litter box each day."

"Eleven o'clock? Come on, Jessie. I have a business to run."

"And I don't? As you know, I do my best writing first thing in the morning. You," I pointed, "will not be here."

He huffed and puffed as I continued laying out the rules as they occurred to me. "Since you're now in the neighborhood—my neighborhood—you might think of popping in at The Stone Fountain. Do not."

"But that bar is where everyone hangs out around here."

"Exactly. My friends and I enjoy it, and I intend to keep it that way."

Ian almost—almost—mumbled out a "Bitch."

"Wilson and his friends like The Stone Fountain also," I informed him. "One assumes you wish to avoid employees of the Clarence Police Department right now?"

Ian curled his lip. "How's that little May-December romance going for you?" he asked, and I reminded him I could revoke his showering privileges before they even began.

"I'll need a key," he said.

After another hearty guffaw I told him to keep dreaming. "Ring the bell downstairs, and I'll buzz you in. And if I'm not here, you'll just have to suffer."

That time I distinctly did hear the word bitch. Snowflake scolded him, and he finally remembered his manners. In fact, he thanked me with what might have passed for sincere gratitude.

He stood up. "Can we start now?"

"No. Tomorrow."

He began to protest, but another firm meow from Snowflake shut him up, and he headed toward the door.

"Wait," I called out, and he turned around.

"Snowflake has one more question before you leave."

"What, what, what?"

I took a deep breath. "She's wondering if you have enough money for food."

He blinked twice. "Things aren't that desperate," he said quietly and shut the door behind him.

I sat and stared into space for who knows how long.

Chapter 4

Seductive attire Karen Sembler-style usually means replacing her white "Sembler Assembly and Carpentry" tee-shirt for a black V-neck, no logo. But I still had to smile when she arrived at my door that evening. She had balked at my suggestion to dress provocatively for our night out. But bless her heart, not only had she changed her shirt, she had also arranged her usual tangle of auburn hair into an elaborate chignon.

I didn't need to look down to know she was in jeans and work boots. I've never seen Karen in anything but jeans and work boots. Unless she's working—in which case she adds a rather daunting tool belt to the ensemble.

Karen was staring at my hair, searching for words, when Candy Poppe, resplendent in a sapphire blue mini dress, arrived. She brushed past us and made a bee-line for the coffee table, where she unceremoniously dumped an enormous pile of junk. I hadn't bothered to tell Candy to dress sexy, since the woman knows no other option, but I had requested she bring up all of her cosmetics and jewelry.

Relieved of her burdens, Candy spun around on her stilettos and almost fell over. "Oh my gosh, Jessie." She held onto the couch for support. "What happened to your hair?" When she realized how unflattering that sounded, she tried again. "I mean, what did you do to your hair?" That didn't quite work either. "I mean, gosh, Jessie, did you get your hair done today?" She tilted her head and attempted a smile.

Karen tapped me on the shoulder. "It looks like you dipped your head in an inkwell, girlfriend."

I thanked her for noticing, and while they stared at me aghast, I explained my new do and the plan for the evening. Their eyes got quite wide when I mentioned the Wade On Inn. And they got even wider when I dug into my jeans pocket and pulled out a handful of twenties. I gave each of them a hundred dollars from the money Wilson had allotted.

"What's this for?" Karen blinked at the cash in her palm.

"Gambling," I said with my brightest smile. "While we search for the killer, we can wager on the pool game. Won't that be fun?"

My friends frowned alternately between my hairdo and the money they each held. The headache that had been threatening since Ian's visit hit me full force, but I kept on smiling.

"It'll be fun," I repeated.

Ignoring me altogether, they embarked on a detailed debate about what was more disturbing—venturing into the Wade On Inn to catch a killer, or being seen in public with me and my new look.

I left the room in search of an Advil.

They were discussing sixties sitcoms when I returned from the bathroom. I interrupted a dispute about The Addams Family and pointed to Candy's cosmetic case, or perhaps I should say Candy's cosmetic duffle bag. "Help me with my makeup, Sweetie?"

"Gosh, Jessie." She hazarded another glance at my hairdo. "I don't know."

I begged. Surely she had something in that satchel to rectify my appearance? Barring that, maybe a couple extra layers of mascara would help my disguise. Karen said something about my needing all the help I could get, and Candy finally acquiesced.

Thus I sat at my dressing table and let my young friend do her magic. I kept my eyes closed for most of the operation and stalwartly ignored Karen, who sat behind us on the bed, humming the theme song from The Addams Family and snapping her fingers at the appropriate intervals.

***

"Okay, Jessie," Candy said eventually. "You can look now."

I opened my eyes and the three of us stared at my reflection. Aghast again.

We had agreed that my fair coloring and pale eyebrows looked awful under such dark hair, so Candy had opted to darken my eyebrows, lashes, and lids with shades that worked well with her own olive complexion and brunette locks. Funny how a plan that sounded so logical in the abstract, could go so awry in the actual execution.

Grim reality hit me. "It's not The Addams Family," I said. "It's The Munsters."

"That's it, Jess!" Karen clapped her hands. "You look just like Eddie Munster!"

"Help me," I pleaded.

But both my friends seemed mystified as to how they might accomplish that. Snowflake was also puzzled. She stared at my reflection from her spot beside Karen, looking oh so smug in her pristine white coat.

"Jewelry!" Candy exclaimed, and we all jumped. "More jewelry will help, Jessie. I just know it will."

Bless her heart, she actually smiled at my reflection before scurrying over to the coffee table to retrieve her bigger-than-a-bread-box jewelry box. She dropped it on the bed, and Snowflake supervised while she and Karen rummaged around, pulling out this and that unlikely item for my perusal.

I watched with growing apprehension. "Wilson thought your jewelry might help my disguise," I told Candy.

Karen held up something akin to a rhinestone-studded dog collar. "This should do the trick."

I resigned myself to my fate and took off my own jewelry, which suddenly seemed remarkably understated. I took out the diamond stud earrings my parents had given me when I graduated from Duke, and un-clipped the diamond pendant necklace I bought myself when I landed my first book contract. And finally, I took off the antique bracelet that I had purchased only a month earlier, after Windswept Whispers hit the New York Times bestseller list, a first for Adelé Nightingale.

Meanwhile Candy was decorating me in rhinestones. "I know this isn't really your style," she said as she hooked the dog collar on me. "But it can't hurt, can it?"

"Help me," I tried again.

"Sorry, Jess," Karen said. "But now you look like Eddie Munster in drag."

I was busy sighing dramatically when Candy slipped a pair of glasses, something else she harbored in that jewelry box, onto my face.

"Sweetie." I straightened the wire-rimmed spectacles. "I do not wear glasses, and I certainly can't wear someone else's if I want to see straight at the pool table." I thought a minute. "You don't wear glasses either?"

"Contacts," she said. "But look through them, Jessie. They're just clear glass." She smiled down at me, and it did seem as if my vision hadn't changed a bit. "I wore them for a Halloween party last year. I went as a librarian."

Keeping an open mind—Lord knows, I was keeping an open mind—I checked my reflection. Pince-nez. I swear to God, Candy Poppe had plopped a pair of pince-nez onto my nose.

Karen confessed that she had run out of words to do justice to my new look.

Being a writer, I helped her out. "I look like a near-sighted Eddie Munster in drag," I concluded. Much to my chagrin, no one argued.

"At least I won't have to worry about getting picked up at the Wade On Inn," I mumbled optimistically. "No man in his right mind would hit on me."

Ever-helpful, Karen reminded me that murderers aren't usually in their right minds as Candy started rummaging around in my underwear drawer.

Okay, now I was really alarmed. "What are you doing in there?" I forced myself to ask.

She pulled out the push-up bra she had talked me into the last time I was in Tate's and held it aloft. "Let's try this!"

"Oh boy," Karen said.

Perhaps I should mention Candy Poppe is the world's best bra and underwear saleswoman. She works at Tate's Department Store, and most every woman in Clarence goes to her for their underclothing needs. Even Karen admits to sporting a heck of a lot of lace beneath her rugged exterior due to our neighbor's influence.

"I admit you're not looking your best with your new look and all," Candy was saying. "But at least you can play up that fantastic figure of yours." "Playing up" one's figure is Candy Poppe's euphemism for pushing up a few key aspects thereof.

I winced at the ridiculous lacy thing, pink no less, that Candy was jiggling before my pince-nez.

"I'd wear the bra if I were you." Karen pointed at my hairdo. "You need all the help you can get right now."

"That's it!" I stood up, yanked the bra from Candy, and gestured for Karen to take the hot seat.

"Oh, no," she said, pointing to the various ointments, tubes and compacts littering the table. "Kiddo here isn't coming near me with that stuff. What you see, is what you get."

She tried hiding behind Snowflake, but Candy was not so easily deterred. She pulled her off the bed and toward my dressing table. "We all have to look like we belong at the Wade On Inn," she insisted.

"And if I can go out looking like this, you can at least put on some damn mascara," I added.

"Good point," they said in unison.

While they argued over the appropriate shade of blush to compliment Karen's porcelain skin tone, I turned my back and slipped out of my sweater. Giving myself some credit, I had already decided on something low-cut and slinky for my outing to the Wade On Inn. Once upon a time flashing cleavage had been one of my standard pool-table ploys. My cleavage wasn't what it used to be, but perhaps the headache-inducing bra would help.

"Wearing things like this might keep me in the running with Wilson," I said as I got dressed.

"What's that, Jessie?" Candy was fiddling with Karen's eyebrows when I turned around.

"Tiffany Sass is that." I re-donned the silly glasses. "You've seen her at The Stone Fountain."

"The knockout who works with Wilson?" Karen asked behind closed eyes. "The guys start spilling stuff when she's around. Is that her?"

I plopped down on the bed. "The girl—and I do mean girl—and my beau are completely smitten with each other."

"Smitten?" Karen shook her head, but Candy scolded her to keep still. "Where do you come up with this stuff, girlfriend? Wilson's smitten with you."

Candy agreed. "You two are madly in love, Jessie. Anyone can see that."

I reminded my friends what I do for a living. "Adelé Nightingale knows smitten when she sees smitten."

"Speaking of the men in your life," Candy asked coyly. "Did you talk to Ian yet?"

"Ian Crawcheck is not a man in my life," I said firmly. "And yes. And don't remind me."

"What's up with Ian?" Karen asked.

"Amanda threw him out and now he wants to move in here!" Candy told her. "You're not gonna let him, Jessie?"

"Only when hell freezes over. But unfortunately it's not that simple."

I explained Ian's predicament and the shower situation while Karen studied me in the mirror. "Wilson won't like it," she said.

"Trust me, I'm not all crazy about it either. But the only thing worse than seeing my ex on occasion would be smelling him, no?"

"Gross," Candy agreed.

She finished with Karen's face and glanced over at me, or more specifically, at my chest. "Oh, Jessie!" she exclaimed. "That bra helps so much! I hope I have a figure as nice as yours when I'm old."

Karen grimaced at her own reflection and then back at me. "Remind me again, ladies. What kind of hustling are we doing tonight?"

***

Looking more or less ridiculous, the three of us made our way down the stairs and out to Wilson's truck. Speaking of ridiculous.

"What happened to your car?" Candy asked as I unlocked the doors.

I was explaining Wilson's logic about our stupid, stupid vehicle swap when Karen grabbed the keys and hopped into the driver's seat.

30

"I'm thinking of trading in my van for one of these babies," she announced happily. "I need something big like this for my business."

I suggested she might consider a newer model, perhaps in a discernible color, and closed her door. Then I convinced teeny-tiny Candy to take the middle seat and climbed in behind her.

"The Wade On Inn, James," I ordered.

I assumed my friends were ignorant of the kind of pool they would witness at the Wade On Inn, so on the drive out I explained the basics of nine ball—that the balls are racked in a diamond shape, and only the one through nine are used.

"What's the goal?" Karen asked.

"Both players pocket the balls in consecutive order, one through nine. The person who sinks the nine ball wins."

She stopped at a red light. "But what about one through eight? No one gets credit for those?"

"Nope. The key is the nine."

"So, like, the eight ball isn't important?" Candy asked. She had seen a lot of eight ball at The Stone Fountain.

"Correct," I told her and explained that in nine ball the eight simply goes in after the seven and before the nine.

"This sounds pretty stupid." The light turned green, and Karen hit the gas. "Isn't it just luck, whoever gets to pocket the nine?"

"Oh, no," I said. "Nine ball involves a lot of strategy. Especially on the leave. After each shot you need to leave yourself a good shot on the next ball. But if you miss, you mustn't give your opponent an easy shot."

"But how can you know if you'll make a shot ahead of time?" Candy asked.

"Exactly, Sweetie. That's where the skill comes in."

"And we're supposed to bet on all this?" Karen sounded skeptical.

"People love betting on nine ball," I insisted. "You can bet on the game itself, or on each individual shot. Money changes hands very rapidly. You'll see."

"Gosh, I won't know what I'm doing," Candy said.

Karen was also concerned, so I gave them some pointers on how to handle their money. We even practiced a few scenarios.

"It's not rocket science," I promised. "If we show some smarts, we should end up richer for our efforts."

I explained to my co-conspirators that my alias would be Tessie Hess. It would be easy for them to remember since it was so close to my real name. "And if you goof and call me Jessie, I doubt anyone will catch it. Besides, Tessie is my mother's name," I reminded them. "I like it."

Karen turned onto Belcher Drive and immediately hit one of the many potholes that line the road to the Wade On Inn. "What about Kiddo, here?" she asked. "After what happened with Stanley's murder, shouldn't she have an alias, too?"

Candy jumped a little. "Gosh, Jessie, Channel 15 and Jimmy Beak picked on me a lot last month. What if someone recognizes me?"

"There's no law against you wandering into the Wade On Inn with your out-of-town friend who likes to shoot pool, is there?" I patted her knee. "Just be yourself. The key to any good hustle is to stay as close as possible to the truth. That way it's easier to act out when things get intense."

"Are things gonna get intense?" she asked.

"Yes, Sweetie." I frowned as we passed a junk yard littered with vehicles looking much like Wilson's truck. "I think they might."

Chapter 5

"Tell me again, why I agreed to this?" Karen grumbled as she wrestled the truck into a parking space. It hadn't rained in two days, but the unpaved lot at the Wade On Inn was still so muddy she had to use a low gear to avoid getting stuck. "What a dump."

"Gosh, I've always thought the Wade On Inn is kind of pretty," Candy argued as we climbed out of the truck.

Karen glanced up from locking the doors and conceded that the building was interesting.

Interesting and beautiful, actually. The Wade On Inn is a huge old stone structure originally built as a grist mill.

"The setting is nice, too," I said. "Just listen." I tilted my head toward the sounds of the waterfalls. "If you forget about the sleazy bar, it's almost idyllic."

"Yeah, right," Karen said. We held onto each other to keep from slipping, and the three of us tiptoed forward. "Take a look at this parking lot, Jess."

Okay, so I had to admit that our immediate surroundings were not exactly picturesque. For instance, Wilson's truck fit right in with most of the other vehicles. They, too, were ugly old junkers, several with plastic sheeting taped over this or that busted out window. But at the corner closest to Shinkle Creek and the waterfalls, the cars were decidedly newer and shinier.

I stopped to take a closer look. Why would people with the best cars park in the darkest, muddiest section of this crime-ridden place, where the overhead lights weren't even working?

Candy must have read my mind. "This is where people using the hotel park." She spoke loudly enough to be heard over the rushing waters. "It's kind of impolite to notice the cars, okay?"

She looked at me imploringly until I finally understood. This was the illicit sex section of the parking lot, where teenagers parked their parents' cars, and where adulterers parked theirs. I wasn't supposed to recognize these cars, much less attempt to deduce who was in the hotel.

Leave it to Candy Poppe to know the proper Wade On Inn etiquette. She's such a sweetie now, but back in her high school days she was a juvenile delinquent. She had likely spent many an evening at that hotel.

As Candy pulled me away, I asked Karen if she had ever been to the Wade On Inn.

"Are you kidding?" she said. "I've never had the guts."

About then, the door opened. A big guy picked up a smaller guy by the seat of his pants and threw him into the parking lot.

"And stay out," he shouted as the poor soul landed at our feet.

The three of us gingerly stepped around the human heap and proceeded to the doorway, where the bouncer's considerable bulk blocked our entry. He looked like a football player who had seen better days, and he took his time studying each of us in turn. As he lingered over Candy's legs, I noticed a book tucked into the waist of his jeans. Was that really a Bible?

The Bible-toting bouncer took one baby step aside, and we entered the cramped entranceway single file. Karen reached for the door with an arrow pointing up, but Candy and I said "No," in unison and gestured to the door with a rather ominous-looking arrow pointing downward.

"Upstairs is where the hotel is," Candy explained. She opened the door leading downstairs. "But we're going this way."

Karen whimpered as if we were ushering her through the gates of hell itself. But a glimpse of the marvelous stone slab staircase lighted with wrought iron lanterns piqued her curiosity, and she led the way.

***

"But this is great!" Karen looked around in delight as she reached the bottom stair.

We had entered into a spacious room with thick stone walls on three sides. The bar lined the wall behind us, and two enormous fireplaces, which likely hadn't been used for a century, faced each other from across an expansive wood-plank dance floor.

The pool table stood in the place of honor, in front of the wall of the floor-to-ceiling windows overlooking Shinkle Creek and the waterfalls. With the bright overhead lamp above it, one could either watch the game itself, or the reflection of the game in the windows.

"I've put this room in several of my books," I said. "Minus those windows, it's my model for any and all the dungeons."

"You must write about some pretty nice dungeons." Karen was still wide-eyed. "And I love the music!"

"Excuse me?"

She pointed upward. "It's the Wicket Brothers. Lucas and Carl Wicket. I love their stuff!"

It's funny what you learn about a person when you set out to catch a killer together. It's also funny how the mind works. I might have remembered the architecture to a tee, but I had forgotten, or more likely repressed, the fact that the Wade On Inn plays country and western music. Incessantly.

I blinked twice and tuned in to the Wicket Brothers, who were agonizing over the trials and tribulations of two guys loving the same gal. I tucked the idea away for the next time I suffered from plot plight and followed Candy to the bar.

"A Corona with lime for my friend," she told the bartender and pointed toward Karen. "And a bottle of Korbel for Tessie and me, please." She turned around and winked.

"Say what?" the bartender asked.

I stepped forward. "On second thought, we'll just take a pitcher."

Candy looked at me as if I had lost my mind. She knows I don't like beer, and had made a solemn vow when my divorce was finalized to celebrate every day of the rest of my life with a healthy dose of champagne. I mumbled something about when in Rome.

"Oh!" Candy caught on. "Oh, yeah! A pitcher of beer!" She winked again and then swung around to the bartender, who I swear bore an uncanny resemblance to Lily Munster.

She had beautiful black eyes, dark red talons, and long dark hair with a dramatic streak of grey running through it.

Karen asked what she had on tap, and Mrs. Munster listed four cheap choices before slapping both palms on the bar. "Name your poison, ladies?"

I tried not to cringe when Karen did so.

While the bartender filled our pitcher with something that promised to be lukewarm and flat, we found a couple of barstools, and my friends sat down. I set my cue at Karen's feet but remained standing in order to study the crowd.

Some of these people had to be undercover cops. In fact, a woman sitting near Karen looked familiar. I couldn't quite place her, but Wilson must have introduced us at some point. The head full of blond curls was a nice touch, though. Clearly she had taken pains not to look cop-like.

Goldilocks the Cop glanced up and scowled. I refrained from waving and looked away, secure in the knowledge she was watching out for us.

The only other person who caught my attention was the teenage girl sitting at the farthest end of the bar doing her homework.

Doing her homework?

I checked again, and sure enough the girl was concentrating on two textbooks and had a notebook spread out in front of her. She was indeed doing her homework. On a Friday night? At the Wade On Inn?

The bartender must have noticed me staring. "That's my daughter Mackenzie," she said as she set down our pitcher. "I can't get her to take her nose out of those books. Even on weekends, she's supposedly got tons of homework." She shook her head. "The kid gets straight A's."

"You must be proud of her," I said.

"A's in math, even." She glanced back at me. "Unn-believable."

I smiled and reached my hand across the bar. "Tessie Hess," I made sure to say.

"Elsa Quinn. I own this dump." She shook my hand and stepped away to check on her daughter.

The child might have been a lot more studious than her mother, but they did look alike. Mackenzie had long dark hair, minus the grey, and painfully thin arms.

Karen filled our glasses and began a dissertation on the Wicket Brothers. And while Candy learned everything she ever wanted to know about Lucas and Carl, I continued my perusal of the Wade On Inn.

At either side of the room, in front of the fireplaces and surrounding the dance floor, were groups of small tables surrounded by rickety-looking chairs, all seats taken. The bouncer sat on a barstool at the foot of the stairs. Occasionally he glanced up from his Bible to check on the dancers, although I really couldn't understand why.

Only one woman seemed to be having any fun at all. She staggered about, apparently oblivious to the fact that she lacked a partner. Suddenly she stopped short, and I perked up my ears.

Thank you, God—Lucas and Carl had finally given up. But the blessed silence lasted only a brief moment before a group of female singers began spouting off about their own angst. Stumbling slightly, the Drunken Dancer returned to her solo swaying.

"Who's this?" I asked over my shoulder.

"Raven Claw," Karen answered. "I love their stuff."

I ventured a small sip of the pale yellow substance in my flimsy plastic cup and finally got around to studying the pool table crowd across the room. A young guy with curly blond hair similar to Goldilocks the Cop's was playing against a little old black man while a bunch of onlookers watched.

No one was talking much, which was a good indication a lot of money was riding on the game. That didn't surprise me, but the pair of old ladies sitting amongst the railbirds did. They had identical blue-rinsed hair, one held a cane, and the other a cowboy hat.

I was puzzling over that when Candy tapped my shoulder. "Are you gonna play, Tessie?" She spoke loudly, just as I had instructed her.

Karen stopped humming along with Raven Claw and assumed her role also. "Our friend J—I mean, my friend

Tessie here's a fantastic pool player," she announced. "I bet she could beat anyone in this place."

Candy banged a fist on the bar. "That's right, Karen," she said. "Tessie can beat anyone. Gosh, I just know she can."

Okay, so my friends are not great actresses. But at least they were attempting to follow the script we had practiced earlier.

Playing my own part, I shrugged at no one in particular and mumbled something about being out of practice.

"Don't be shy, Tessie," Karen scolded. "You're a real good player, and you know it." She nodded at anyone who was watching her, but most people—most men anyway—had their eyes on Candy.

She smiled sweetly to her new fans. "Karen's right," she said. "Tessie never, ever loses, okay?"

Several men mumbled a mesmerized "Okay," as Karen caught my eye.

"Now?" she mouthed.

I offered the slightest nod, and she up and pulled her wallet from the pocket of her jeans and slammed it on the bar. That went just as planned, but I almost fell over backwards when Candy lifted her money from somewhere deep down in her cleavage. Trust me, that was not in the script, and trust me, I was not the only person who noticed.

"Oh boy," Karen said as several men practically toppled off their barstools.

***

"Now, let's see." Candy hopped off her own barstool and was making a show of counting out the five twenties I had given her earlier. "I have a hundred dollars, and I'm willing to bet forty that my friend Tessie can beat anyone in here." She fanned herself with her cash and looked around. "How about you, Karen?"

Karen announced that she, too, was willing to put forty dollars on me. "Heck," she said, getting into the spirit. "Let's make it sixty!"

It was my turn for some bad acting. "Oh, but ladies." I backed away and batted my eyelashes in various directions. "I haven't played in, like, forever. I'm really not that good."

Continuing my reluctant act, I took another step backwards, and bumped into what felt like a very large person. I cringed and turned around, expecting to see the bouncer.

But instead I had my nose in the broad chest of the blond guy who had been shooting pool a moment before. I almost didn't recognize him since he now wore a cowboy hat. I peeked over his shoulder. Sure enough, the hat was missing from the old lady's lap.

"Jeepers, ma'am." Cowboy Hat smiled. "You think you can beat Avis even?"

Jeepers?

He continued, "I just lost three games in a row to him. Shucks, he's good."

Shucks?

"Who's Avis?" I asked and braced myself for the answer.

"Avis Sage." Cowboy Hat pointed to the old black man who still had command of the table, and I closed my eyes and prayed for strength.

Avis Sage was a hustler from way back when. He might be playing at the Wade On Inn these days, but once upon a time, he had visited my childhood home and shot a few games against my father. And me. But surely my brilliant disguise and several decades of aging would keep me safe from recognition?

"The only guy who could beat him around here is dead," Cowboy Hat chirped happily as he handed Elsa an empty pitcher.

She made a show of slamming things around behind the bar and handed him his refill. "Take this, and this conversation, back to the pool table, Bobby," she ordered.

I glanced around to see who else was disturbed by Bobby's line of conversation and noticed Elsa's daughter. Mackenzie wasn't disturbed, exactly, but she was staring at the wannabe cowboy. And she had lost all interest in her homework.

Once again, Candy took charge. She tucked some of her money away from whence it came, lifted the other forty over her head, and led what amounted to a conga line across the room toward the pool table.

"Here goes nothing," Karen whispered. She grabbed our pitcher, slung my cue case over her shoulder, and joined the end of the line. I stepped around Cowboy Hat and tagged along.

"I'd be careful if I were you," he said from behind me.

I stopped and turned at the edge of the dance floor. "Oh?" I asked. "Why's that?"

"Shucks, ma'am. We've had some trouble in here lately. Two people were killed." He gestured toward the pool table.

"Playing pool?" I acted shocked and lied that I was from out of town. "My friends should have warned me about this."

"I reckon they should have."

I blinked twice and held out my hand. "Tessie Hess," I said. "And you're Bobby?"

"Bobby Decker." He ignored my hand and tipped his cowboy hat. "You'd best be careful, ma'am. You hear?"

I studied him some more. "I've always been a cautious player," I said eventually. "How about you?"

"I reckon I'm not the cautious type." Bobby smiled again, and I noticed his chipped front tooth for the first time.

Chapter 6

Candy's conga line parted, and Avis Sage stepped forward as I approached the pool table. He bowed and said it was a pleasure to meet me, and since the old guy didn't seem to recognize me, I returned the sentiment.

Of course, Tessie Hess was also a stranger to everyone else gathering around, but that didn't seem to discourage people from placing their bets on me. Tens, twenties, and fifty-dollar bills practically flew through the air as everyone offered their opinion about my alleged talents.

But no one was flashing more money than the blue-haired old ladies. When I heard the amounts being discussed, I paid closer attention. Doreen, I surmised, was the heavyset one with the cane. Ethel was equally ancient, but thin.

Avis Sage tapped me on the shoulder and asked if I cared to make a wager.

"Maybe." I gestured toward the old ladies. "But not on those terms."

"Tessie's cautious," Bobby the wannabe cowboy explained.

"Oh, but she's so good!" Candy bounced a bit, and her enthusiasm worked to unearth a few more wallets.

"I think my friends are a bit overconfident," I told Avis.

"The old man understands, Miss Tessie. How about we start with a twenty?"

I said that seemed reasonable and placed a twenty on top of the overhead light, the standard spot for holding the players' bets. Avis reached deep into the pocket of his baggy trousers and pulled out his own money.

"Get out of the way, Bobby," the woman standing with Karen scolded. "Some of us want to see this game."

I glanced at Karen, and she introduced me to her new friend, Melissa Purcell. Like Karen, Melissa was about forty, but she was taller and darker, and lacked Karen's flawless complexion.

"Your friend's been bragging about you," Melissa said. "You really that good?"

"Fair," I said humbly. "How about you?"

"I still have a lot to learn."

Bobby grunted. "I reckon that's the truth."

Melissa ignored Bobby. "Maybe you can teach me some tricks, Tessie?"

I suggested she might want to watch me play first and turned back to Avis Sage, who had two balls set up for the lag.

I noticed the puzzled look on Karen's face, and realized I should have explained this ritual beforehand.

In a serious game, players often lag for the break. The opponents stand side by side at one rail, and each shoots a ball at the opposite rail. The player whose ball lands back closest to where they are standing wins the break.

And the break is crucial in nine ball. A good player might sink the one ball and run the whole table before their opponent even gets a chance to play.

Karen handed me my cue and wished me luck.

"Yeah, Tessie." Melissa winked. "Good luck."

***

Lucky me, I won the lag. And then I had the pleasure of watching someone named Spencer rack for me. Like the old ladies, Spencer was not the kind of person I had expected to see at the Wade On Inn. He was a clean-cut, classically handsome, yuppie-type, replete with a cleft in his chin and a dimple in his smile.

Spencer was by far the best-looking man in the place. Indeed, when he glanced up and flashed me a dimple, I decided he might be the best looking man I had ever seen.

"He's too young for you," Melissa told me.

"Well, darn."

"And he's too old for your friend." She jerked her head toward Candy, to whose side Spencer had gravitated.

I told her she might have a point and bent over to take my shot. Nothing much happened, but I did make sure to hide the one ball from the cue ball.

I stepped back for Avis Sage, and under his guidance, the cue ball found the one anyway. He also sunk the two

42

ball. And the three. And the four. You get the picture. He ran the table and won the game.

"Did you see that?" Doreen banged her cane on the floor. "I just lost over a hundred bucks! In the blink of an eye!"

"But I just won a hundred!" her friend Ethel exclaimed as she admired the bills being dropped into her lap. "No one will ever convince me playing bridge is more fun than this."

"Are you good bridge players?" I asked.

"Better than you are at pool," Doreen said.

Ethel told me to ignore her senile old friend and rack them up. "I'll bet on you this time, Tessie. Two hundred!"

"And you call me senile?" Doreen said, and they laughed heartily.

Avis Sage was also raring to go. "The first to three for fifty, Miss Tessie? What do you say?"

I agreed to the match and racked the balls while the onlookers negotiated their bets. Poor Candy and Karen were again confused, but they would catch on. The first to three simply meant Avis and I would continue to play until one of us had taken three games. The first to three would win the match and the money.

"Don't be disappointing me, buddy," Spencer the Handsome tore his eyes from Candy to speak to Avis. "I don't like losing to Melissa."

"Jeepers, me neither," Bobby said from Candy's opposite side.

Candy squirmed away from her fan club and reminded everyone what a good player I am. "You're smart to keep betting on her," she told Melissa.

Melissa frowned. "I am smart," she said.

The music switched to another talent-challenged country and western band, and Avis bent over to take aim.

He got off to a good start, but he missed the six ball and left the table wide open. Melissa patted me on the back and told me to show the crowd what I was made of.

I stepped up to the table and did so.

***

In fact, I won that game and the next. News of my skill at tricky bank shots spread quickly, and more spectators wandered over to wager on game three.

I was in the middle of a good run when the bouncer stepped up to the table and shook his Bible at me. Then he placed it on the rail and thumped it. Literally.

"Woe to you, scribes and parasites and hypocrites!" he announced.

Scribes? But even if this guy had somehow guessed I'm a writer, that quote still didn't sound quite right. I squinted at Candy, but she also seemed confused.

Not Avis Sage. He picked up the Bible and handed it back to the bouncer. "The Gospel of Saint Matthew was one of my dear mother's favorites," he said. "I believe the word is Pharisees, Henry. Jesus didn't much like those Pharisees."

"What's the difference?" Henry the bouncer said and pointed a finger in my direction. "Now is the judgment of this world!" he informed me.

I blinked twice. "Oh?"

"Would you give it up, Henry?" Melissa said testily. She turned to me and rolled her eyes. "Henry's been a Christian for a whole month. So he thinks it makes him some sort of expert."

"Pastor Muckenfuss says it's up to every Christian to wrestle sin from the world," Henry defended himself. "Pastor Muckenfuss says the good Lord needs my help."

"Then the good Lord must pretty be hard up." Melissa shooed him away and waved me back to the table. "Go ahead," she told me, but somehow I had lost my momentum. The game ended up going to Avis, putting the match at two to one.

I racked for the next game while the railbirds searched their wallets for more cash. Everyone appeared to be enjoying themselves, and Ethel the skinny old lady commented that the Wade On Inn might have found itself a replacement for Fritz Lupo.

"A girl can hope," Doreen agreed.

"Who's Fritz?" I jumped on that perfect opportunity. "Does he play here?"

"He's the guy who just got killed," Melissa said. "Don't you watch the news, Tessie?"

"Tessie's from out of town," Karen reminded everyone.

Bless his heart, Avis Sage broke and ran several balls, allowing me the chance to stand back and soak in the conversation.

"Angela Hernandez was shot, too," Doreen said helpfully, and the guy sitting next to her shuffled uneasily in his seat.

I glanced down and finally took notice of the quiet young man sitting beside the old ladies. He must have been right there the whole evening, but what with the flamboyance and energy of Doreen and Ethel, I hadn't even seen him.

He looked up and offered a benevolent smile. In his wire rim glasses, goatee, and sandals this guy looked more suited to a library reference desk than the Wade On Inn pool table.

"I hope you aren't losing your life savings on me?" I asked him.

"Jeepers. That ain't likely." Bobby Decker once again startled me from behind. "Kevin never bets more than five bucks a game."

Kevin took off his glasses and cleaned them with a handkerchief he pulled from the pocket of his trousers. "I'm cautious," he said, still studying his glasses.

Cautious and extremely shy apparently. "Play me a game?" I asked and waved to where Avis was working on the five ball.

Kevin shook his head. "I'm just a spectator. I have no talent at the pool table."

"That's never stopped Melissa," Spencer the Handsome mumbled just as Avis missed his shot at the seven ball.

I stepped up, cleared the table, and won the match.

Ethel squealed in unadulterated glee, and the other winners hooted and hollered. The losers grumbled almost as loudly as they forked over their cash.

"There was a double murder in here?" I asked Avis as he shook my hand. "What kind of place is this?"

"Oh, Miss Tessie." He held onto me and ignored the ruckus around us. "Losing those two just about broke the old man's heart. The Fox is gone."

"The Fox?" I asked, still feigning ignorance.

"Fritz Lupo's nickname," Bobby Decker answered. "And Avis here?" He tipped his cowboy hat to Mr. Sage. "I reckon we call him the Wiseman."

Oh, my Lord—I reckoned they did. I had completely forgotten Avis Sage's moniker from the days of yore.

Avis waved a dismissive hand. "The Wiseman's just the old man nowadays. Pay no attention to Bobby."

Sorry, sir, but paying attention was exactly what I intended to do. I turned to Bobby and asked him to tell me about the murders.

With a shucks here and a jeepers there, he did so. None of the story was news to me, but I pretended otherwise, until he gasped and stopped his narrative mid-sentence.

"It's Isabelle Eakes!" he exclaimed and pointed upward.

"Excuse me?"

"Isabelle Eakes and the Cornhuskers," Karen clarified. "I love their stuff."

"Me too!" Bobby shouted out. And as the Cornhuskers chimed in with Isabelle in a rousing chorus about the joys of being a farm girl, he whisked Karen off to the dance floor.

Melissa Purcell shook her head in disgust. "Leave it to Bobby to avoid the rest of the story."

"Why's that?" I asked.

"Because he was sleeping with Angela, that's why." Spencer the Handsome spoke loudly and Kevin the Quiet groaned quietly.

Candy and I blinked at each other as Melissa spilled some more startling news. Evidently Bobby Decker the wannabe cowboy was also the person who had found both the bodies. "Right on his own property," she added.

"Bobby lives around here?" Candy asked.

"Downstream. In a trailer." Spencer snickered at that last word.

"Oh, for goodness sake!" Doreen poked poor Mr. Sage in the butt with her cane and ordered him rack them up. "Get this show on the road, old man. Let's see what else Tessie has up her sleeve."

"Play me a game?" Melissa jumped in front of me.

When I agreed, Avis stopped collecting the balls and took me aside. He told me to give her the six. "And the break," he added.

"Are you serious?" I asked. By spotting Melissa the six, I would be offering her a much easier game. She would only need to pocket up to the six ball to win, while I would still need to pocket through the nine.

Avis nodded firmly, and only when I had offered Melissa the six and the break, did the crowd start placing their wagers.

She looked around at all the people clamoring to bet against her. "I'm not that bad," she mumbled.

"The only thing she's good at is forcing the rest of us to watch her play," Spencer told Candy.

Melissa stamped her foot. But when Spencer looked up and offered her one of his dimple-laden smiles, the woman practically melted before my eyes. I, however, was growing a bit tired of Spencer and his dimples.

***

"Let's try again?" Melissa begged me the moment she had lost. "Maybe I can pick up a few pointers this time?"

But the crowd would not tolerate watching Melissa any longer. Doreen poked Spencer's bottom with her cane and ordered him to play.

"Spencer bending over the table is a sight to behold," Ethel told me. "Don't let him distract you, Tessie."

I mumbled that I would try to control myself, and Kevin the Quiet held up a five dollar bill. "I have faith," he said.

While Spencer was preoccupied shooting a game with me, Candy slipped away. She ended up back at the bar sitting with Mackenzie Quinn. The two of them seemed to hit it off and were deep in conversation every time I looked up.

"What's she doing with Elsa's kid?" Spencer asked me.

I had no idea. I also had no idea what Karen was up to, although it appeared that she and Bobby Decker were leading a line dance. The entire floor had filled up, and even the lone Drunken Dancer was making an attempt to jive with the others.

The next time I checked, Karen was with Henry the bouncer. I do believe they were doing the Texas Two-Step.

I had planned to lose to Spencer, but that proved impossible. Bobby Decker tore himself away from the dance floor just as the nine ball fell. He handed his cowboy hat to Ethel and challenged me to a game.

After dealing with Spencer and Melissa, I wasn't expecting much. But Bobby was actually a good player, and we ended up shooting two matches.

"Ooo-eee," Avis exclaimed anytime Bobby or I made a particularly impressive shot. "Looks like the old man needs to practice."

"You need to practice and I need lessons." Melissa said after one such shot. "Who taught you to play?" she asked me. "Where are you from?"

Much to my chagrin, that question got everyone's attention.

"Umm," I said and desperately tried to think of a place these people had likely never been. "I learned in Hawaii."

"Jeepers," Bobby mumbled.

"Hawaii!" Melissa said. "That sounds so exotic!"

It did indeed. But of course I had no idea, since I had never actually been to Hawaii.

"I live there." I dug my grave even deeper. "In Honolulu. I'm a waitress," I continued on for who knows what reason. "At, umm—at a resort."

"Me, too!" Melissa exclaimed.

Doreen guffawed. "If Hastie's Diner is a resort, then the Wade On Inn is a five-star hotel."

"Harmon used to take me to Hawaii," Ethel mused. "He took me to all kinds of nice places to keep me in the dark."

"Who's Harmon?" I asked, endeavoring to change the subject.

"Ethel's gorgeous-to-a-fault dead husband," Doreen answered. "And she certainly was in the dark."

Spencer mentioned he would like to take his wife to Hawaii and began interrogating me about places to stay and things to do.

"You might want to check out the beaches," I suggested brilliantly.

Chapter 7

"What happened to your hair?" Gina Stone asked as she swept by me with her drink tray.

Ahhh. It was good to be home. Or at least back at The Stone Fountain, where the Korbel was cold, the music was stellar, and Wilson was waiting. I breathed deep and soaked in the sweet sounds of The Rolling Stones, and by the time I thought to answer Gina, she was long gone.

Her husband Matthew was another matter. He stood riveted at his station behind the bar. "Jessie?" he asked in a hoarse voice. "Is that really you?"

I mumbled something about it being my publisher's idea, and fielded the same question from a few others, as my friends and I maneuvered our way toward the far end of the bar.

Candy was locating our usual barstools, and Karen and I were having a friendly dispute over the musical talents of Carl Wicket versus Mick Jagger, when I spotted Wilson. I stopped dead in my tracks.

For there at my friendly neighborhood pool table was Wilson Rye, hovering ever so intimately over the voluptuous young body of Tiffany Sass. Their left hands were outstretched together, guiding the cue they shared, while their right hands gripped the lower end of the stick, down near Tiffany's curvaceous right hip. Mick Jagger may not have been getting much satisfaction, but my beau certainly was.

"Oh boy," Karen whispered.

"Gosh," Candy contributed as I took off my pince-nez and dropped them into her outstretched hand.

I glared full force at my soon-to-be ex-beau, but Wilson didn't even flinch.

At least my pool-playing buddies Kirby and Gus recognized me. But then again, they were not lucky enough to be groping Tiffany Sass, which must have been distracting indeed.

Gus glanced at Wilson and Tiffany, and then at me. "Oh boy," he agreed with Karen.

Kirby saluted me. "Play a game?" he asked.

"I would love to, Kirby," I said. "That is, once Captain Rye wraps things up."

Ahhh. It seems Wilson did recognize my voice. The cad did a quick double take, and lickety-split, popped his happy torso into vertical position.

He cleared his throat and spoke to Tiffany as she struggled to stand upright. "We're about done here," he told her.

"Oh really, Wilson?" I said. "It looked to me like you were just getting started."

Everyone within earshot made a great big effort to direct their attention elsewhere, but Tiffany remained unfazed. She smoothed down her blouse and actually looked me in the eye.

"Oh hi, Jessie," she said, all perky-like. "I almost didn't recognize you with your new hair." I curled my lip as she continued, "The Captain was showing me a few tricks."

"Yes, Tiffany," I said. "I noticed that."

I grabbed the cue stick from my dumbfounded beau and stepped up to the table as Ms. Sass settled her pert young derriere onto my damn barstool.

Poor Kirby. Even in the best of circumstances his lack of pool-playing talent rivals Melissa Purcell. And that night he couldn't help but be distracted by my new hairdo and foul mood.

I wasn't in my best form either. I mean, I had already shot pool for hours. And how was I supposed to concentrate with my soon-to-be ex-beau hovering over Tiffany Sass? First, at the pool table, then at the bar, and by the time I had finished my game against Kirby, they were cozying up together in one of the booths. Even with Karen and Candy chaperoning from the opposite side of the table, Wilson was barely managing to keep his middle-aged hormones in check.

Testimony to my infinite maturity and self-control, I refrained from screaming and walked over.

***

"That accounts for one of your hands," I mumbled as Wilson glanced up and gave me the glass of champagne he had waiting for me.

I was busy glaring, and he was busy pretending not to know why, when Lieutenant Densmore joined us. No doubt Tiffany would have offered to sit on the Captain's lap to make room for us all, but Wilson stood up.

"You two go on home," he told Russell and Tiffany. "We'll talk in the morning."

Tiffany scooted herself out of the booth, and I watched my beau watch his staff depart.

Only when the Sass ass was out of sight did he turn to me. "All of us sitting together like that would have attracted attention."

"Tiffany does seem to attract attention," I agreed and took the seat opposite Karen.

When Wilson sidled in next to me, I pushed myself farther into the corner. He stared at my hair, but made zero comment. The man is not a complete idiot.

Candy broke the silence. "We've been talking about Lester Quinn, Jessie. It's so sad."

"Quinn? As in Elsa and Mackenzie?"

"The husband and father," Karen said. "Candy found out he was shot a few years ago. Right at the Wade On Inn."

"He was killed," Candy elaborated. "Mackenzie doesn't remember it, but she told me about it."

I scowled at Wilson. "Did you know about this?"

He nodded and reminded me about the shoot out Fritz Lupo had been involved in years earlier. "Lester Quinn was the guy who ended up dead. Elsa and Mackenzie, who was about two at the time, witnessed the whole thing."

"Wilson!" I practically shouted. "Why didn't you tell me the details before?"

"The less you knew, the less chance you would go in there with pre-conceived notions." He tilted his head toward Candy. "And our brilliant friend here did a good job discovering the details all on her own. I take it you got sick of hanging around the pool table?" he asked her.

"I got sick of Spencer Erring," Candy answered. "Mackenzie was lots more interesting. And guess what?"

She sat forward and waited until we asked what.

"Mackenzie used to talk with Angela Hernandez all the time! Did you know that, Wilson? She's taking Spanish in school, and she used to practice with Angela. They talked about boys. In Spanish!"

Wilson also sat forward. "What boys?"

"Gosh, we didn't get into the details."

"My guess would be Bobby Decker the wannabe cowboy," I said. "I think Mackenzie has a crush on him. And apparently he and Angela Hernandez were an item."

"What!?" Karen seemed shocked. But one glance at my beau informed me he was less so.

"You knew about this, too?" I asked.

"Preconceived notions," he reminded me. "But yes, Bobby Decker used to brag about sleeping with Angela. He's changed his story now that she's dead."

Karen took a large gulp of her Corona.

"Bobby's also the person who found both the bodies," I said, and she emitted a slight squeak. I tapped Wilson's hand. "And we all know from personal experience what Captain Rye thinks of the poor souls who happen to find dead bodies on their property."

"I suspect them." He was studying Karen. "You have something to tell me about Bobby Decker?"

"She danced with him." That was Candy.

"She likes the music," I added.

"Especially Isabelle Eakes and The Cornhuskers," Karen said. "So when Bobby asked me to dance, I said sure."

"The Cornhuskers?" Wilson asked.

"I love their stuff." She twisted her Corona, and I noticed she was blushing. "Bobby didn't tell me he found the bodies, but he did say he lives nearby."

"And?" the rest of us asked in unison.

"And." She continued admiring her beer. "And he invited me out to see his place sometime. To show me his guitar."

"His guitar?" I said.

"Hey, I don't plan to take him up on it."

"Why not?" Candy asked. "Bobby's kind of cute."

"Bobby Decker is a suspect," Wilson reminded her before glancing at me. "And his trailer makes my place look like the Taj Mahal."

I grimaced at that downright frightening notion. Wilson's little cabin—or shall I say shack—on the banks of Lake Lookadoo might have spectacular views, but the furniture is anything but. Ditto on the plumbing.

I spoke to Karen. "Do not go there," I said sternly. "Trust me on this."

She shrugged. "Whatever he lives in now, Bobby's family used to own everything out that way. Something like four hundred acres, including the Wade On Inn."

"No way," Wilson said. "Decker's family never owned the Wade On Inn. Elsa's family is solely responsible for that hell-hole."

"Maybe," she said. "But the Rice family owned it back when it was still a working mill. Bobby's mother was a Rice before she got married."

"Well, I'll be damned." Wilson was clearly impressed with this new info."Are you willing to keep dancing with the cowboy?"

"Hey, I like the music."

He turned to Candy. "And you'll keep talking to Mackenzie Quinn?"

"I'll see what she knows about Bobby and Angela, okay?"

"And anything else she cares to mention," Wilson suggested. "Mackenzie Quinn seems like a good kid. Amazing, considering the environment she's grown up in. She's been doing her homework in that bar since grade school."

"It hasn't done her any harm," I said. "According to Elsa, she's a straight-A student."

"But they live there, too, Jessie. The Quinns live on the third floor over the hotel, which gives that poor kid a bird's eye view of everything that goes on out there."

"Do you think one of them saw the shootings?" Karen asked.

"Not that they're telling me." Wilson groaned. "No one out there has told me much of anything."

"They like to keep to themselves," Candy said.

"They protect each other," Karen added.

Wilson raised an eyebrow. "They also kill each other."

Chapter 8

"Puddles!" Candy exclaimed, and we all jumped. "I'm sorry, Wilson, but I have to go." She stood up as I explained her puppy-sitting arrangement with Peter Harrison.

"Well then, let's go rescue Mr. Harrison," Wilson said. "I mean Puddles," he corrected himself. "I haven't met him yet."

Karen told him he was in for a treat, and the four of us walked home to retrieve Puddles from a weary and worn Peter Harrison.

The poor old guy. As if spending an entire evening with Puddles weren't exhausting enough, he also had the added shock of seeing me in my new look for the first time. Luckily Wilson was there to catch him when he just about fainted.

But Peter quickly recovered his jolly smile, made some excuse about being a bit tired due to the lateness of the hour, and swore to Candy that her puppy had been no trouble at all.

"Only one piddle all evening," he said brightly.

Puddles made up for lost time the moment we got him out to Sullivan Street. As the puppy rounded the fire hydrant for the third time, Wilson reminded us we still had a lot of ground to cover.

"I know it's late," he said. "But what else did you ladies notice tonight?"

"Karen noticed the bouncer." Candy bent down to tell Puddles what a good boy he was. "She danced with him, too."

We started walking down Vine Street, deserted at such a late hour, and Karen described her conversation with Henry Jack the Bible-toting bouncer. "He goes to some new church," she told us. "The Zion Tabernacle of Praise and Prophecy."

"You know this how?" Wilson asked.

"Umm, Henry might have invited me to go to church with him."

Wilson chuckled. "Is there anyone out there who didn't ask you for a date, Ms. Sembler?"

"Hey, I'm a good dancer."

"When Henry wasn't flirting with Karen, he was thumping his Bible at me," I said. "Apparently his pastor, a guy named Muckenfuss, has ordered Henry to wipe out sin at the Wade On Inn."

"Muckenfuss?" Wilson asked.

"Isn't it great? I guarantee an evil Lord Muckenfuss will make an appearance in my next book. Especially since he has Henry convinced that all pool players are going straight to hell."

Speaking of hell, about then we passed 209 Vine, and I glanced up at the second floor window. The lights were out in Ian's office. That lumpy couch must have been comfy enough after all.

"Something up there?" Wilson asked, and I shifted my attention back to Puddles, who had managed to twist his leash around one of Candy's stilettos.

"Maybe Henry Jack killed those people," she said as she struggled to disentangle herself. "You know, if he thought they were sinners?"

Wilson bent down to hold Puddles, and Candy freed her foot. He glanced up at Karen. "You willing to keep dancing with him?"

"Oh sure," she said. "I'm way better at dancing than I am at gambling."

He stood up. "Don't tell me you were all betting?"

"It was fun," Candy answered as we turned toward home. "Jessie taught us what to do."

Wilson frowned at me for good measure and asked how my evening went. "Tell me everything, Little Girl Cue-It." He put an arm around my shoulder and kissed the top of my head. "Except how you managed to get your hair that color."

I reminded my soon-to-be ex-beau that my disguise was his idea, and that I did not appreciate being addressed by my childhood nickname. "Only Daddy got to call me that."

"The Wade On Inn?" he prompted, and I told him it wasn't at all what I expected.

"Everyone seemed so sweet and innocent." I began counting the regulars off on my fingers. "Bobby Decker the wannabe cowboy with his shucks here and jeepers there, Elsa the adoring mother, Mackenzie the stellar student." I waved my hands. "Quirky old ladies, yuppies, poor Melissa Purcell just hoping to play better someday. I swear it seemed almost wholesome."

"Excuse me?"

"Of course, my favorite was Avis Sage." I smiled at the thought of Mr. Sage after all these years. "What a sweet old man."

"That sweet old man is my prime suspect."

"What!?" my friends and I said in unison, and even Puddles yipped at the idea.

"We're talking about the little old black guy?" Karen asked. "The one who's no bigger than Kiddo here?"

"That little old black guy is a shark from way back," Wilson said. "He has a record a mile long."

"Yeah, right," I said. "A bunch of silly gambling misdemeanors from way back when he knew my fa—"

Oops.

Wilson stopped. "Your father?" he said and we all stopped. "Are you telling me Avis Sage knew your daddy?"

"Umm," I answered and appealed to my friends for support. But they were both taking an inordinate interest in the storefront window of King's Bakery and Confections.

"The display case is empty," I pointed out, but they kept staring at it anyway. I gave up and told Wilson to have at it.

"Please tell me Avis Sage didn't recognize you."

"He didn't recognize me. He hasn't seen me since I was ten." I pointed to my hair. "I have changed a bit since then."

"You're a little scary. You know that?"

"Maybe, but Mr. Sage certainly isn't."

"Avis Sage has a serious heart condition and huge medical bills. His health depends on him winning at that pool table. He couldn't afford to be losing to Lupo. Or Hernandez."

I thought about Avis. He was good, but dare I say, he had lost some of his edge over the decades?

"He wouldn't have the strength to push dead bodies into those waterfalls," I argued.

"Yeah, right," Wilson said as we started walking again.

"Speaking of scary muscle men." I was a tad sarcastic. "There's always Kevin to consider." I had to describe Kevin's goatee and glasses before Candy and Karen even remembered him.

"The guy in sandals?" Karen asked. "That really does make him scary. Right, Jess?"

Okay, so men in sandals is one of my pet peeves. And much to my chagrin, Clarence, North Carolina is a city chock-full of men in sandals. Trust me, they all look ridiculous.

"What's a quiet, unassuming guy like that doing at the Wade On Inn?" I asked. "He looks like he belongs in a library."

"He does," Wilson said. "Kevin Cooper's a librarian at the University."

"And Melissa Purcell's a waitress at Hastie's Diner," Karen added as we moseyed our way back to Sullivan Street. "She invited us to visit her sometime."

Wilson squeezed my hand. "Don't even think about it," he said before addressing Karen. "Keep on Melissa's good side? She's been a regular out there for as long as Avis Sage. There might even be some history between her and Fritz."

"Right now she has her eyes on Spencer," I said, and Karen asked if any woman didn't.

"He is incredibly handsome," I agreed, but Candy begged to differ.

"He's creepy. He kept bragging about his wife's money, at the same time that he's hitting on me." She wrinkled her nose.

"Spencer Erring's married to a very rich woman," Wilson explained. "Dixie Wellington-Erring's family owns that chain of high-end grocery stores."

"Wellington Market?" I asked. "They have a great selection of champagne."

"So how was playing with Mr. Incredibly Handsome?"

I reported that Spencer's a terrible player and an even worse gambler. "He lost a lot of money tonight."

"His wife's money."

"The old ladies are also good at losing money," I said. "They seem to take great pleasure in it."

"Ethel Abernathy and Doreen Buxton." Wilson identified the old ladies and went on to name their sons, George Abernathy and Paul Buxton. "As in A and B Developers," he said ominously, and we all grimaced.

A and B is the largest real estate developer in the county. The company is always in the news or in court, fighting for permits to build this or that project. They seem bent on putting shopping malls and parking lots on every square-inch of open land.

"And you're right, Jessie," Wilson continued. "Ethel and Doreen are working on losing every nickel of the family fortunes before they die."

"They're just having fun," I argued.

"Those old ladies started showing up at that bar, and now we've got two murders on our hands."

"I can't picture them tossing people into Shinkle Creek," Karen said as we finally headed home.

"Ethel and Doreen are nothing but trouble," Wilson insisted. "Their sons built Cotswold Estates Retirement Home to keep them safe. But since Ethel still drives, the old ladies venture out to the Wade On Inn whenever the mood strikes."

"Who knows?" I said, feeling a sudden affection for the feisty old duo. "I might be tempted to do the same thing when I'm their age."

"Something I can look forward to," Wilson mumbled.

Chapter 9

Hard to imagine, but Puddles still had one more piddle left in him before we made it into our building. Even harder to fathom, Wilson still had the energy to nibble on my neck while I was trying to unlock my door.

I might have giggled in my complete state of exhaustion, but when he reached out to help me with the door handle, the image of him guiding Tiffany Sass's cue stick flashed before me.

I slapped his hand away and twirled around. "I am tired," I said firmly.

"We need to talk, Jessie." He pointed down the stairs where we had dropped off my neighbors. "Alone," he added.

I glanced at the stairwell. "Go to bed, Sweetie," I called down. And sure enough, I heard Candy close her door.

"You can make us some tea," I said. I led him inside and collapsed on a barstool at my kitchen counter. "I really am tired."

He put on the kettle while I slipped off my shoes and gestured for Snowflake to join me.

"Okay," I said as she hopped into my lap. "Let's talk."

"You can begin by explaining what possessed you to take along those two." Wilson again pointed downward.

"Oh, probably genius."

"Nice try, Jessie." He set the tea cups on the counter. "You want to imagine my reaction when Kim Leary called to inform me she never signed up for protecting three civilians? 'Three?' I said to her. 'What do you mean three?' But I had a pretty good idea who she was talking about even before she described your partners in crime."

He banged a teaspoon down. "'It's like trying to guard the Three Stooges,' Kim told me." He threw his hands in the air. "What the hell did you think you were doing?"

"Are you," I pointed across the counter, "actually accusing me," I pointed to my innocent self, "of causing problems? You had to know I wasn't going to set foot in the

Wade On Inn alone. Especially after you made a point of emphasizing how dangerous it is."

"We never agreed you should bring along an entourage."

"Come on, Wilson. It would have looked mighty strange for a woman my age to wander in there all by herself. It would look like I was interested in a lot more than a pool game."

I waited for an argument, but clearly he was unable to counter my very sound point.

I continued, "And even you can't deny Candy and Karen pulled their own weight tonight. I wouldn't have found out nearly as much on my own."

The teapot whistled, and we both jumped.

"I will agree," he said as he poured the water, "that your friends did a great job. Densmore and Sass will be busy for days following up on what they learned."

"Sass?"

"But having three of you to protect has my people a little on edge. Can't you see that, Jessie? I don't have the staff for this."

"Sass?"

"It makes Kim Leary's job a whole lot harder."

I sighed and gave up on getting any sort of response about Tiffany La-Dee-Doo-Da Sass.

"So this Kim person is the undercover cop who's watching out for us?" I asked. "She's cute as a button, by the way. I just love the Goldilocks disguise."

"Excuse me?"

"No one would ever suspect she's a cop. I felt extremely safe every time I peeked over at all those blond curls."

It suddenly occurred to me that Kevin the quiet guy, the supposed librarian, was also one of Wilson's people. Lord knows his gambling stakes were pathetic enough to be sponsored by the Clarence Police Department.

"I'm a bit less confident in Kevin Cooper," I said. "I don't see him protecting me if the culprit turns out to be Bobby or Henry. Or even Spencer for that matter."

Wilson slid my tea across the counter. "Kevin's a librarian, Jessie."

"Yeah, right."

"Would you stop worrying about who's there to protect you? That's my job, which you've now made a whole lot harder."

I assured my beau I would be extremely careful not to blow anyone's cover. "I won't even speak to them unless I have to." I winked at Snowflake. "I suppose I'll just have to pay attention to Spencer Erring and his lovely dimples instead."

"Which brings us to our good friend Candy." Wilson leaned on the counter. "What does Carter think about his girlfriend hanging out at the Wade On Inn?"

"They broke up again."

"What's that, like the tenth time?"

"Apparently Carter doesn't like dogs. But don't be such a chauvinist, Wilson. Boyfriend or not, Candy has every right to spend her evenings any way she sees fit."

"Candy Poppe causes a testosterone-induced riot wherever she goes. The woman needs a chaperone at the grocery store, for God's sake."

Okay, good point. Candy has been known to procure a date or two while browsing the produce aisle. I sipped my tea. And the dairy case.

"She had Karen and me chaperoning her tonight," I offered.

"Gee, I feel so much better now." Wilson stared at my rhinestone dog collar. "You're having way too much fun with this."

"I'm having too much fun? After that cozy little scene I witnessed between you and Tiffany, you're accusing me of having too much fun?" Wilson tried to speak, but I was on a roll. "If you're hiring chaperones, you might think about getting one for Tiffany Sass. Tiffany Sass!" I threw my hands up. "Sheesh!"

"What about Tiffany?" I kid you not—the man actually said those words.

"Do not toy with me, Wilson Rye. What's going on between you and that girl?"

"Come on, Jessie. You know there's nothing going on."

We locked eyes. And I must admit that those baby blues, intense even in un-intense moments, were a little unnerving. "I saw you groping her," I said. "Lord only knows what would have happened if I hadn't arrived when I did."

I looked at Snowflake, who was now sitting on the counter between us and following the argument. "You two were very close to getting yourselves arrested by one of your own officers." Wilson started chuckling. "For lewd and licentious behavior," I continued.

"Lewd and licentious? You're overreacting, Jessie."

I reminded my beau that I never overreact. "But I was tempted to take notes. You know, for my next book?" I squinted suspiciously. "And what kind of name is Tiffany Sass, anyway? She sounds like one of Adelé Nightingale's heroines, for Lord's sake."

"She has the looks for it."

I glared like I have never glared before.

"Jessie!" he said. "There is nothing going on between me and Sergeant Sass." He leaned across the counter, but I backed away from an attempted kiss.

"First of all." He stood back up. "The girl is young enough to be my daughter, as you keep reminding me. It would be completely unethical, even if I weren't her supervisor. What do you take me for?"

"Dammit," I mumbled.

"You have nothing to worry about." Again, he tried sounding sincere. "I'm in—" he hesitated.

I folded my arms and continued glaring. "You're in what, Wilson?"

He looked at Snowflake for support, but for once the cat seemed to be on my side. The two of us waited for an answer.

"I'm involved with you." His voice had gotten all husky. "Very involved," he added.

I decided to pet Snowflake.

"What the hell are you wearing?" he asked eventually.

I knew where his eyes were aimed, but I stifled a grin and jiggled my earrings. "They're Candy's. Do you like them?"

He frowned and continued staring at my chest.

"Remember we decided my diamonds would stand out too much at the Wade On Inn?" I asked.

"I'll tell you what's standing out, darlin.' And it ain't those earrings."

"You've seen this sweater before."

"That sweater," he reached across the counter and brushed my newfound curves with the back of his hand, "has never looked like this before."

I reminded my beau that women at the Wade On Inn tend to dress a little flashy. "So Candy suggested I wear my first-ever push up bra." I leaned forward. "Do you like it?"

He took a deep breath. "Lord, give me strength."

Eventually he looked up. "How much did you win tonight?"

"Not nearly enough to endure all the country music." I hopped down from the barstool. "I need a shower," I said and headed toward the bathroom.

"How much did you win, Jessie?" Wilson followed me. "I need to know for my report."

I turned around at the tub and pulled off my sweater. "You better not be reporting this, Captain Rye."

Chapter 10

Sarina Blyss couldn't sleep for thinking of her handsome stranger. She lay in bed, gazing at the ceiling, and envisioning the kind gentleman who had given her a ride into town earlier that week. Oh, how she wished their journey had never ended!

But alas, they had arrived in St. Celeste. And what with making Mrs. Dickerson's acquaintance, and being bustled into her dress shop, Sarina hadn't the opportunity to thank the stranger, or even learn his name. Indeed, by the time she thought to turn and bid the gentleman goodbye, his carriage had disappeared.

Sarina discovered the reason for such haste when Mrs. Dickerson called her attention to her ripped bodice. Oh dear! What must the handsome stranger have thought? Sarina was ever so grateful when the older woman offered to mend the damage.

The kind lady guided her behind a screen and instructed her to disrobe. And all the while she sewed, the seamstress sputtered indignantly about dastardly scoundrels who were wont to take advantage of every pretty girl they had the honor to meet.

Hidden behind the screen, Sarina stifled a giggle. But then she realized Mrs. Dickerson was referring to her own handsome stranger. The woman thought that the stranger had—. That he had—. Oh, dear!

Sarina protested vehemently and insisted her stranger had been ever so kind, but Mrs. Dickerson refused to listen, or to enlighten her as to who the gentleman might be. She returned Sarina's frock with a stern admonition to put the man completely out of her mind.

Sarina promised to try, and as she buttoned her dress, she was even so bold as to mention that she herself was an accomplished seamstress. And come to learn, Mrs. Dickerson was in search of an assistant!

Thus Sarina Blyss had found employment on her very first day away from home. Lodging also. For Mrs. Dickerson insisted she take up residence in the room above the dress shop, where she could keep a protective eye on her.

Sarina lay in bed, marveling at her vast good fortune. Despite her promise to Mrs. Dickerson, when she finally did close her eyes, her handsome stranger occupied her every dream.

***

I was filling Sarina's night with some scintillating dreams indeed when the buzzer from downstairs rang, and I remembered my own less than vast good fortune—namely Ian Crawcheck. I took a pre-emptive Advil and buzzed him in.

"What took you so long?" he asked when I opened my door.

I pointed him toward the bathroom, reminded him about Snowflake's litter box, and returned to my desk. But I had barely gotten Sarina back into the dress shop the next morning, where she was about to encounter the vile constable of St. Celeste and face criminal charges of all things, when my phone rang.

"I'm not disturbing you and Wilson, Jessie?" It was Candy.

"I only wish," I said. "Ian's here."

"Did you kiss and make up?" She gasped. "With Wilson, I mean. You seemed kind of mad last night."

I told my nosy neighbor not to worry.

"So you did kiss and make up?"

"Something like that," I mumbled. "Did you call for a particular reason, Sweetie? Aren't you at work?"

"I'm on break. We're having a sale on push-up bras. You should come see."

"No time," I said and explained that I needed to get some writing done. "What's up?"

"I have an idea about the Wade On Inn. You know, about the murders?"

Candy sounded excited, but I confessed I hadn't given the Wade On Inn much thought that morning. "I've been too preoccupied with the fascinating goings on in St. Celeste. Sarina Blyss's luck is about to run out. Her altogether evil sister-in-law Agnes is now claiming ownership of the golden necklace."

"Huh?"

"So Constable Klodfelder is going to arrest poor Sarina for thievery. Of her own jewelry!"

"Huh?"

"I'm still working out the details," I admitted, and bless her heart, Candy told me it sounded interesting.

"Kind of like Cinderella, but with an evil sister-in-law?"

"Exactly. But what about the murders? You think you've actually figured it out?"

"I do!"

I glanced at the closed bathroom door and stood up to pace. "You are kidding?" I said. "What? Who?"

"Well," she began. "It occurred to me today when I was helping Mrs. Marachini. She's one of my best customers, Jessie. She's really rich, and she comes in almost every week and buys, like, tons of stuff. She likes things with polka dots, especially red polka dots. I always save her sizes for her—"

"Candy," I interrupted before I learned the rich lady's cup size. "Does Mrs. Marachini have an idea about the murders?"

"Gosh, I don't think so. But she's always complaining about her no-good husband, Mr. Marachini. He wastes all her money. He gambles, just like Spencer."

The sound of Candy eating something reminded me it was almost time for lunch. I wandered over to the kitchen and started assembling a peanut butter sandwich.

"I take it Mr. Marachini loses his wife's money somewhere other than at the Wade On Inn?" I asked as I spread the Skippy.

"Well, yeah," she said. "But don't you see?"

"Not really."

"Like, duh! Wilson says Spencer's been losing his rich wife's money, right? So maybe he got mad at Fritz and Angela. You know, since he lost so much money to them? Or—" she waited for me to fill in the blank.

"Or." I did my best to think like Candy Poppe. "Or maybe Spencer's wife did it?"

"Exactly!" Candy shouted, and I almost dropped the jelly. "Since she was mad about the money. It makes perfect sense, doesn't it?"

I squinted at Snowflake. "Umm," I said. "I appreciate you thinking about this. But Dixie Erring hasn't even been to the Wade On Inn, has she? How would she know who Angela and Fritz were?"

"I bet she was mad enough to kill anyone she saw coming out of the bar." Candy sounded quite confident. "I bet she was waiting in the parking lot for them."

"Is she likely to continue on this killing spree?" I asked doubtfully. "I mean, why stop with those two, since Spencer's still gambling?"

Candy hesitated. "Gosh, I guess I didn't think of that."

"And now that he's losing money to me, am I in danger?"

"Gosh." She hesitated some more. "I sure hope not."

I told her not to be too alarmed. "We'll mention your ideas to Wilson tonight," I said as I sliced my sandwich. "I'm sure he'll be interested."

"What are you wearing tonight, Jessie?" I could almost hear Candy bounce over the phone. "Can I help with your makeup again?"

I agreed that was an excellent plan and reminded her to bring her jewelry, too. We hung up, and I looked at Snowflake.

"I am one brave woman," I told her. Ian emerged from my bathroom. "Very brave," I corrected myself.

Ian strolled over to the kitchen and curled his lip at the sandwich poised on the counter. "I see you've finally learned how to cook."

I blinked twice at his wet hair and ordered him to sit down and eat. "I just thought of another chore for you," I said.

And for this one, he would need his energy.

***

Dear Karen. She called just as Ian took his first bite. Perfect timing, since I needed a few minutes to decide how best to present his new task to him. Or more accurately, I needed a moment to think of a good lie.

"What's up?" I asked her as I poured Ian a glass of water.

"It's Bobby Decker, Jess."

"Oh?" I slid the glass across the counter.

"He and his family have too much history with the place," Karen continued. "It can't be just a coincidence that his ancestors used to own the Wade On Inn and half of Belcher Drive."

"Maybe?" I said.

"I'm thinking the good old boy routine is an act— Bobby's tougher than he lets on. Did you notice the chipped tooth? I bet he got that in a fight."

"Did he tell you that?" I noticed Ian studying me and turned my back to him.

"Bobby was sleeping with Angela Hernandez," Karen added.

"We're not sure about that," I reminded her.

"Yeah, but either way, I bet she had something on him. Something he didn't want other people to know."

"But what about—" I was going to say motive, but remembered the audience behind me, and cleared my throat. "What would his reason be for the other," I hesitated, "incident."

"For Fritz Lupo?" Karen thought a moment. "I don't know yet, but I bet we'll think of something. And Bobby found the bodies, right?"

"Yes," I said slowly.

"That's evidence against him right there. Remember what happened to you when Stanley died on your couch?"

"Don't remind me," I mumbled.

"Wilson almost arrested you," she reminded me. "Bobby must not have known cops are automatically suspicious of people who find bodies. I bet he thought he was throwing them off track. He planned it."

Ian asked for another sandwich. For a guy who has always insulted my inept cooking, he certainly was relishing his PB and J.

I got out some more bread and considered Bobby Decker. How could he have anticipated the bodies of Angela and Fritz floating downstream and landing precisely on his own property? It seemed rather unlikely.

I put the knife down and stared at my ex.

"Jess?" Karen asked. "Are you still there?"

I snapped out of it. "I'm preoccupied with *An Everlasting Encounter* right now," I lied. "But I'll keep your ideas in mind, okay? We can talk this evening."

"Let's just hope my feet hold up for another round of dancing. So, Jess." Karen shifted her tone of voice. "Did you and Wilson kiss and make up last night?"

"Everything's fine," I said firmly.

"So you did kiss and make up?"

I told her she was giving me a headache.

"Candy's the one who does that," she said and hung up.

***

"And you," I muttered to Ian.

"And me what?" he asked between bites.

"You give me headaches, but you'll make it up to me this afternoon." I winked at Snowflake, who was keeping her distance over on the windowsill. "I have an errand for you out at the Wade On Inn."

Ian choked.

"I'm working on a scene, you see."

"No," he squeaked. "I don't see." He gestured for more water, and I refilled his glass.

"This scene involves waterfalls, and I'm picturing the ones at Shinkle Creek." I tapped my chin and scowled up at the skylight—Adelé Nightingale pretending to contemplate this supposed scene. "I want my description to be accurate, of course, so I need you to take some photographs."

Ian put down his sandwich.

"I'll want quite a few shots, from as many different angles as you can manage without falling in," I continued.

"Especially of those largest falls near the edge of the parking lot. While you're at it, take a few pictures of the parking lot itself, okay? I'll want to get the perspective just right—"

"Are you crazy?" Ian interrupted. "Since when are your books based on accuracy? And what kind of idiot do you think I am? Risking my ass to get you some stupid pictures? Do you know what's happened out there? Someone's likely to shoot me just for the fun of it."

"A girl can hope," I mumbled, but then I noticed the sincere look of panic in Ian's beady little eyes.

I took a deep breath and gave him a pep talk, claiming no one would likely be hanging around there mid-afternoon. "Hopefully you can take your pictures and get away unnoticed."

"Why the hell can't you do this yourself?" he asked.

Okay, good question.

"Umm," I stalled. "I'm working on a deadline." That sounded plausible, so I kept going. "I need to get *An Everlasting Encounter* done by next week or my publisher will kill me. I simply don't have time for traipsing out to the Wade On Inn this afternoon."

"Oh, and I do?"

I tilted my head. "Business has picked up that much since yesterday, has it? It is the weekend, Ian."

He groaned and asked why he should do me this huge favor.

"Because you want to use my shower facilities."

"That's blackmail, Jessie."

"No, it's bargaining." I considered the bargain. "And to make the deal a little fairer, I'll make you lunch again tomorrow. That is, if you do this favor for me today."

Ian looked at his empty sandwich plate. "BLT's," he grumbled, and I actually smiled. Bacon, lettuce, and tomato sandwiches for lunch might be the only thing my ex and I could still agree on.

"Deal," I said.

"I want that apple-smoked bacon from Wellington's," he said, and this time I was the one who almost choked.

"Bacon from Wellington Market it is."

He squinted at me, considering the offer. "What am I supposed to tell anyone who sees me taking pictures out there? You know, before they shoot me?"

"I don't know. Tell them you're bird watching."

"Bird watching!?" he shouted as I scurried away in search of my binoculars.

I walked back to the kitchen and handed them over. "Do you have a camera?" I asked, and he held up his cell phone.

Chapter 11

Ian finally left, but I still had the disapproving glare from the cat to contend with.

"What?" I asked defiantly and set about making a sandwich for myself. I, too, needed to keep up my energy. Because, deadline or not, I certainly wasn't planning on writing all afternoon.

First stop on my extended walk? The University of Clarence Library. I climbed the slate stairs leading into the massive building, seriously doubting I would find Kevin Cooper anywhere therein. Librarian, my foot, I said to myself.

The expansive space I entered was filled with people wearing spectacles and sandals, and looking a lot like Kevin. But just as I suspected, the man himself was not at the reservation desk, or the circulation, or reference desks. I walked upstairs to make extra-double sure, as Candy would say, and that's where I spotted him.

I stopped short. Maybe he really was a librarian? But Kevin was not stationed at a counter doing anything librarianish. Instead he was sitting at one of the large tables provided for the students. I slipped behind the nearest bookcase and commenced spying.

He seemed to be transcribing something onto his laptop. I couldn't see it, but he must have had a tape recorder on his lap, which in turn was attached to the ear buds in his ears. He typed at a furious pace, but every so often he switched off the machine on his lap and stared up at the ceiling, deep in thought.

What the heck was he doing?

I grabbed a book from the nearest shelf, took the long route around the back of the stacks, and sat down at the table directly behind him. I kept my head down and my nose inside my miscellaneous book, but I was listening intently, hoping to hear what was coming from that machine attached to his ears.

Nothing but indecipherable chatter.

Well, that was altogether unacceptable. Eventually I got up the nerve to turn around. Ever so cautiously I glanced over his shoulder at his computer screen.

Aha! I caught a glimpse of Avis Sage's name just as Kevin turned to face me. The tips of our noses practically touched.

Oops.

He glanced down and turned off all of his doohickies. I waved at his ears, and he removed the wires.

"Why does Wilson have you working here?" I asked once he was wire-free. He made every effort to look perplexed as I continued, "Is hanging out in here part of your cover?" I pointed to his tape recorder. "Why aren't you doing that down at the station?"

"Huh?"

"The police station, Kevin. I know what you're doing."

"You do?"

"Well, yeah. You're transcribing what went on at the Wade On Inn last night." I again pointed to the tiny tape recorder. "I didn't realize Wilson wanted it verbatim like that."

"Wilson?" Kevin continued acting confused, but he wasn't much of an actor.

I rolled my eyes and waited patiently.

"Tessie, right?" he said. "Sorry, but it took me a minute to place you. We met at the bar last night?"

I continued rolling my eyes. "Yes, Kevin."

"How's your vacation going? Clarence must be a lot different than Honolulu."

"Honolulu?" I repeated before it dawned on me. "Oh! Oh yes—Honolulu." I winked and said I was enjoying my vacation. Then I assured him it was not my intention to get him in any trouble with his boss and stood up to leave.

"I'll see you tonight?" he asked.

"I'll be there."

He pointed to his apparatus. "You won't mention this to anyone, will you, Tessie?"

I may have giggled. "Of course not," I said. "I have no idea who you are and vice versa, correct?"

"Correct," he said and offered yet another puzzled expression.

***

Ricky Wellington's expression was one of glowing approval. His smiling face beamed down at me as I perused a display of chai tea near the cash register. No tea for me. I was already laden with a basketful of unnecessary and inordinately expensive treats for my friends and family, courtesy of Wellington Market.

Snowflake and Wilson's cats would be getting organic catnip toys, my mother, a jar of lavender hand cream, Karen, a box of chocolate and sea salt covered almonds, Candy, an eyeliner made from pure Egyptian kohl, whatever that was, Puddles, a jingle-bell ball of his very own, and Wilson, two packages of fresh tagliatelle noodles, which I hoped would live at my condo until he found some yummy use for them.

Ian, of course, could look forward to a couple of sandwiches made with his favorite bacon and prepared by his least favorite person. And I, a fancy bottle of unusual champagne. I would need it, what with serving my ex-husband lunch two days in a row.

Indeed, about the only thing I hadn't obtained during my shopping spree at Wellington Market was any insight on Spencer Erring or his in-laws. The photograph of Spencer's father-in-law near the checkout counter was not exactly enlightening. All I could say for certain was that Dixie Wellington-Erring's father was almost as handsome as her husband.

Ricky Wellington did look a bit smarter than his son-in-law, and mighty prosperous in his three piece suit, but really that was all.

I made it up to the cashier, and as I emptied my basket of goodies onto the counter, I attempted some less than idle chitchat. Pointing to the picture of Mr. Wellington I asked if they were a local family. "Wellington Markets is a southern chain, isn't it?"

"The company's based in Atlanta," the cashier informed me as he rang up my items. "Mr. Wellington lives there."

"But why did I think he has family in Clarence? A daughter, maybe?"

"And a son—Ricky, Jr."

"Ricky, Jr.?" I tried hiding my enthusiasm at learning something new, however small and inconsequential. "So there are two Wellington children in Clarence? Do they ever come in here?" I asked. "Do they work here?"

I stalled in finding my credit card and glanced around the store, deftly avoiding the annoyed looks from the people in line behind me.

The cashier told me the ridiculously high total and waited for me to slide my card. "The Wellingtons must get their groceries somewhere else," he said. "And they definitely don't work here."

"I wonder where they do work?" I tilted my enquiring head at the cashier, and then toward the shuffling and sighing people behind me, and then at the photo of Ricky Wellington, Sr.

The cashier waved a hand in front of me. "Paper or plastic, ma'am?"

***

"Goldilocks Whoever-She-Is seems way tougher than Kevin Cooper," I told Snowflake as I dressed for my second night at the Wade On Inn. I wiggled into another tight sweater, this one in pink. "But if he's carrying a gun along with that tape recorder, I guess I'll be safe enough."

I pressed my index finger to my lips when I heard Candy and Karen at the door and reminded the cat that none of us were supposed to know who the undercover cops were.

My friends were dressed much as they had been the previous evening, but this time Karen had control of the jewelry box, and Candy was carrying a Tate's shopping bag in addition to her cosmetic case.

I eyed the Tate's bag. "What's in there?" I forced myself to ask.

Candy jiggled the little pink bag before my eyes. "It's another push up bra, Jessie! I told you we were having a sale." She pointed to my chest. "You can't wear that one all week," she scolded and pulled out a gloriously red contraption.

"Kiddo's got some more gems in here, too." Karen held up the jewelry box and led the way to my dressing table.

***

They weren't exactly gems, but the enormous seashell earrings and matching necklace my friends selected for me that evening were priceless. And as we entered the Wade On Inn I could tell Henry the bouncer was duly impressed with my nautically-inspired ensemble.

Elsa Quinn noticed also. "Those from Hawaii?" She pointed to my ears as Candy ordered a pitcher of unpalatable beer.

"Eddie Munster goes Hawaiian," Karen mumbled.

"How do you know where I'm from?" I asked Elsa. It couldn't be a good thing if the regulars were talking about me?

"From Henry." She jerked her head toward the pool table. "He keeps me posted on what he hears over there."

"Have you ever been to Hawaii?"

"Heck no. I can't afford anything like that."

"You'd like it." I spoke with confidence, despite the fact that I had no idea what I was talking about.

"No kidding," Elsa agreed. "Sitting on a beach, drinking something other than beer and thinking about something other than my bank balance? Sounds good to me."

She knocked on the bar and left us, and I searched around for familiar faces. Goldilocks the Cop was in her assigned seat nursing a drink, and Mackenzie was at the opposite end of the bar.

She must have finished her homework for the weekend, since she had her head in a Kindle. I assumed she was reading a classic—the kind of intellectual and edifying stuff I had enjoyed when I was young and studious, just in a different format.

I turned back to Candy, who was pouring our beers and doing her best to ignore the red-headed guy who had sat down next her, apparently for the sole purpose of ogling her cleavage. She handed me a glass which I promptly handed off to Karen. If only the music at the Wade On Inn were so easy to avoid.

A glutton for punishment, I took a moment to listen to what sounded like a whole chorus of men gargling with gravel as they sang—and I use that verb loosely—about a tractor pull. I blinked twice and double-checked. Yep, a tractor pull.

"Who's this?" I asked.

"Boomerang!" You guessed it—Karen loves their stuff. She took a gulp of beer and handed me her half-full plastic cup. "Here goes nothing," she said and headed to the dance floor, where Bobby Decker was waiting with open arms.

Candy also got down to business. She held out an index finger and lifted the Red-Headed Ogler's chin, forcing him to look her in the eye. "My friend Tessie here, is a fantastic pool player," she told him. "Come see." And with that, she dropped his chin and hopped off her barstool.

"Let's go, Tessie," she urged. She grabbed our pitcher, and despite the red-head's lack of cooperation, the two us of meandered our way toward the pool table. This took a while, since Candy stopped at every other table along the way to brag about what a great player I am.

Exhibit A, I stood by silently while my friend gathered interest, and by the time we were halfway across the room, she had four men following us and grabbing for their wallets.

Here goes nothing, I thought to myself. But just as I was passing by Karen and Bobby, someone tapped my shoulder.

I turned around to witness an elaborate Fred Astaire-type tap dance maneuver. But this guy was no Fred Astaire. He was about twice the size of Bobby and sported a leather vest which I believe went out of style in the seventies. He had a bandana tied around his head, and various chains of unknown purpose hanging from his person. Expert sleuth that I am, I deduced he was a biker.

"Wanna dance?" he asked. "It's Boomerang!" Mr. Leather and Chains pointed to the ceiling and did another little jig, promptly toppling over the Drunken Dancer.

I mumbled a "No, thank you," and together we helped the poor woman up. While she staggered back into swaying position, I escaped to the pool table.

Chapter 12

Evidently it was the night to stroke my middle-aged, menopausal ego. First the attention from Mr. Leather and Chains, and now this—Spencer Erring actually looking up from his game against Avis Sage to flash half a dimple in my direction.

"That man is way too handsome," I said to the old ladies as I sidled on over.

Doreen fanned herself with two fifties. "Spencer is the spitting image of Harmon when he was that age."

"Harmon was Ethel's husband, correct?"

"Her gorgeous-to-a-fault dead husband," Doreen elaborated.

"Doreen knows all about Harmon's faults," Ethel said, and the two old ladies laughed with their usual gusto.

"Spencer's especially fetching when he's bending over the pool table," Doreen said. "His backside is even better than Harmon's."

Despite the fact that I had never seen Harmon's derriere for accurate comparison, I chose to agree with Doreen.

"Spence is too young for you," Melissa informed me. She turned to Doreen and Ethel. "And he's way too young for you guys."

"But let me guess," Ethel said. "He's just right for you?"

Melissa shrugged. "We're both forty. It's perfect."

"Perfect," Kevin grumbled. He took off his glasses and began the cleaning routine. Kevin was no match for Spencer, however, and all us women turned to watch the game.

Spencer lost to Avis and commenced flirting with Candy. Bless her heart, she shooed away all the men she had gathered earlier and gave him her undivided attention.

"He's too old for your friend." Melissa was still on topic. "He should know better by now."

"Oh?" I said. "Does Spencer have a thing for younger women?"

"Don't they all?"

We watched as Candy pulled a twenty from her cleavage and brushed the tip of Spencer's finely chiseled nose with it. They both giggled, and I marveled at the drastic improvement in my friend's acting skills since the previous evening.

I sighed dramatically. "The man in my life is smitten with a younger woman," I said. "She's even younger than Candy."

"Smitten?" Melissa patted my shoulder and waved to Avis. "Tessie's back. She wants to play me a match."

The crowd groaned, and it was decided I should play Avis instead. I stepped up to the table, and we agreed on a match to five for fifty.

"You've been playing here a long time?" I asked him while we waited for the railbirds to conduct their own wagering.

"I've called this table home since way back when, Miss Tessie."

I knew the answer, but asked anyway, "Did you ever go out on the road, sir?"

"A long time ago. But the old man's not up to travelling anymore." He patted his chest. "The ticker's no good."

Old sharks with faulty tickers. I swallowed hard and tried to ignore the stinging in my eyes.

"Now, don't you be worrying about the old man." Avis was studying me. "Doctor gave me some medicine."

He patted his chest again, and we stepped forward for the lag, which he won. Melissa volunteered to rack, and while she did the honors, I brought the conversation around to Fritz Lupo.

"Did the guy who just died ever go out on the road?" I asked. "I understand he was a good player?"

"The Fox was talking about travelling again." Avis smiled fondly at the pool table. "Fritz was lucky."

"Oh?"

"I don't mean no disrespect, Miss Tessie, but if he had to die, he picked the best way. Have a good night at the table and die right afterwards."

"So, he played well that night?"

Avis nodded and broke. He sunk the one ball and ran the whole table, a repeat of our first game the previous night. This time though, I made use of my leisure to ask around about Fritz. Apparently, he had won over a thousand dollars the night he was killed.

"Considering how drunk he was, it was impressive," Ethel said.

"Drunk?" I gave Candy a meaningful look, and she got the idea.

"Gosh, I thought people don't do well if they drink too much." She batted her eyelashes at Spencer, and he shrugged his broad shoulders.

"Fritz was even worse off than her." He pointed to the Drunken Dancer. The poor woman had once again fallen over, and Bobby was helping her up. "Melissa had to help him out."

Melissa agreed. "Fritz was a goner all right."

"You brood of vipers!" Henry Jack exclaimed as he popped over from his post near the stairs.

He waved his Bible aloft. But as he listed a whole smorgasbord of sins, including fornication, theft, adultery, avarice, deceit, licentiousness, pride, and folly, I had to wonder just how many vices were actually represented by the gang at the Wade On Inn. Apparently I wasn't the only one confused by all the options.

Henry looked around at the perplexed faces of his audience. "Pastor Muckenfuss says intemperance is the work of the devil," he concluded, simplifying matters considerably.

Avis Sage thanked him kindly for the sentiment.

"Would you stop encouraging him?" Melissa scolded. "Next thing we know he'll have Pastor Muck-In-Face in here preaching to us himself."

"No, Mel." Henry shook his head vigorously. "Pastor Muckenfuss says the Wade On Inn is my responsibility." He again lifted his Bible, and was threatening to regale us with some more sins, when Candy stepped forward.

"My friend Karen's looking for a new dance partner," she told him, and as if on cue, the music switched.

"It's Lila Dewees," Henry said. "She's my favorite!"

Candy smiled sweetly and walked him arm in arm onto the dance floor. She left him in Karen's capable hands and continued onward, landing herself back at the bar and next to Mackenzie. Wilson might insist Candy Poppe needs a chaperone twenty-four-seven, but she certainly was handling the Wade On Inn crowd with aplomb.

***

Meanwhile, I played some pool. I took game two and three of the match. But as Mr. Sage worked on clearing the table in our fourth game, I returned to Melissa and the topic of Fritz Lupo.

"Avis tells me Fritz Lupo was planning a road trip," I said casually.

"No way," she said.

"Oh, yeah, Mel." I jumped and turned around and into Bobby Decker's chest. "He was gonna take Angela with him."

I frowned. "Did Angela play that well?"

"No, she did not." That was Melissa.

"I think Angela was a good little player," Ethel said, and Doreen tapped her cane in agreement.

"Good enough to go out on the road, though? I've never had the nerve to do it myself," I lied.

Bobby grinned and enlightened me that not all pool-players are as cautious as I.

"Fritz and Angela had themselves a plan," Avis said. He sunk the nine ball and stepped back for me to rack.

I held off. "So the two people who got killed had plans to leave town together?" I feigned shock. "Do the cops know about this? I mean, it sounds like it could be important."

"Oh, for God's sake," Spencer said. "Angela was not about to take off anywhere with Fritz Lupo. Bobby just wants it to look that way."

Bobby twisted his cowboy hat. "I keep telling you guys Angela wasn't really interested in me. Jeepers, it was just a joke." He fumbled with his hat so much it toppled off his head.

"Now I'm really confused," I admitted honestly as I finally began racking.

Kevin Cooper leaned over and handed Bobby his stupid hat. "Angela wasn't going anywhere," he told me.

Bobby swung around to Kevin. "How would you know?"

"I know a few things." Kevin spoke quietly, but with certainty, and I wondered what else the Clarence cops knew that Wilson was keeping from me. For instance, you would think this road trip Fritz and Angela had planned would have been worthy of mention?

Avis Sage looked up from breaking. "I told the Fox to go along while he still could. Take it from the old man, Miss Tessie, have fun while you're young."

Speaking of having fun, Karen took a break from the dance floor about the time I won the match against Avis and was negotiating a new match against Bobby.

I swept by her. "Bobby," I whispered.

She caught on. She held up a twenty and bet it on the wannabe cowboy, and Melissa wasted no time in wagering her own money on me. "You should be ashamed of yourself," she scolded Karen. "Betting against your friend."

Karen said something about being loyal to her dance partner, and Bobby tipped his hat to her before handing it to Ethel.

Lo and behold, Bobby won the game. I reminded him that Melissa would like to play. While the two of them bickered about the details, I caught Karen's eye and tilted my head toward Spencer.

We drifted over in his direction, but he didn't even notice, since he was too busy watching Candy. She was still at the bar, deep in conversation with Mackenzie.

Karen stepped straight into his line of vision, and asked him point blank what a nice guy like him was doing in a place like the Wade On Inn.

"I like the music."

"No, Spencer, I like the music." She tapped his chest. "You don't seem like the Wade On Inn type."

"And these people do?" He waved toward the old ladies and Kevin.

"What are you doing here?" Karen asked again. "And don't tell me it's because of The Feeters."

Okay, I just had to interrupt. "The Feeters?"

"Rupert and Bunny." She pointed to the dance floor but kept her eye on Spencer. "I love their stuff."

Karen and I stood in front of Spencer, arms folded, and pretended to comprise a formidable front.

He held up his hands in mock protest. "I just like it here, ladies. I like the company."

Kevin Cooper guffawed. "What company you talking about?" he asked, and Spencer's head snapped.

"All the company. I like everyone here."

"Yeah, right." Kevin took off his glasses to better smirk. "Your wife okay with that?"

Spencer hesitated and then spit it out. "Dixie and I are separated, if you must know."

"She still footing your gambling bill?" Kevin asked, and I bit my lip. Why, oh why, was this cop provoking people? He was on the verge of blowing his cover, for Lord's sake.

"Spence, honey." Doreen tapped his bottom with her cane. "If Dixie ever cuts you off for good, you just call on me. Money, booze, sex? Name it and it's yours."

"Would you stop it with other women's husbands, Doreen?" That was Ethel. She had decided to try on Bobby's hat, and while everyone was busy laughing, Spencer escaped to the bar.

Chapter 13

Thank you, God, it was The Grateful Dead night at The Stone Fountain. We entered the bar just as Jerry Garcia was trucking home, back where he belonged.

I, too, would have felt at home, but Wilson was missing. I checked the booths, I checked the bar, I braced myself and checked the pool table. The good news? He wasn't entwined with Tiffany thereupon. The bad news? He wasn't there at all.

I declined a game with Kirby and took my seat at the bar between Candy and Karen. Lieutenant Densmore arrived just as Matthew's new bartender Charlie located the Korbel.

"That goes on Captain Rye's tab," Russell instructed him.

"And where is Wilson?" I took my champagne from Charlie and turned to face the Lieutenant.

Russell backed up a step. "Umm," he said.

I raised an eyebrow. "Umm?"

"Is Wilson okay?" Candy asked.

Russell backed up even further, his eyes darting back and forth between the three of us. "As far as I know?" he said finally.

"Well then, where is he?" Karen demanded. "I'm tired, Russell. I need to go home."

Charlie came back with her Corona and started pouring. "You guys looking for Captain Rye?" Russell was waving at him, but bless his oblivious heart, Charlie kept talking. "He was here earlier, Jessie. But they left a while ago."

"They?" My voice was exceedingly calm. No, really.

"He and Tiffany," Charlie chirped. "Actually, it was quite a while ago." He handed Karen her glass and walked away.

I blinked at Russell over the top of my pince-nez.

"Umm," he said.

I may have glared, but considered it undignified to inquire any further about my no-good, gallivanting, soon-to-be ex-beau, or Miss Tiffany La-Dee-Doo-Da Sass.

Russell must have noticed my self-restraint. He relaxed a bit and suggested we take a booth and chat.

Candy hopped down from her seat and said that gosh, she had a lot to report. Karen yawned and allowed Russell to steer her in the right direction. I grabbed the Korbel bottle and followed.

Once we got situated, he turned to me. "Are you okay, Jessie? You don't look so good."

"Watch it, Russell."

Candy scolded me for scolding Russell. "I don't think he meant it like that, Jessie." She looked at the Lieutenant. "Did you?"

"Not at all," he hastened to defend himself. "But I know you're tired. The Captain appreciates how hard y'all are working."

I rolled my eyes at the thought of Wilson Rye, the ever-appreciative, and Karen yawned yet again.

"I have got to go get some sleep," she said. "Let me tell you what I learned so I can go home?" Lieutenant Densmore nodded, and she informed him she had worked on Bobby Decker and Henry Jack.

"Henry's real excited by that Zion Tabernacle place," she said. "He's inspired by Pastor Muckenfuss."

Russell grimaced. "That's not good," he said. "I've been checking into Muckenfuss."

I asked what he had learned, but he ignored me and told Karen to continue.

"Don't quote me on this," she said. "But I'm pretty sure Henry's got a crush on Elsa Quinn."

"Why?"

"I asked him why he works at the Wade On Inn if he's so worried about sin, and he said he owes it the Elsa. He's worked there since way back before Lester Quinn got shot." Karen offered each of us a meaningful glance. "He blames Fritz Lupo."

"Oh?" I asked.

"Oh, yeah. Henry told me point blank Fritz Lupo was the one who should have died that night. His exact words."

"I think I have something horrible to say." Candy began chewing her knuckle.

"Go ahead," Russell encouraged her.

"Well," she sang. "Mackenzie thinks so, too."

"Thinks so, too, what?" Karen asked.

"Mackenzie blames Fritz for her father's death. She pretty much told me exactly what you just said, Karen. That Fritz should have died that night instead of Lester." Candy worked on her poor knuckle. "She's pretty mad about it."

"How mad?" Russell asked suggestively.

"Oh, come on," I protested. "I can't believe that innocent child is a killer. She's way too young to remember the night her father died, even if she was there."

Candy spoke to her champagne glass. "Teenagers aren't always so innocent, Jessie."

I blinked twice. Candy Poppe knew from whence she spoke.

She continued, "When we were talking about the guys Angela liked, Mackenzie said Angela and Fritz were friends, but that she herself hated the guy."

Karen interrupted and asked if she could finish up and go home.

Russell took out a notepad and jotted something down as he spoke. "Did Henry Jack give you anything else, Karen? Maybe on Elsa Quinn?"

"When I asked him if he and Elsa were involved, he got real nervous. He twirled me around kind of fast and we bumped into this woman who dances all by herself."

"She falls down a lot, huh?" Candy said.

"It's sad," Karen agreed. "We had a heck of a time getting her back on her feet. Then the music changed to Chester Straney, and we got into a line dance. I lost track of Henry."

"What about Bobby Decker?" Russell asked. "You danced with him, too?"

"Bobby was kind of interesting." Karen took a sip of her beer.

I smiled at Russell and gestured towards my friend. "Tell Wilson he should hire this woman."

"I'll bring her an application tomorrow night."

"No thanks." She stifled another yawn. "Cops stay up way too late."

"Bobby Decker?" Russell reminded her.

"He's unemployed, but boy he has big dreams. He's planning on buying back the Wade On Inn and all the property his great-grandfather lost to Elsa's family and turning it into a ranch."

"That explains the cowboy hat," I said.

"But the guy's broke, Jess. Like, completely."

"So how does he think he can do this?" Candy asked.

"That's just it, Kiddo. He can't. But he says Elsa's about to sell the place real cheap. Bobby's sure the bank will be so impressed with this dude ranch idea that they'll loan him gobs of money." Karen yawned for good measure. "He also thinks his mother will be so proud of him she'll move back to Clarence."

"Is the mother an issue?" I asked.

"She is to Bobby."

"Mrs. Decker moved to Charlotte a few years ago to be near her other son," Russell informed us. "The one with a job, and a wife and children."

Speaking of children, I had just spotted Tiffany Sass in the doorway. Tagging along behind her was my soon-to-be ex-beau.

***

Tiffany caught sight of us and smiled all pleasant-like. Wilson, on the other hand, took one look at the expression on my face and lost his grin.

Candy might have picked up on the tension, but poor Karen was too busy falling asleep to notice my love life unraveling before her half-open eyes.

Wilson glanced down at her. "Walk Ms. Sembler home?" he asked Russell.

Russell said it would be a pleasure, and the two of them departed as Wilson took the seat next to me. He then spoke to Tiffany. "You can head home, too, Sass. We've had a long day."

I tried to ignore the implications of that unsettling statement. I also tried to ignore Tiffany, who lingered over me for who knows what reason.

"I like your seashell jewelry, Jessie." The girl had yet to stop smiling. "Pinks and pastels suit you."

Pinks and pastels suit me? I either smiled vaguely or curled my lip. Who really knows?

Candy mumbled something about it being her jewelry, and after an excruciating exchange of fashion tips between the two young women, Tiffany finally left.

This, of course, was when Wilson got around to noticing me. He sat back and took a long, hard gander at my outfit. Apparently he was not all that enamored with the seashells. I kicked him under the table, and he snapped out of it.

"Did you have an interesting evening?" he asked.

"Did you?" I asked back.

Wise-woman Candy Poppe interrupted us. "Karen did great tonight," she told Wilson. He tore his frown from me as Candy reiterated what Karen had learned from Bobby and Henry.

"What's the deal with Pastor Muckenfuss?" I asked. "Russell didn't tell us."

"Take the title 'Pastor' with a grain of salt. Theodore Muckenfuss is a high school dropout, has zero theological training, and has spent about half his life in jail."

"How come he has his own church?" Candy asked.

"Take the word 'church' with a grain of salt, too," Wilson said and explained that the Zion Tabernacle was located in an abandoned warehouse down the road from the Wade On Inn and very close to Hastie's Diner. "The only thing Muckenfuss did to establish this church was stick a sign out front—a piece of plywood with a cross spray-painted on it."

He shook his head. "He's pulled this stunt before. He ran one of these pseudo-churches in New Orleans until Hurricane Katrina hit. Then he moved to Orlando."

"What brought him here?" I asked.

"It's more like what drove him out of Orlando. He hightailed it out of Florida after three teenagers in his congregation shot out the windows of a Jewish synagogue."

Candy mumbled a "Gosh," and I added an "Oh, my Lord."

"Yep." Wilson nodded. "Muckenfuss told those kids it was up to them to make their city safe for Christians."

I cringed. "The guy's an anti-Semite?"

"He's anti-everyone, Jessie. From what Densmore's gathered, Muckenfuss hates Jews, immigrants, gays, blacks, Catholics, Hispanics, Asians, working women. You name it."

"Was Angela Hernandez an immigrant?" Candy asked.

"Second generation. And that's a good question."

I cringed again. "Are you suggesting Muckenfuss brainwashed Henry Jack into killing people because he disapproves of Hispanics?"

Wilson insisted it had possibilities and helped himself to my champagne.

"We need to warn Karen," I told Candy as Wilson replenished my glass. "Next to Bobby Decker, Henry's her favorite dance partner."

Wilson addressed Candy. "What about the cowboy? Did you ask Mackenzie about him?"

"Mm-hmm. We talked about boys, just like you said to, and Mackenzie thinks Bobby's real cute. But she swore to God and crossed her heart that Angela didn't like Bobby."

"So he was lying about their fling?"

"Mm-hmm." Candy bounced a bit. "But Angela did have a boyfriend at the Wade On Inn."

"Who?" Wilson and I asked in unison.

She sighed. "I'm still working on that, okay? It was an older man. That's all Mackenzie would say."

Wilson mentioned that every man at the Wade On Inn would seem old to Mackenzie, and I suggested in might have been Fritz Lupo.

"The two of them had plans to go out on the road and do some hustling together."

Wilson raised an eyebrow. "So those afternoon lessons he was giving her had a purpose?"

"Apparently so. Although not everyone agrees on that. Bobby and Avis Sage think they were about to head off, but Melissa, Spencer, and Kevin insisted Fritz and Angela had no plans to go anywhere." I sipped my champagne. "You need to talk to Kevin, Wilson."

"Why's that?"

"Because he's about to blow his cover. He was purposely provoking people tonight. That's not how an undercover cop should act."

"The quiet guy in glasses is a cop?" Candy was incredulous.

"Oh, yeah," I answered without thinking. "So what do you think, Sweetie? Was Fritz Angela's older man?"

"No. Mackenzie says Melissa's the one who liked Fritz."

"Melissa? But she has a crush on Spencer."

Wilson interrupted and suggested we move on from the love triangles. "Anything else from the Quinns?" he asked Candy.

"Angela saved Elsa from trouble with the IRS," she said. "Did you know that, Wilson? Angela was this great bookkeeper, and she helped Elsa so she wouldn't have to sell the Wade On Inn."

"So Bobby Decker might be telling Karen the truth?" I asked. "That Elsa's on the verge of bankruptcy?"

"No, Jessie," Candy corrected me. "Angela fixed things."

"But what if Elsa can't find a replacement for her?" Wilson asked. "Elsa Quinn's a disaster at finances. Densmore's checked the tax records."

A fleeting thought of my ex-husband's new bookkeeping business crossed my mind, but I dismissed it. Ian could use the work, but I was growing rather fond of Elsa.

I took a deep breath. "So why can't Tiffany Sass be given these boring jobs, like background checks on Pastor Muckenfuss and tax checks on Elsa Quinn?"

"Because, Jessie, Denmsore lives to uncover that kind of information. Sergeant Sass has other talents."

You can imagine my glare?

Chapter 14

"Speaking of talent." Wilson held my eye. "How much did you win tonight?"

"I did quite well. Thank you for asking."

"You learn anything interesting?"

"Fritz Lupo won a ton of money the night he got shot."

"And he was drunk," Candy added.

"So where's the money now?" Wilson asked.

I thought about it. "No one mentioned that. It wasn't found with Fritz?"

"Nope."

"Do you think he was robbed?" I asked, suddenly intrigued by the money.

"I've said all along this was about a bet gone bad."

I sighed. "You were right about Avis Sage, too. He told me he has a bad heart. He's content, though."

"Content as long as he's winning," Wilson mumbled. "What else?"

"Well, Ethel and Doreen still puzzle me. There's some odd history between those old ladies. Something other than their sons being business partners."

"Tiffany Sass and I paid a visit to A & B Developers," Wilson said.

"Oh? I'm surprised they were open on a Saturday night."

He ignored the sarcasm. "Abernathy and Buxton could be involved in this mess."

"You think they killed people just to scare their mothers away from the Wade On Inn?"

"A and B are brutal about getting what they want," he reminded me.

"But murder?" Candy asked, and he shrugged.

"We had to check it out," Wilson explained. "But George Abernathy and Paul Buxton both have alibis for the nights in question." He looked back and forth between Candy and me. "Anything else?

"Melissa Purcell's hard to read," I offered. "She's so testy, but at the same time, she seems desperate for friends. She adores Spencer."

Candy sat forward. "Should we tell him my theory now, Jessie?" She didn't wait for my answer, but plunged on in and announced that Spencer's wife did it.

"Did what?" Wilson asked.

"Like, duh! The murders! You know, since Spencer gambles so much? I bet his wife is pretty mad about it. Just like Mrs. Marachini."

"Who?"

"The polka dot lady," I explained, and before he could even think of a response to that, I suggested we stick to Spencer's wife.

Wilson surprised me when he told us he had already checked into Dixie Wellington-Erring. "She has an alibi. At least for the second night in question."

"She's thrown Spencer out," I said.

"He told you this?"

"Oh, yes. And if you ask me, it's no wonder. The man is a professional flirt."

Candy groaned. "All the women like Spencer except me."

"You either love him or you hate him," I said.

"What about you?" Wilson asked me. "Do you love him?"

I raised an eyebrow. "Never fear. Spencer's too young for me."

"Everyone but Avis Sage is too young for you, darlin.'"

***

"So enlighten me, Captain Rye," I said as I unlocked my door a bit later. "Where were you and Tiffany tonight?"

I folded my arms and waited, determined to hold my ground on the threshold with much more resolve than I had shown the previous night.

Wilson shook his head. "Can't tell you that."

"Can't or won't?"

"Both. I don't trust you."

I guffawed. "You don't trust me? Now that's rich."

"I'll tell you what's rich—Ian Crawcheck being spotted in the Wade On Inn parking lot this afternoon." He reached for my elbow and moved us inside. "We need to talk."

I mouthed a four-letter word to Snowflake and allowed my soon-to-be ex-beau to steer me into the kitchen before pulling away.

"Let me guess." I took a seat at the counter. "You have someone staking out the parking lot?"

"Very good." He turned on the stove and slammed my poor tea kettle onto the burner. "Officer Richardson called in that some fool pretending to be bird watching was out there taking pictures of the premises."

"I told Ian to be discreet," I mumbled.

It was Wilson's turn to use that four-letter word. "Richardson didn't recognize him. But he ran the plates and called me." Wilson slammed the cups onto the counter. "'Should I arrest him?' he asks me."

I grimaced. "Did he?"

"Nooo. Crawcheck should already be in jail for the crap he pulled last summer. But no, we did not arrest him."

He took a very long, deep breath. "What were you thinking, Jessie? And what the hell does your ex-husband know about what's going on at the Wade On Inn? And your involvement in it?"

"Nothing," I said, and before he popped an artery, I related the story I had used to lure Ian out there. "Trust me, Wilson. He really doesn't know what I've been up to. He has no idea he was helping with our investigation."

"Our investigation!" Wilson practically shouted the 'our.'

"Shall we check out his pictures?" I asked. "I'm sure he sent them, but I haven't had a chance to look."

I hopped off the barstool and started moving toward my computer, but Wilson told me to stop. "You're a little scary. You know that?"

"Do you want to see the pictures or not?" I asked from the middle of the room.

"Not." He beckoned me to sit back down and handed me my cup. "Believe it or not, my people took lots of photos themselves. I know what the crime scene looks like, for God's sake."

"But I don't," I argued. "I haven't had a good chance to study that spot where the bodies were dumped. It's always dark by the time I get out there."

Wilson continued frowning as I continued arguing. "I wanted to see if it would be possible for an old person to push two bodies into the waterfalls."

"I already told you, Jessie. It is possible. Why can't you believe me?"

I mumbled some lame excuse about liking to get a clearer idea on my own.

"What's the deal with you and your ex-husband, anyway?" he continued with the pesky questions.

I petted Snowflake, who had joined us at the counter. "I suppose you know about his new business? And its location?"

"I do now. I did some checking after his stunt this afternoon. Tell me why he's set up shop in your backyard."

I had no idea, but I bit the bullet and explained the showering arrangement. Despite Wilson's huffs and puffs, I was even honest enough to mention the lunch I had served Ian that day, and the lunch I was planning to give him the next.

I did, however, consider it wise to skip the details about the fancy bacon from Wellington Market. I also decided to leave it to some other time before presenting Wilson with the goodies I had purchased for him and his cats. It was, perhaps, not the best moment to mention my excursion to Wellington's?

"How long is this deal going to last?" Wilson pointed toward my bathroom. "I'm not all that crazy about Ian Crawcheck running around naked in here."

Okay, so I may have grinned. Just a little. Then I assured my beau I had no intention of ever seeing Ian in the buff again. "And don't worry. His lowdown, conniving, and altogether despicable new wife Amanda is bound to ask him to come home sooner or later."

I mumbled something about how late it was getting and led Wilson to the door, where he couldn't resist the urge to scold me one more time about my status as an amateur and a civilian.

"Concentrate on the pool table," he said. "Leave the rest of the investigation to me."

"To you and Tiffany Sass, you mean. Where were you two tonight?"

"I'm not telling you that, Jessie. The less you know, the better."

"This, after I've been so forthright about Ian. Goodnight, Captain." I tried to shut the door, but he stopped me.

"What?" I snapped.

"I was just going to thank you for doing such a great job of disguising yourself." He glanced at the top of my head.

"Make one comment about my hair, Wilson Rye, and I swear to God, I will never speak to you again."

"No really, Jessie. It's great." He continued staring and frowning. "But—"

"But what?"

"Well," he sang. "With your hair like that you remind me of someone." He squinted. "Someone from an old sitcom, maybe?"

I closed my eyes and prayed for strength. "Eddie Munster?"

"That's it!" he exclaimed and clapped his hands.

When I opened my eyes he was pointing to my necklace. "Eddie Munster goes Hawaiian," he said.

I shut the door.

***

"What?" I asked to the cat as I made a bee-line for my computer.

She was watching me with those baleful gold eyes, no doubt wondering what possible excuse I could have for treating the charming Wilson Rye with such disdain.

"The man's been out gallivanting with Tiffany La-Dee-Doo-Da Sass all night. I have a right to know where they were."

I pointed to the computer and sat down. And I had a right to check out Ian's pictures. After all, if he risked life, limb, and arrest to get the stupid shots, the least I could do was take a look.

While the internet booted up, I took off Candy's seashells and placed them on the windowsill. Snowflake jumped up and tapped at them while I studied the photos Ian had e-mailed.

Unfortunately, Wilson was right. It would probably require some strength to toss a body over the safety railing which separated the Wade On Inn parking lot from the depths of Shinkle Creek. But almost anyone would be capable of shoving a dead body underneath that barrier. Even Avis Sage. Or even Ethel, or Doreen.

So much for narrowing down the list of suspects. "Well darn," I said to Snowflake and closed my computer.

But then a new idea occurred to me, and I called my mother.

It was after one a.m., but Mother is a night owl. She picked up on the first ring, and I immediately told her there was nothing wrong. She may stay up until all hours, but she knows I usually do not.

"But something is wrong, Honeybunch," she argued. "Is Wilson okay? Snowflake?"

I thought about my soon-to-be ex-beau and lied, "Everyone's fine, Mother. But I do have a favor to ask of you. A big favor."

Chapter 15

The dress shop was spinning. Or at least that's how it felt to Sarina Blyss. The stricken girl trembled in stunned silence as Constable Klodfelder listed the criminal charges against her. Not only was Agnes Blyss claiming ownership of the golden necklace, but she was also insisting Sarina did not even exist!

The Constable turned his corpulent face to Mrs. Dickerson and explained that her new seamstress was not at all who she claimed to be, but was in truth one Daisy O'Dell—a lowly servant girl, formerly in the employ of the Blyss estate. According to Agnes, Sarina, nay Daisy, had not only left her position without giving proper notification, but had also absconded with the Blyss family's most valued possession!

The Constable pointed a stubby finger at the prized jewelry, and with no further warning, pounced. Sarina recoiled in horror but was unable to stop the vile man from yanking her treasure from her. Shocked and indignant, she clutched the empty spot where her necklace had been while the Constable leered at her trembling bosom.

He jammed the trinket into the pocket of his soiled trousers, admonished the girl not to give him any trouble, and propelled her out the door of the dress shop.

Sarina felt the man's beefy paw grope her bottom, but despite such rough handling, she somehow found the strength halt in the doorway and proclaim her innocence to her employer.

But Mrs. Dickerson only sputtered about how difficult it was to find honest help these days. She watched without protest as the Constable threw Sarina into the back of his cattle cart and drove away.

Sarina blinked back tears as the figure of Mrs. Dickerson receded into the background. Indeed, the ordeal was so terrifying that the lovely damsel could but assume she was being taken to the gallows!

***

Just how the dashing Duke of Luxley was going to deliver Sarina from such a fate was something Adelé Nightingale had yet to decide. Luckily my mother's arrival saved me the trouble. I buzzed her in and rushed downstairs to help with her luggage.

"Goodness gracious, Honeybunch. What happened to your hair?" she offered by way of greeting.

I told her it was nice to see her too and led her to the elevator.

"Thank Karen for me?" she said as we rode up.

The elevator in our building had been forever on the blink. But after some issues a few weeks earlier, Karen finally got herself licensed to repair it. Even though I always use the stairs, I was happy the thing was in operation for my eighty-two year old mother.

She found a seat on the couch and greeted Snowflake while I made tea. When I glanced over from the kitchen, the cat was rolling around on her back, purring in ecstasy as my mother rubbed her tummy.

"How was the drive?" I forced myself to ask.

Mother didn't answer, which could mean almost anything—that she didn't hear me, that her habitual lead foot had almost caused an accident or two, that she had acquired a speeding ticket, or that her drive up from her home in South Carolina had been uneventful. Trust me, that last possibility was the least likely scenario.

"I'm afraid I was half asleep when you called last night," she said. "Tell me again what you need me to do, Jessie?"

I repeated the plan. My mother was going to infiltrate The Cotswald Estates Retirement Home and get the lowdown on Ethel Abernathy and Doreen Buxton.

"There's something fishy about those two," I said as I poured our tea. "It may have something to do with Ethel's deceased husband Harmon, but they're being very cagey about it. Wilson's concerned about their sons also."

"You met Ethel and Doreen at this Wade On Inn establishment?"

I handed her a cup and sat down with Snowflake between us. "I'm not sure I would call the Wade On Inn an

'establishment.' Two people have been shot out there."
Mother grimaced and I continued, "Wilson insists the
murders are related to a bet that went wrong at the pool
table. But I'm wondering if the history between the old
ladies might be relevant."

"And you say Avis Sage plays there? I can't believe
you've run into him after all these years." Mother offered
the skylight a benevolent smile. "Bless his heart."

I reached over and held her hand. "Were you listening
last night when I mentioned Fritz Lupo?"

"Yes." She squeezed hard. "The Fox is dead. Oh, but
that makes me feel old."

"He was a good player, wasn't he?"

"Not as good as your father. But, yes, Fritz was good.
And such a nice young man."

I mentioned that Fritz Lupo was in his sixties when he
was killed, and Mother mumbled something about how time
flies.

"Wilson actually has you shooting nine ball at this
dangerous bar?" she asked. "I'm surprised he's allowing
such a thing. That darling man loves you so much."

I frowned. "Wilson Rye is far from darling. And it's
far from love."

She let go of my hand. "He is darling. And it is love.
Listen to your mother."

I decided not to argue and reiterated what I hoped she
would accomplish at The Cotswald Estates.

"I made an appointment for you," I told her. "You're
meeting with the weekend manager, a woman named Tracy
Brody. She's going to show you around and introduce you
to a few residents. Then she's going to leave you on your
own in the dining room for their Sunday brunch. I told her
you wanted to try the food."

"I'm to act interested in moving there, correct? And
I'm to sit with Ethel and Doreen at lunch and see what I can
discover?"

"Exactly. So, you're willing to give this a try?"

"Willing?" She clapped her hands. "I can't wait! I've
never been a detective before."

We drank our tea and worked out the details of her impending excursion. Mother wrinkled her nose when I mentioned her alias was Martha Smith.

"I'm sorry," I said. "But I had to think up something quick when I was on the phone with Ms. Brody this morning."

I explained my own alias at the Wade On Inn. "You can't very well be Tessie. I don't want Ethel and Doreen to wonder why they all of the sudden know two Tessies."

"It's so sweet you've been using my name, Jessie. I'm flattered."

"Well, just remember you're Martha Smith. And if it comes up, I told Ms. Brody my name is Susan Smith."

"Martha and Susan," Mother repeated carefully. "Got it."

She sipped her tea. "Now then, how will I recognize Ethel and Doreen?"

As Karen would say, oh boy. I hadn't thought about the fact that the dining room of The Cotswald Estates would be chock full of old ladies.

"Okay." I thought about it. "Doreen is heavy-set. And Ethel is even thinner than you."

Mother frowned. "I'm going to a retirement home looking for a skinny old lady and a fat old lady? That's not very helpful, Jessie."

I tried harder. "Doreen uses a cane."

Mother was still frowning. "And?"

I thought some more. "And they're very loud," I said. "They're loud even in a barroom setting. I imagine you'll hear them before you actually see them. And look for two women with remarkably blue hair," I added. "Their hairdresser must use the same rinse on both of them."

I admired my mother's lovely and natural white hair. "Thanks for not going that route yourself."

She was checking out my hairdo also. "I don't like to criticize," she said. "But that color really doesn't suit you."

"I know that, Mother. But it's part of my disguise. I can't be recognized at the Wade On Inn."

"The blond was so becoming," she mused and continued staring at my head.

I promised her I would go back to blond as soon as possible.

"Thank goodness! Now then, let me freshen up a bit, and I'll be on my way." She stood up and made her way toward the bathroom.

I glanced at Snowflake. "If Wilson ever finds out about this, he'll kill me."

The cat did not argue.

***

Mother looked marvelous when she emerged a few minutes later. She started rummaging around in her suitcase.

"I think I should wear pumps, don't you, Jessie? I need to look like I can afford a place like Cotswald Estates."

I helped her find the shoes, which, I noticed, matched the purse she had brought with her. Then I crossed my fingers, handed her the directions to The Cotswald Estates, and led her to the door.

"How do I look?" she asked as I gave her a good luck hug.

I held her at arm's length and studied her. My mother looked like Queen Elizabeth. I mean, exactly. Especially since she was wearing her most perfect old-lady powder blue skirt suit, replete with matching shoes and purse.

"You look like a little old lady," I told her and walked her to the elevator. "A very charming little old lady."

Mother stepped in and pushed the button. "And you look like Eddie Munster."

I told her she was giving me a headache, and she disappeared.

***

Speaking of headaches, Ian arrived shortly after Mother left. He handed me the binoculars, snarled for good measure, and headed to the shower. But he stopped short at the suitcase blocking his path.

"Who's here?" he demanded.

"Not that it's any of your business," I said as I pulled various ingredients for his gourmet lunch out of the fridge. "But Mother is visiting."

"Tessie!" He jumped and looked all around. "Where is she?"

I smiled to myself and assured him my mother was not on the premises at the moment. I must say it was rather rewarding, how the thought of sweet little old Tessie Hewitt could send big, bad, Ian Crawcheck into serious panic mode.

I got busy frying bacon and had the BLT's waiting when Ian emerged from the bathroom.

He sat down at the counter and plunged in with gusto. I myself remained standing on the opposite side and ate with a little less enthusiasm. I suppose we could have sat down at the table, but breaking bread with my ex was surrealistic enough without making it any sort of pleasant occasion.

"You got the pictures?" he asked.

I nodded and mumbled a thank you.

We kept eating, but curiosity got the better of me. "Did you have any trouble out there?" I asked. "Did anyone see you?"

"Some teenage girl ran out the front door and started screaming at me. Weird."

I bit my lip. "Did you talk to her?"

"I didn't plan on it, but she stormed right up and asked me what I thought I was doing, like she owned the place or something."

I stopped eating while Ian continued, "The kid gave me a hell of a time, but I already had your damn pictures, so I told her to cool her jets and made a run for it." He sneered. "For such a sweet looking thing, she was tough. She actually chased me to my car. I jumped in and locked the doors before she attacked." He shook his head. "Weird."

I cleared my throat. "Did anyone else notice you?"

"No," he said and drank some water. "The teenager from hell was crazy enough, thank you."

I stifled a smile. Wilson's team really was good at undercover surveillance. Evidently even Mackenzie Quinn didn't know the cops were watching the place.

"So what's this scene that's so all-important?"

"Scene?"

"Earth to Adelé Nightingale." Ian dug into another sandwich. "The scene at the waterfalls? The reason I risked my life at the Wade On Inn?"

"Oh, yeah." I waved a hand. "That scene."

Of course, there was no waterfall scene whatsoever in *An Everlasting Encounter*. All the heavy action in my current masterpiece was occurring in the lavender field.

"Well, let's see." I thought fast, and the tropical paradise of Hawaii came to mind. "My heroine," I appealed to the skylight for ideas, "is Delta Touchette. She's, umm, being held captive deep in the jungle—"

"Since when do they have jungles in Europe?"

I pursed my lips. "I'm branching out from medieval Europe for this one. We're somewhere in the South Pacific. Anyway," I continued, "Delta's assailant must get rid of her, and all evidence of her, as he is being chased by the law—a Tarzan-type character named, umm, Skylar Staggs. He's the hero."

"Tarzan?"

I contemplated Tarzan. "I think Tarzan lived in Africa, but Skylar has the same skill set—swinging from vines, diving from cliffs, that sort of thing. So, the evil kidnapper, whose name I am still working on, has decided to throw Delta to certain death into the waterfalls of the Goochie Leoia Gorge—"

"Come again?"

"Goochie Lee-O-I-A," I repeated as the name started to grow on me.

I shrugged. "That's as far as I've gotten." Well, that certainly wasn't a lie! "Skylar will arrive just in time to witness the villain tossing Delta into the watery depths. Skylar will dive in after her, and inevitably we'll have a hot and heavy love scene in some verdant grove of banyan trees at the bottom of the waterfalls—"

I glanced up to see my ex smiling at me in a most disconcerting fashion.

"Not we, we," I clarified. "Delta and Skylar."

"I've missed this," he said, and I frowned accordingly.

"Finish your lunch and get out of here," I ordered.

"No, really, Jessie. You have a great imagination. You're always so entertaining."

I blinked twice and repeated my request that he go away.

Chapter 16

Lavinia Barineau stood in the doorway of the drawing room and frowned at her son, who continued staring out the window at nothing. Whatever had gotten into her normally active and robust offspring? Indeed, Trey had been daydreaming the entire week.

It wasn't healthy, Lavinia surmised, and it could cost him his title. For Trey's father had stipulated in his will that his son must marry by age twenty-eight, or lose his inheritance.

Lavinia knocked briskly and moved into the room. And before even offering her son a proper good morning, she reminded him his birthday was only one short week away.

Trey listened politely as his mother discussed the Barineau family traditions. Gentlemen were to marry and settle down properly, she insisted. She folded her arms and inquired, not for the first time, as to which St. Celeste maiden he had in mind.

When Trey's only response was to return to the window, poor Lavinia lost her patience. She stamped her foot and scolded that unless Trey made a decision soon, Luxley Manor would pass to his cousin Hubert. Hubert might not possess Trey's charm and good looks, Lavinia said, but at least the man had the decency to be married with two children and another one on the way.

Trey Barineau smiled at his distressed mother and promised he would find himself a bride forthwith. And with that, he rang for the groom and directed him to saddle up his most trusty steed.

***

I, too, determined immediate action was called for. I saddled up Wilson's truck and drove to Hastie's Diner. After all, I reasoned, I couldn't very well send my elderly mother off sleuthing if I wasn't willing to do a bit of it myself. Wilson wouldn't approve. But he seldom follows my logic, impeccable though it may be.

He had mentioned that Hastie's Diner is a dive, and on that we could agree. Even the parking lot screamed greasy spoon. I parked in one of the many empty spaces and tried to blame the lack of customers on it being a Sunday afternoon.

A few sleigh bells hanging from the door handle announced my arrival, and Melissa Purcell saw me instantly. She stood up from the counter, where she and another equally unbusy waitress were leaning, and waved furiously.

I smiled brightly and ventured forth to be introduced to Tammy. She was not exactly thrilled to meet me. But when I reached my hand across the counter, she did manage to lift her head and wobble it slightly. Then she resumed staring glassy-eyed at the front door.

Melissa grabbed a coffee pot, which almost shouted lukewarm and stale, and led me across the room to one of the many unoccupied booths overlooking the parking lot.

"Sit over here, Tessie." She waved to a seat where the vinyl wasn't torn. "The coconut cream pie is really good today, so save room."

She hovered over me as I sat down, and began reciting all the calorie-laden possibilities for my dining pleasure. When she got to the description of the meat loaf plate, I interrupted and told her I had already eaten lunch. Her face dropped, but I kept smiling and said the coconut cream pie sounded just right.

"Dessert it is, then," she said. "Maybe it will put some meat on your bones."

I also asked for tea instead of coffee, and she walked off.

While Melissa was thus occupied, I might have tuned in to the stimulating conversations of the other clientele. But nothing was happening at Hastie's Diner that could even remotely pique my interest.

The only other customers were two men who made my mother look young. They were playing gin rummy on one of the Formica tables in front of the old-fashioned juke box, which was playing country and western music.

Dare I say, I actually I recognized the pseudo-harmonizing of Carl and Lucas Wicket? Apparently they had gotten themselves a new long-haul rig that they were quite pleased with.

Melissa came back laden with tea for two. She plopped down two brown mugs, pulled two sets of silverware rolled up in paper napkins from her apron, and took the seat across from me.

"It's great Clarence is having such good weather for you," she began as we simultaneously dunked our tea bags into the two mini stainless steel pitchers she had also carried over. "You must have great weather where you're from. I bet Hawaii is beautiful."

I didn't have to respond before she changed the topic and asked after Candy and Karen. "Why didn't they come with you?"

"They're both at work."

"On Sunday?"

"Candy's in retail and Karen's self-employed. But at least she let me borrow her truck." I pointed out the window, and Melissa stared aghast at Wilson's jalopy.

The sea of empty spaces surrounding the truck was just as depressing, and she groaned audibly. "We're having a slow day," she apologized. "So it's perfect you came in."

"Does it ever get busy in here?" I asked rather skeptically.

"Used to." Her gaze wandered back to the window and the deserted car lot across Belcher Drive. A sign announcing "Big Daddy's Used Cars and Trucks" was still up, more or less, but Big Daddy had clearly gone out of business ages ago.

"Nowadays I barely bring home enough tips to make my rent." Melissa sighed and poured a package of milk-like substance into her tea. "Do you make good tips, Tessie? Is your age a problem?"

I considered the challenges of Tessie Hess, the fifty-two-year-old cocktail waitress from Honolulu and chose to be upbeat. "Not really." I smiled. "The work is seasonal—some months I do really well."

When Melissa asked which months, I decided I should be the one asking questions. "If it's so dead in here, why don't you look for another job?" I whispered.

"I have been," she whispered back. "I've been after Elsa to give me a job, like, forever."

"You actually want to work at the Wade On Inn?" After I said it, I realized how negative that sounded. "I mean, I haven't noticed any waitresses there, have I?"

"Exactly." She glanced at Tammy and remembered to keep her voice down. "Elsa claims she can't afford to hire me. So everyone has to traipse up to the bar and get their beers from her." Melissa shook her head. "It's, like, totally ridiculous."

I was busy agreeing when an unnecessarily loud bell rang, and we both jumped.

"Are you planning on serving that lady any actual food?" the man I assumed was Mr. Hastie bellowed from behind the wait station. He continued to bang his palm down on the bell thingy until Melissa stood up and yelled at him to hold his horses.

The whole place, meaning all five of us, watched as she went behind the counter and hacked off a good quarter of the coconut cream pie. She brought it back to the booth and again sat down.

"So tell me, Melissa." I slid the desert in her direction and gestured for her to help me with it. "Have you been going to the Wade On Inn a long time?"

"Only like forever." She plunged her forked into a corner of the thing, and I worked on the opposite side.

"The place must have an interesting history," I said. "My friends warned me it was a bit rough."

"Maybe. But Henry's pretty good at keeping people in line."

"Elsa has the money for a bouncer but not a waitress?"

"She managed to find the money to hire a bookkeeper for a while there, too." Melissa frowned and dug into a gob of whipped cream.

"But I guess she really does need a bouncer," I said. "Especially after those shootings last week?"

My comment inspired a discussion of the murders, but I didn't learn anything I didn't already know.

Ever the optimist, I pressed on. "Didn't I hear something about some other trouble a long time ago? Another shooting? Also involving this Fritz-guy?"

"Lester Quinn got killed," Melissa said without hesitating. "Right in front of Elsa and Mackenzie. It was an accident."

"But that's so awful. Were you there?"

She nodded and swallowed some more whipped cream. "Avis and Henry, too. Henry's always saying Fritz was the one who was supposed to die."

I pretended to think about that. "You don't think Henry killed Fritz?"

"It wouldn't surprise me," she said and smiled as I gasped. "He blames Fritz for Lester's death. And he's," she hesitated, "real devoted to Elsa."

"Did Elsa blame Fritz?"

"Elsa never blames anyone for anything. She's what you call naïve." Melissa pointed to the pie and told me to eat up.

"What did you think of Fritz?" I asked as I dutifully tackled the remaining two-inch layer of whipped cream.

She began fidgeting with empty package of fake milk. "Fritz and me go way back. We—well, you know?"

I made a point of watching her shaking hands. "This is upsetting you," I said. "Maybe we should change the subject."

Melissa assured me it wasn't necessary. "It's been over between me and Fritz for a long time."

"What about you and Spencer?" I ventured.

She looked up from the pie. "We're cooling it for a while until he gets his divorce."

I put my fork down and stared, wide-eyed. "You aren't the reason he left his wife?" I asked breathlessly.

She grinned, pleased with my reaction. "He'll deny it. But yeah."

I imagined Spencer would deny it because it wasn't true. But why not see what other fantasies Melissa Purcell was harboring?

"Love is so strange isn't it?" I asked. "Take Bobby Decker, for instance."

"What about him?"

"Well, I'm confused about him and the girl who died. Were they sleeping with each other or weren't they?" I asked point blank.

"Oh, absolutely. Bobby's scared out of his mind the cops are gonna say he killed her."

I cringed. "So, like, you and Bobby were never—" I cut myself off and twirled an index finger in the air, since Melissa seemed to enjoy the coy routine.

But this time she offered a straightforward denial and told me Bobby was not her type. "I hate that aw shucks and jeepers routine, don't you?"

I was thinking of my response when the damn bell behind the lunch counter started ringing again. I looked up to see a crazed Mr. Hastie furiously banging his bell, making an ungodly racket that drowned out Isabelle Eakes and all the Cornhuskers combined.

"Earth to Mel," he bellowed. "Move your sorry butt and get back to work!"

Melissa sprang up and scurried to the counter without a backward glance.

***

Our gallant hero spurred his horse to a fast gallop and hastened toward St. Celeste.

The Duke of Luxley had tried to uncover the truth about the mysterious damsel before, but on each of his previous visits to Winnie Dickerson's dress shop, the proprietress had stood her ground at her doorstep. Sputtering vague accusations regarding his character, the girl's honor, and what had transpired in that lavender field, Winnie had stoutly refused him entry.

Trey resolved to do better this time, and was astonished when Mrs. Dickerson actually welcomed him into her shop. Indeed, she sat him down at a table littered with an abundance of fabric and lace and told him everything that had transpired since he had delivered Sarina Blyss to her doorstep.

Sarina Blyss! What a beautiful name! Trey smiled wistfully, but Winnie was saying something else now.

Something about the lady's true identity—that she was in actuality a girl named Daisy O'Dell, a former chambermaid.

Mrs. Dickerson explained to the stunned and shocked Duke how the girl had been hauled off by Constable Klodfelder that very morning. Arrested for thievery.

Thievery! Trey sprang to his feet. The lady of the lavender fields was innocent, and it was up to him to prove it! To secure her future as Sarina Blyss Barineau, the Duchess of Luxley!

***

I jumped when the phone rang.

"I found out what you wanted, Honeybunch."

"You did? But that's fantastic." I gave Snowflake a thumbs up, and told my mother to come on home and tell me all about it.

"Oh, but I can't say much of anything right now." She lowered her voice to a whisper. "Doreen might overhear me."

I scowled at the cat. "You're still with Doreen?"

"Mm-hmm. In her guestroom. She and Ethel gave me such a pleasant tour of Cotswald Estates. This place is just lovely. But I still like living at The Live Oaks," Mother continued. "I'd miss my friends far too much if I moved up here. And of course I'd never want to get in your way. Especially now that you've found yourself a new beau."

"Mother," I interrupted. "You can come home now." I reminded her I was heading back out to the Wade On Inn that evening and wanted to hear what she had learned beforehand.

"We'll have a nice dinner together," I said. "I took some of Wilson's lasagna out of the freezer."

"My, that does sound good."

Why was she hesitating? "We'll have a nice meal," I insisted. "And then you and Snowflake can rest while I go out. You've had a long day, no?"

"Well, yes. But I'm afraid the plans have changed a bit."

Somehow I knew not to blame the stomachache I was getting on that stupid coconut cream pie.

"Mother," I said sternly. "Why are you in Doreen Buxton's guestroom?"

"Because we're resting up for tonight."

"Tonight?" I squeaked.

"You'll never guess what's happened, Jessie!"

I was getting a vague and altogether horrifying notion.

"Doreen and Ethel have invited me to join them at the Wade On Inn! Isn't that marvelous?"

Chapter 17

While I pulled the receiver from my ear and stared at it in stunned dismay, Mother took the opportunity to hang up on me. Of course, I tried calling her back. But of course, she had turned off her cell phone.

I took an Advil for the enormous headache I had suddenly acquired and called my friends. Clearly we needed a strategy session before venturing out again, but this newest crisis was far too grave to discuss over the phone. Both Karen and Candy agreed to come over for dinner, especially after I enticed them with promises of Wilson's lasagna.

They were at my place at seven o'clock, and I opened the door before they even knocked. "My mother will be at the Wade On Inn tonight."

"Your mother?" Karen stared at me, aghast. "Wilson is gonna kill you."

Candy started chewing her knuckle.

I whimpered only slightly and dragged them inside, where they were momentarily distracted by the heavenly aromas.

"Lasagna," I reminded them. "I planned on serving it to Mother." I waved my arms. "But she's not here because she's on her way to the Wade On Inn." My voice went up a couple of octaves. "With Doreen and Ethel!"

"The Wade On I—" Karen shook her head vigorously. "You're losing me, Jess."

"Gosh, Jessie. Why is your mother even in Clarence tonight?" Candy asked.

I grimaced. "It's kind of a long story."

I had them sit down, and while I served dinner, I explained what had seemed like a perfectly reasonable plan to have my mother visit The Cotswald Estates and befriend Ethel and Doreen.

Candy interrupted with a few "Gosh, Jessies," and Karen felt compelled to remind me that Wilson was going to kill me, but I soldiered on.

"I thought it would be a good idea to find out more about Ethel and Doreen." Even as I said it, the idea didn't sound so good after all. "I thought their secrets might have something to do with the murders. And I thought my mother would be the perfect person to visit the old ladies. You know, since she's an old lady herself?"

I stopped talking and waited for a response. Any response.

"Would you guys please say something?" I begged.

After another long pause Karen spoke up. She pointed to her plate. "This is delicious lasagna."

I whimpered and appealed to Candy. "Wilson even mentioned George Abernathy and Paul Buxton last night. Right, Sweetie?"

"But, Jessie," she argued. "He also told us A and B both have alibis. Don't you remember?"

Karen agreed with Candy. "Even if A and B were involved, how was your mother hanging out at Cotswald Estates going to help?"

"Umm," I answered.

"Do you really think the ancient history between those old ladies is important?"

"Probably not." I sighed at my untouched plate of lasagna.

When I looked up, my friends were exchanging a meaningful glance.

"Umm, Jessie," Candy ventured. "Karen and me were wondering about you and Wilson."

"Oh?"

"Is everything okay?" Karen asked. "You seemed pretty ticked off last night."

"Puddles and I noticed he didn't stay very long," Candy added.

I asked her if she didn't have something better to do than spy on her elders, and Karen came to her defense.

"We're concerned, Jess. That's what friends are for, right?"

I sighed dramatically. "I'm worried about this thing he has going with Tiffany Sass."

"Jessie!" they both squealed, and Candy continued, "Wilson loves you! He just works with Tiffany is all."

"I am not a fool, Sweetie." I sat up straight. "I have my pride, and I intend to keep it this time."

"You mean about Ian?" Karen asked.

I dropped my fork, which had yet to make it to my mouth.

"But, Jessie," Candy said, "Wilson's way more trustworthy than Ian ever was, okay?"

"And you know this how? You've met my ex-husband maybe three times?" I turned to Karen. "And I don't believe you've ever had the pleasure."

"No," she agreed. "But I know Wilson, and Kiddo's right."

I mumbled something about Tiffany La-Dee-Doo-Da Sass under my breath and changed the subject back to my mother—surprisingly, the less touchy topic.

"Let's just hope she understands enough to pretend she doesn't know me," I said. "And let's just hope no one sees the family resemblance. And let's just hope I don't walk right up to her and wring her scrawny old neck in front of the entire Wade On Inn crowd."

"Gosh, Jessie." Candy glanced at my hairdo. "I don't think anyone will guess you guys are related."

Karen also scowled at me and reminded me how short my mother is. "Even if you do have the exact same nose and eyes."

"I wonder how long we can pretend we don't know each other," I continued fretting. "And how we'll keep our names straight all evening. Mother's alias is Martha Smith."

"And you're still Tessie Hess? Gosh, this is getting confusing," Candy said.

We all agreed with that understatement, and as we cleared the table, we also agreed to make it a short evening.

"I'm tempted to just walk in there, toss her over my shoulder, and carry her out," I said as I loaded the dishwasher.

Candy handed me the remaining plates. "I hope Wilson won't be too mad when he finds out about this."

"He's gonna kill you," Karen reminded me for the umpteenth time, and I asked if anyone else would like an Advil.

***

"Another great outfit," Elsa Quinn complimented me a bit later, and I had to agree my friends had outdone themselves on my behalf once again.

My new red bra had inspired my ensemble that evening. I was wearing a red blouse, and Karen had hunted around in Candy's jewelry box until she discovered what she insisted were the perfect earrings to accessorize my get-up. I was far too preoccupied to argue when I had agreed to hang what looked like Christmas tree ornaments from my unsuspecting earlobes.

Speaking of red, Candy found herself a seat between Mackenzie and the Red-Headed Ogler, whose eyes immediately attached themselves to Candy's cleavage.

Karen ordered a pitcher, and I lingered at the bar to actually drink a bit. Perhaps some beer would give me the courage needed to turn around and face the pool table and my mother. My mother. At the Wade On Inn. I took a large gulp of the watery yellow substance and concentrated on the barflies.

Despite my bizarre outfit, no one was paying particular attention to me, except for Goldilocks the Cop. She stared aghast, likely admiring my stunning attire. I resisted the urge to wave and tuned in to the conversation between Elsa and Karen.

Unfortunately they were discussing the music. Thus I ascertained we were listening to the wondrous sounds of Heidi Perkins and the Pink Flamingos, who were chirping some ridiculous ditty about their beloved pink cowboy boots.

Karen informed me she loves their stuff, and I grimaced accordingly.

"Are you planning on dancing all night again?" I asked her and winked at Elsa. "Karen's been making lots of new friends in here."

"She's made quite an impression on my bouncer," Elsa agreed. "I've never seen Henry have so much fun."

"Melissa tells me he's worked here a long time?" I asked, oh so cleverly guiding the conversation in useful directions.

"Oh yeah. Henry's a fixture around here. I don't know what I'd do without him."

"I think the feeling is mutual." Karen tilted her head and tried looking coy, but Elsa wasn't following. "He likes you, Elsa," she said bluntly.

"Noooo thank you." She took a step backward. "Henry's a loyal soul and all. But a guy who wants to take me to church? He's all yours, honey."

She was about to wander away, so I quickly asked another question. "I've heard Fritz Lupo was nice looking. What about him?"

Elsa stopped short. "You ladies have something against my hard-earned independence?" Karen and I shrugged in unison, and she took the bait. "First of all, Fritz is dead. So, I'm guessing there's not much chance of a romance there. And Fritz wasn't exactly my type, if you know what I mean."

She knocked on the bar and walked away before I could inquire further.

Okay, so much for procrastination. I took a deep breath and turned around to locate my mother. She was nestled between Ethel and Doreen, clutching her Queen Elizabeth purse in her lap and looking about as pleasant and pleased as a person can look at the Wade On Inn.

"Help me," I begged Karen.

"Oh boy," she whispered as she, too, took in the surrealistic scene.

Courage, I scolded myself and stalwartly began my trek across the room. But my legs refused to cooperate, and I stumbled about halfway to the pool table. I knew I must have been really bad off when the Drunken Dancer caught me before I fell. Mr. Leather and Chains also came to my rescue. He popped onto the floor and asked me to dance.

Now, here was a situation Karen could help me with. She stepped around me as the music changed. "It's Lila DeWees!" she exclaimed. "I love her stuff."

She grabbed Mr. Leather by the hand and swept him away, his sundry chains clinking and clanging to the beat of the music. The guy was a walking tambourine.

There was no turning back now. I took another deep breath, focused on the pool table, and made it to Melissa's side without further ado. My plan? I would engage Melissa in a lengthy discussion of the tactics and strategies of nine ball, keep my eyes on the pool table, and my back firmly directed at my mother.

Yep, that was the ticket—I would keep my back to the old ladies and ignore them.

"Tessie!" Doreen poked me in the butt with her cane. "Don't you want to meet our new friend?"

A spot underneath the pool table looked ever so inviting, but I reminded myself about the courage thing and turned around.

"This here's Martha." Doreen tapped my mother's knee. I clenched my teeth in a smile-slash-grimace and acknowledged my mother. "Martha's from South Carolina," Doreen was saying. "But she wanted to see the Wade On Inn."

"She's never been to a bar like this," Ethel added and formally introduced me to my mother, one Martha Smith.

Don't ask me how, but evidently I survived the moment.

In fact, I must have held out my hand, since Mother shook it and told me how pleased she was to make my acquaintance.

"I'm anxious to see you play, Tessie." She refused to let go of my hand. "Ethel and Doreen tell me you're a very good player. So I'll be placing all my bets on you tonight."

I closed my eyes and prayed for strength.

***

Then, somehow, I shot some pool.

I muddled through, winning a dozen or so games, while my mother the lunatic made herself at home. She hooted and hollered and carried on with Doreen and Ethel. When I made the mistake of playing Spencer Erring, she admired his perfectly shaped backside along with the rest of the female railbirds and reluctantly accepted Melissa's assessment that she was way too old for him. When I played Melissa, she encouraged her to listen to my advice.

"Of course, I don't know Tessie all that well," Mother, a.k.a. Martha, announced. "But I can just tell she's a good teacher." She turned from Melissa to me. "Are you a teacher, Tessie? Is that what you do? Don't ask me how, but I can usually guess these things." Mother smiled, waiting for my answer.

Bless her heart, Melissa responded for me. "Tessie's a waitress, just like me," she said, and then listened closely as I offered her the lesson Martha was insisting on.

With a lot of coaching from yours truly, Melissa did sink a fairly difficult bank shot, and my mother made a show of standing up and high-fiving her. Apparently she had forgotten her money was riding on me.

When I played Bobby Decker, Martha Smith asked if she might have the honor of holding his cowboy hat. Taking a lesson from one of Adelé Nightingale's more ludicrous heroines, she blushed demurely when he tipped said hat and handed it over.

Oh, yes. Mother found time to charm just about everyone. She discussed her favorite books with Kevin Cooper, and her favorite Bible passages with Henry Jack.

The trickiest moment occurred when Avis Sage wandered over to chat. I braced myself for any sign of recognition, prepared to throw her over my shoulder and race up the stairs and out the door if need be. After all, Mr. Sage had sat at my mother's dinner table on at least one occasion. But luckily three or four decades had altered her looks, and he remained clueless as to her true identity.

I remembered how to breathe again and got back to my game.

At some blessed point she stood up and announced she was leaving. "My daughter Suzie must be worried sick about me." She giggled. "I am sure she won't approve when she finds out where I've been all this time."

"Do yourself a favor, Martha," Doreen spoke up. "Don't tell your children anything about how you spend your time, or your money."

"It'll only give you headaches," Ethel added.

With that, the three old ladies delved into a lengthy discussion of the trials and tribulations of dealing with adult children. I rolled my eyes only once, I swear to God, before getting back to the pool table.

I was aiming at the eight ball by the time Martha Smith remembered she was supposed to be leaving. She made a show of yawning and picked her way across the room and toward the stairway, where Henry Jack escorted her up the stairs and out the door.

I quickly won the game, collected my winnings, and made some lame excuse that I also needed to get some rest. After bidding everyone a hasty goodnight, I waved to Karen on the dance floor. She caught on and abruptly twirled around to follow me to the bar. We collected Candy and got the heck out of there.

***

It goes without saying Mother was driving way too fast, and she had a head start on us. But Karen kept her wits about her and struggled to catch up.

It couldn't have been easy—what with Wilson's truck determined to hit every pothole on Belcher drive, and Candy gripping the dashboard with all fours and whining that we were all going to die unless she slowed down. I myself was giving the exact opposite advice, incessantly screaming that Karen not let the maniac get away.

Bless her heart, she didn't. And we all breathed a collective sigh of relief when Mother actually stopped at a red light. Karen pulled up behind her and we relaxed for a brief moment.

Brief is the word. Mother peeled out a split second before the light turned green, Karen muttered something I didn't quite catch and hit the gas.

Just then, my cell phone rang. I should have known it was Wilson by the angry ringtone, but I pulled the phone out of the glove box and checked anyway.

"Yep. It's Wilson," I announced.

"He's gonna kill you," Karen informed me as she rounded a sharp curve at about ninety.

Chapter 18

"Tell me that wasn't your mother." My soon-to-be ex-beau was in a most unpleasant mood.

"How did you find out, Wilson?" I tried sounding only mildly curious.

He yelled that it was his job to find out.

"Did Goldilocks call you?" I asked as my mother blew through a stop sign.

I glanced at Karen. "Stay with her," I ordered.

She tapped the brakes, gave a cursory glimpse in each direction, and kept following.

"Or Kevin?" I asked Wilson.

"What the hell was your mother—your mother!—doing at the Wade On Inn?"

I reminded Wilson I was in his truck. "Everyone in this cab can hear you."

"Good! Then maybe one of you will answer me."

No one else volunteered, so I decided it was up to me. "Mother spent the day with Ethel and Doreen," I explained. "She was trying to learn their deep dark secrets."

"What!?"

"She met them at The Cotswald Estates, and somewhere along the line they asked her to join them at the Wade On Inn."

"What!?"

While Karen, and now Candy, filled me in on the startling revelation that Wilson was going to kill me, I provided him with further details.

"Trust me," I concluded. "This trip to the Wade On Inn was not part of the original plan."

"Plan!?"

"Yes, Wilson, plan. But I never told her to go to the Wade On Inn. I am innocent," I proclaimed.

"Like hell you are!"

"Where's she going, Jessie?" Candy pointed ahead as Mother made an unexpected left turn.

I held my hand to the phone. "I have no idea and can guarantee she doesn't either. She gets lost all the time." I spoke to Karen. "Follow her, and let's just hope she finds Sullivan Street before morning."

Karen mumbled an expletive I had never before heard her say and floored it.

Meanwhile Wilson continued shouting obscenities in my other ear.

"Listen to me, Wilson," I yelled back, and much to my surprise, he did. I resumed my calm voice and assured him my mother must have gotten some great information. "Otherwise she would never have spent so much time with Ethel and Doreen. She doesn't like loud people."

"Did she like the Wade On Inn?"

I ignored the sarcasm. "Yes, I do believe she enjoyed watching me play. She had fun."

"Fun!?"

Mother ran another red light, and this time Candy sputtered out a word I had never before heard her use.

"Have I mentioned I'm getting a headache?" I asked no one in particular.

"Where are you?" Wilson demanded.

"We're following Tessie, of course. And poor Karen's trying to keep us all alive." I flinched as Mother's car hit a curb at warp speed. "Mother really shouldn't drive at night."

"Tell me about it." That was Karen.

"She's a menace," I said.

"Like mother, like daughter," Wilson said and ordered me to meet him at my condo instead of at The Stone Fountain. "That way I can wring your neck in private." He hung up.

When I told Karen and Candy the new plan, they both yawned vigorously and insisted they were not up to a party at my place.

"So you guys are willing to let Wilson kill me, right in front of my dear, sweet, elderly mother, and not try to stop it?"

"Yes," they answered in unison.

***

The car chase from hell finally ended when Mother found her way back to Sullivan Street. She pulled into a parking space, and we watched as she got out of her car and searched her powder blue pocketbook for the key I had given her to my place.

"Stay put," I told my friends. Clearly my mother had no idea we had been following her. "Let her and Wilson duke it out for a few minutes without me."

While we waited for who knows what to transpire in my condo, Karen and Candy reported to me what they had learned at the Wade On Inn that night. Interesting things. Things Wilson might spare my life in order to hear.

***

"Oh, Honeybunch!" Mother exclaimed the second I arrived home. "Wasn't that fun?" She beamed at me from her perch at my kitchen counter.

I mumbled something that resembled the four-letter word everyone had started using, staggered over to the seat beside her, and plopped down.

Meanwhile Wilson was banging around on the opposite side of the counter, presumably making tea. I avoided his gaze and concentrated on Snowflake instead.

The disapproving stare the cat offered clued me in that Wilson had already explained the situation to her. And as usual, she was going to take his side in the argument I was quite certain we were about to have.

Oblivious to all this friction was my mother. She informed me how pleasantly surprised she had been to find Wilson at my place when she got back. "But how did you get here so fast, Jessie?" she asked. "I thought you'd still be playing pool?"

Wilson slammed the tea pot onto the stove, and I jumped accordingly.

"Would anyone else like an Advil?" I asked.

***

"Oh dear," my mother said as I returned to the kitchen. "You're upset with me, aren't you, Wilson?" Apparently she had tuned in to the tension while I was off retrieving the drugs.

He took two Advil and a few deep breaths before replying. "Let's just say you had me worried, Tessie. And let's just say," more deep breathing, "that if you ever set foot in the Wade On Inn again, I'll arrest you." He poured her tea and slid it across the counter. "I have no idea what the charges will be, but I'll think of something."

Mother suppressed a giggle. "Wilson Rye," she said, "you are just darling!"

I grimaced at the darling man. He offered me my tea, frowned for good measure, and asked my mother to tell him about her day.

"Well now, let's see." She slipped off her pumps and sighed in relief. "I drove up this morning," she began. "And after visiting with Jessie for a bit, I went over to Cotswald Estates and got a tour from Miss Brody. My goal was to meet Jessie's new friends Doreen and Ethel. You know, Wilson? From the Wade On Inn?"

Wilson worked on that deep breathing thing again as my mother explained her Martha Smith alias. "Jessie didn't want to arouse their suspicions, so I couldn't very well be Tessie, could I? Wasn't that clever of her?"

Wilson failed to respond, so she continued, "The place is very pleasant, but I'm so happy where I am." Mother then elaborated on how much she enjoyed living at The Live Oaks Center for Retirement Living.

"What happened at The Cotswald Estates?" he asked.

"I had lunch with Doreen and Ethel, just like Jessie suggested."

My beau likely frowned at me again, but I was busy petting Snowflake and pretended not to notice.

"You were right." Mother turned to me. "They were the loudest people in the dining room. We got acquainted and ended up spending the whole day together." She clapped her hands. "It was so much fun being a detective, Wilson! You must love your job."

"Tell me what you talked about, Tessie."

She looked puzzled.

"With Ethel and Doreen," I reminded her.

"Well now, I got that information you were so interested in, Jessie. You know, about their secrets?"

"What!?" Wilson held his hand up in apology. "I mean," he said in a calm voice. "What did you find out?"

"We had a lovely lunch," she replied. "Doreen had the roast chicken, but Ethel insists on eating fish for lunch every day. She tells me those Omega 3's are so important for our health as we grow older."

Bless his impatient heart, Wilson actually asked my mother what she had eaten.

"I had a garden salad and baked potato," she answered and then listed each and every item that was in her garden salad.

One glance in my beau's direction informed me we should be moving on. "So!" I interrupted a riveting description of the citrus vinaigrette. "Tell us what you found out, Mother."

"Found out?" she asked.

"What's the big bad secret between Doreen and Ethel?"

She sipped her tea. "It took me all day to get to the bottom of things. Typical old ladies, we talked about our children most of the time. But I couldn't even mention Jessie." She reached over and squeezed my hand. "I was afraid I would say something wrong and blow your cover.

"Isn't that the correct phrase, Wilson? Blow her cover?"

Wilson closed his eyes, perhaps praying for strength.

Mother spoke to me. "I told them all about Danny and Capers, and the twins. Caitlin and Hailey will be graduating from high school next spring. I can't believe how time flies, can you, Jessie?"

"What did Ethel and Doreen say about their children?" I asked. "We think their sons are angry with them."

"They certainly are, but we didn't get into the details at lunch."

"After lunch?" Wilson had opened his eyes.

"After lunch we went to Doreen's apartment," Mother continued. "There were pictures of her son Paul and her grandchildren scattered around, and I thought it was the perfect opportunity to ask some very pointed questions."

"What did you find out?" I asked.

With a lot more coaxing from Wilson and me, Mother told us what we already knew about George Abernathy and Paul Buxton, and their motive for building The Cotswald Estates. She looked back and forth between us. "But you knew these things already?"

We nodded.

"I thought so," she said. "So I decided to stick around a bit longer to learn more. I wondered out loud if the dinners at Cotswald Estates were as good as the lunches."

"And they invited you to stay?" I asked excitedly.

"They did!" Mother clapped her hands, quite pleased with herself. "And then Ethel mentioned their plans to visit the Wade On Inn this evening. So of course I accepted that invitation, too."

"Of course," Wilson grumbled.

"Ethel went on home to her own place after that, and Doreen showed me to her guest room. She told me we would need our rest. You know? Before our evening out?"

Wilson took another Advil.

I cleared my throat. "You shouldn't have gone to the Wade On Inn, Mother. It was way too dangerous."

"Well now, I am sorry." She sounded fairly contrite. "But I just couldn't resist the chance to see you play." She forgot about the contrite thing. "Your father would have been so proud!"

"You didn't need to go to the Wade On Inn to see your daughter play pool," Wilson argued.

"Leon loved watching Jessie play," Mother waxed nostalgic. "He taught her everything she knows. Did you know that, Wilson?"

"Jessie's mentioned it," he said and shot me yet another ominous glare.

"You were so good tonight, Honeybunch." She squeezed my hand again. "Hustling to catch a killer? Even your father never did that."

She became eerily quiet. "I miss him so," she whispered.

I leaned over and offered her a one-armed hug. "Me, too," I whispered back.

Poor Wilson looked on in dismay until I forced myself to snap out of it. "So, Mother," I said eventually. "What's the deep dark secret between Doreen and Ethel?"

She looked up. "Back in the 1970's Doreen had an affair with Ethel's handsome-to-a-fault husband Harmon."

Chapter 19

"What!?" Wilson and I said in unison.

Mother nodded. "While they were stepping out together one night, they had a terrible car accident. Harmon was killed instantly."

"Oh, my Lord," I said as the bizarre and touching truth dawned on me. "That's when Ethel and Doreen became friends."

"No way," Wilson argued.

"But Jessie's right," Mother said. "Ethel found out about the affair the night of the accident. Doreen ended up in the hospital, and Ethel felt compelled to visit her. And Doreen felt compelled to offer what comfort she could to Ethel, who had just lost her husband, you see."

"No way," he said with less conviction.

"Way," I mumbled without taking my eyes from my mother. "And they've been best friends ever since?"

"Mm-hmm." She turned to Wilson. "Is this useful to you? Did I do all right?"

"All right?" I exclaimed. "You did an amazing job. Didn't she, Wilson?"

"Yes," he agreed, and sincerely thanked her. "But," he added in his sternest, cop-like voice. "You are not to go back to the Wade On Inn, Tessie. Is that clear?"

She giggled and winked at me. "Yes, Wilson, honey. I promise to be good."

He was back to frowning. "One of my undercover officers figured out who you were. Which means someone else could have also."

Mother and I pondered that. "Avis Sage," we said in unison, and Wilson groaned.

"Oh, but I'm sure Avis didn't recognize me." Mother waved a dismissive hand. "I'm afraid I've aged quite a bit since he last saw me. Why, Jessie couldn't have been more than twelve at the time."

"I really doubt Mr. Sage recognized her," I agreed. "But how did anyone, Wilson? I mean, how did they know she's my mother?"

He looked back and forth between us. "How about the face? You two have the exact same face." He frowned at me. "Even if yours might," emphasis on the might, "be a little younger looking."

I stuck out my tongue at him, and Mother covered a yawn.

"Well now, if y'all will excuse me, I'm going to bed." She stood up. "It's been a long day. And I have the drive home tomorrow."

Thoughts of my mother's driving again made me cringe, and I started to protest.

"No, Jessie," she insisted. "You have enough on your plate right now, what with your investigation at the Wade On Inn, and your writing, and with your own romance."

She winked at Wilson and leaned over for a kiss from me. Then she wandered off to my bedroom.

"I'm taking my hearing aids out," she called over her shoulder. "So you two lovebirds can do whatever suits you, and I won't hear a thing. I'm done being nosy for one day."

***

"What the hell are you wearing?" Wilson asked once my mother had turned the corner.

"Clothes." I pointed toward my bedroom and suggested we re-convene on the roof.

Mention of the rooftop garden woke up Snowflake. She jumped down from the counter, was at the door in a flash, and raced up the stairs the second I opened the door. I followed a lot more slowly. And Wilson followed me, sputtering out this and that pesky question about what had possessed me to get my mother involved.

His persistence did not pay off, however, and when I failed to respond, he reached his own conclusion. "You're insane," he announced.

He then moved on to scolding me for making his staff at the Wade On Inn work too hard. "Kim Leary was beside herself when she identified the newest old lady," he complained. "Like she has the manpower to protect yet another inept amateur?"

"So Goldilocks called you from the bar?" I asked over my shoulder.

"Goldi—? Kim, Jessie. Kim called me."

We made it to the roof and sat down on our favorite bench overlooking Sullivan Street.

While Snowflake found a leaf to toss about, Wilson continued his lament. "Kim Leary called the minute she had a chance. 'Jessie's mother?' I asked her. I said she had to be mistaken, but Kim insisted she was pretty sure. And then she demanded a raise. God knows she deserves one after dealing with you."

"I've made a point not to bother Goldilocks in the least," I said indignantly. "And in case you've forgotten, Captain Rye, I'm doing you a favor. And," I argued, "my mother did a fantastic job today. Even if she is a little scary."

"Like mother, like daughter. You still haven't told me why you got Tessie involved in this mess." He threw up his hands in frustration. "What possessed you?"

Okay, so I had no idea what possessed me.

I decided to change the subject and shifted the discussion to Wilson's own adventures. "Where were you tonight?" I made sure my tone was at least as accusatory as his. "With Tiffany Sass, I presume? Just like last night?"

He grinned, and I sat on my hands so as not to slap him silly. "What have you and the lovely Ms. Sass been up to, Wilson? And don't you dare tell me it's none of my business."

"We were at Hastie's Diner tonight." He caught my eye and held it.

"Oh?" I said casually. "Isn't that where Melissa Purcell works?"

"As if you didn't know. Imagine my surprise when Stuart Hastie told us someone had come by to see Melissa earlier today."

"Oh?" More casualness.

"Hastie noticed this, since Melissa seldom has visitors."

"Imagine that." I contemplated running away, but Wilson put his arm across my shoulders and held me down.

"I asked Hastie what this friend looked like, and take a wild guess what he said."

"Umm. Like Eddie Munster?"

While Wilson decided whether to wring my neck or simply take out his gun and shoot me, I asked if he and Tiffany had learned anything interesting at Hastie's.

"You mean, other than about you?"

I shrugged and eventually got some info—Stuart Hastie was worried about Melissa. "He's about to close up shop and retire," Wilson explained, "and he's concerned she'll have a hard time finding another job. Forty-year-old waitresses aren't exactly in high demand."

I mentioned Melissa would like to work at the Wade On Inn.

"She tell you that?"

"She did. But I was more interested in her love life. She claims she had an affair with Spencer Erring, and that she and Fritz were an item a long time ago."

"You believe her?" Wilson asked.

I shook my head. "Especially not after hearing what Candy learned tonight. According to Mackenzie Quinn, Angela Hernandez was the one who had an affair with Spencer. But she dumped him the second she found out he was married."

When Wilson failed to react, I glanced up. "You knew about this?"

"I thought maybe," he said. "You think anyone out there knew?"

"I have no idea," I said honestly. "Mackenzie prides herself on all the secrets Angela shared with her. But let's face it, the regulars at the Wade On Inn seem to know quite a bit about each other."

I reached over to pet Snowflake, who had hopped onto Wilson's lap. "Angela had started dating someone else, after Spencer."

"Who's that?" he asked. "Not Bobby Decker?"

I shrugged and told him Mackenzie had denied that particular possibility. "All she would tell Candy is she'd never guess in a million years."

Wilson suggested we keep working on it and surprised me when he squeezed my shoulder. With affection this time. "You guys are doing great."

I tilted my head back. "Why, Captain Rye, are you actually thanking me?"

"Maybe." He grinned and almost kissed me before I remembered the as yet unresolved Tiffany Sass issue. I sat up, and he cleared his throat.

"What about Karen?" he asked. "She get anything?"

"Henry Jack thinks Bobby's the murderer."

"Because of this supposed fling with Angela?"

Actually it was a lot more complicated than that. I tried to remember exactly what Karen had told me. "Henry insists Bobby actually hated Angela," I said, "since she was helping Elsa avoid bankruptcy. Remember the bizarre dude ranch dream? If Elsa had gone under, Bobby was hoping to buy the place cheap." I shook my head. "Believe it or not, Bobby the wannabe cowboy can't even ride a horse. That's according to Henry anyway."

"So Decker either loved Angela or hated Angela, depending on who you ask." Wilson had started rubbing the back of my neck, and I was getting very, very drowsy.

"Melissa certainly believes Bobby and Angela were together," I said, forcing myself to concentrate. "We discussed everyone's love life over a piece of coconut cream pie."

"Keep eating at Hastie's and you'll get fat."

"Speaking of fat, where were you and Tiffany last night?"

He grinned. "Tiffany is not fat."

"Unfortunately."

"It's killing you isn't it, Jessie?"

"Just answer the damn question. I'm willing to believe you were at Hastie's tonight, but that still leaves last night unaccounted for."

"We went in search of the guy who killed Lester Quinn—name's Andre Stogner."

"He's not in prison?" I asked.

"Nope. He got out on parole last month. And he's back in town."

I thought fast. Could the guy who had meant to kill Fritz Lupo years earlier still hold a grudge?

I asked Wilson.

"That was Sass's theory," he said. "So we went looking for Stogner last night. About the only bar in Clarence we didn't hit was the Wade On Inn itself."

The thought of my beau bar-hopping with the lovely Ms. Sass put a knot in my stomach, but I listened anyway as he explained their escapades. "We finally found Stogner at The Squeaky Cricket," he said. "He swore up and down he'd never set foot in the Wade On Inn again, and had no desire to see Fritz Lupo. He was shocked when I told him Lupo's dead."

Wilson looked at me. "It wasn't an act, Jessie. Tiffany's checked out his alibis for last week. He's not the guy."

"This was all about Angela Hernandez," I said with newfound certainty. "It has something to do with a weird love triangle." I was devising my theory as I spoke. "Fritz was an afterthought."

"But remember Lupo was teaching her the tricks of his trade. And they were planning a road trip together. And that thousand dollars he supposedly won his last night is still missing."

"Yes, but Angela was killed first," I argued.

"Just because the last murder investigation you got yourself involved in had a jealousy theme, doesn't mean they all do."

When Wilson began a riveting dissertation about Fritz Lupo's vice-infested existence, I stood up and stretched. I was too tired to argue.

"How much did you win tonight?" he asked as we walked downstairs.

"Not nearly enough." I unlocked my door, and Snowflake padded inside. "Mother distracted me."

I gave Wilson a quick kiss and shut the door. Frankly, I was relieved I didn't have to decide whether or not to invite him in. My mother was sleeping in my bed, after all.

"Which means we're sleeping on the couch," I whispered to Snowflake.

We found some sheets and a blanket in the closet and tiptoed around in the bathroom. I had my pajamas on and my teeth brushed before I realized Mother was awake.

She sat up suddenly as I pulled a couple of pillows from the bed. "Wilson Rye is the most darling man I have ever met," she informed me and laid back down. "Other than your father, of course."

Chapter 20

Sarina Blyss paced the dirt floor of her jail cell. The poor lady felt thoroughly distressed and utterly forsaken, but Sarina was a stalwart soul. Courage, she scolded herself, and reached for her golden necklace. But of course, her neck was bare.

A gasp of despair seized her, but she quickly recovered and forced herself to think pleasant thoughts. For instance, that loathsome Constable had finally left her alone. She could hear his occasional grunts from somewhere down the long, dark hallway, but she was rid of him. At least for the moment.

But hark! He was approaching! Sarina trembled at the sound of his heavy footsteps. Imagine her shock when he strutted up to her cell and grunted that someone wanted to see her. She rushed to the bars, ever so hopeful her brother Norwood had arrived to put an end to her unjust imprisonment.

Sarina blinked her emerald green eyes and strained to identify the figure rushing down the passageway. But, no. The visitor was much taller than Norwood. Could it be? Could it possibly be?

Yes! No sooner did she recognize him than her handsome stranger was standing before her, demanding entry to her cell. Constable Klodfelder stubbornly refused, but the gentleman insisted the girl needed counsel, and finally Klodfelder obeyed. He unlocked the door and lumbered away.

Sarina rushed forward to greet the handsome stranger, and he swept her off her feet in an embrace that banished all her fears. Thus, in hushed tones they finally introduced themselves.

Trey—his name was Trey!—listened ever so intently as she explained her plight. Indeed, he asked ever so many clever questions. When the Duke—he was a duke!—asked if she could prove her identity, Sarina furrowed her brow.

The old gardener knew her from the day she was born. Oh, but Agnes had fired Mr. Shropshire long ago. Alas, Agnes had dismissed all of the hired help, including the real

Daisy O'Dell, when she decided to make poor Sarina the sole servant of the Blyss household.

Sarina sighed in dismay, and Trey's grateful eyes landed spellbound on her nubile bosom.

***

The would-be lovers were trying to stay focused on the crisis at hand, wracking their not-too-bright brains for ways to prove Sarina's true identity, when Puddles arrived. Oh, my Lord, Puddles. I had forgotten all about my promise to babysit. Candy had to go to work, and Peter Harrison had a doctor's appointment.

I made a hasty apology to Snowflake, who had already settled herself on top of the refrigerator, and opened the door. I put an index finger to my lips, but it was too late. Puddles swept inside, barked profusely at who knows what, and immediately found my bed and my mother.

"Who are you, little guy?" I heard her ask between giggles.

I smiled at Candy. "I do believe she's about to find out."

"I can't stay long, Jessie." She handed me a leash and a sack of toys and called a "Good morning" toward the bedroom.

"Is that you, Candy?" Mother came around the corner, holding a subdued, and dare I say, calm Puddles under her arm. "I do apologize for not saying hello last night. But we didn't want to blow our cover, did we?"

Candy stepped inside to give the real Tessie a hug, and they spent a moment agreeing on how much "fun" the Wade On Inn was. Mother seemed hopeful for a more lengthy discussion, but Candy had to leave. She promised us Puddles had just piddled and even claimed he was almost housebroken.

***

I turned to my mother the moment Candy left. "Shall we hazard a guess what 'almost housebroken' might mean?"

She giggled again. "It does sound a little dangerous, doesn't it?"

I glanced apprehensively at Puddles, but the puppy was now sitting quietly at my mother's feet, licking her toes. "I'll make some fresh coffee," I said. "You're getting breakfast in bed."

"Bagels?" Mother asked hopefully. I shooed her away, and she and Puddles made their way back to the bedroom.

Snowflake and I listened to them cooing at each other while I puttered around in the kitchen. Eventually the cat felt confident enough to hop down from her perch.

"Ooh!" Mother was delighted when I approached the bed with our breakfast tray. But I almost dropped the whole thing when I beheld the scene before me. Tessie was propped up on pillows, about as I expected. But my cat and Puddles were curled up together at her feet—Snowflake, pure white and Puddles, pure black. It was pretty darn cute.

I flinched when Puddles lifted his head to lick Snowflake's nose, and almost dropped the tray again when the cat actually purred.

"You're a miracle worker," I said as I settled myself on Wilson's side of the bed.

Wilson's side of the bed? Perhaps I was getting a bit too accustomed to Wilson Rye's company.

Mother was studying me. "Something's wrong, Jessie?" Actually, it was more of a statement than a question. She continued staring deep into my soul. "You're upset with Wilson," she concluded.

I pointed to the pets and repeated the miracle worker observation, but Mother was not to be distracted. She informed me there is no other woman, and I spilled my coffee.

"How do you do that?" I jumped up to get some paper towels.

"Do what?"

"You know what," I called from the kitchen. I returned to the bedroom and sopped up the mess. "How do you always know what I'm thinking?"

"Intuition, I suppose." She poured me a fresh cup from the thermos, and I sat back down. "You think Wilson's interested in another girl?"

"Girl's a good way to put it. Her name's Tiffany Sass."

"Oh, dear. She sounds like she belongs in one of your books."

I groaned out loud.

"Tiffany works with Wilson, does she?"

I groaned again and then told my mother everything—from the basics of Tiffany's perfectly perky figure, to the pool table scene at The Stone Fountain, to the fact that she and Wilson seemed to be spending an inordinate amount of time together.

"Don't be scandalized," I concluded. "But I am quite sure the girl—and I do mean girl—would jump into Wilson's bed at a moment's notice."

"No, Jessie."

"Trust me, Mother. You haven't met her."

"Well now, that's true. But I do know your beau, and Wilson would never do anything to hurt you." She pointed her bagel at me. "That's his shirt?"

I looked down and cringed. I was dressed in my usual writing attire, one of Wilson's discarded dress shirts and a pair of cut-offs. Before Wilson, I had worn Ian's old clothes. But the day after we started sleeping together, Wilson had given me a bunch of his own shirts and suggested it was time to get rid of the others.

"How long have you been wearing Wilson's clothes?" my mother asked me.

"Since we started," I hesitated, "keeping company. I guess it bothered him to see me in Ian's shirts."

"Of course it did. The man adores you."

"Then why is he spending so much time with Tiffany La-Dee-Doo-Da Sass?" I asked in my most obstinate voice.

"Well, let's see." Mother pursed her lips at me. "Because they work together?"

I argued that this was no excuse, but she would hear none of it. "I know a thing or two about faithfulness," she said. "Surely you remember how many nights your father was away when you were little?"

"Daddy never cheated on you."

"I know that, Jessie. But your father was a pool shark. Think about the places he spent his nights." She offered me one of her stern, motherly looks. "Leon Hewitt had ample opportunity to be unfaithful."

"Daddy never cheated on you," I insisted again. "He loved you way too much."

"Exactly." She relaxed and smiled. "Just like Wilson loves you."

I told her she was giving me a headache and changed the subject. I thanked her again for her work the previous day, but Mother pooh-poohed her efforts.

"I'm afraid I wasn't much help," she said. "Surely Doreen's affair with Harmon Abernathy had nothing to do with those dreadful murders?"

"But at least my curiosity is satisfied." I spread some cream cheese on the remaining bagel and handed Tessie half. "And ruling out the old ladies does help. Trust me, Tiffany Sass is way too young to infiltrate The Cotswald Estates like you did."

I glanced sideways at my mother and thought about her flawless intuition. "So," I asked, "did you notice anything odd last night? Did anyone at the Wade On Inn catch your attention?"

"Spencer," she said without hesitating.

"What about him?"

"I don't trust him, do I?"

"His wife must not either," I said. "He had an affair with the woman who got killed, and supposedly with Melissa."

"Melissa and Spencer? I don't think so."

"Neither do I. But why would she lie about it?"

"I should say Melissa lies quite a bit. She likes her little fantasies. She's not a very good pool player, is she?"

"She's pathetic. But you have to give her credit for trying." I sipped my coffee. "Okay, so who else?"

"What's that?"

I reminded my mother she was providing me with the benefits of her stellar intuition. "Who else did you notice last night?"

"How about Kevin?" she asked.

"Kevin Cooper?" I was a bit surprised. "But he's so quiet."

"Because he's hiding something."

Like I said—flawless intuition. "Kevin's an undercover cop," I explained. "He's one of the people Wilson has protecting me out there."

"No. I don't think so."

I squinted and thought back. Had Wilson ever actually confirmed Kevin Cooper is a cop?

"If he's not a cop, then why's he secretly taping us?"

Mother's eyes got wide, and I described my visit to the library. "He was transcribing the previous night's conversations at the pool table onto his computer."

She suggested I might want to learn more about that, and I agreed I certainly might.

"Thinking about the pool table reminds me of something else Ethel mentioned." Mother waved a hand. "Oh, but I'm sure Wilson already knows about it."

"What's that?" I asked.

"About the gun?"

"Mother!" I almost shouted. "What about the gun?"

"Wilson knows where it came from, doesn't he?"

"No." I sat up straight. "The gun's missing. We think it's somewhere at the bottom of Shinkle Creek—that's the river behind the Wade On Inn."

"Maybe so." Mother petted Snowflake, who had deserted Puddles in hopes of finding a stray dab of cream cheese on the breakfast tray. "But Fritz kept a gun under the pool table."

"What!?" That time I did shout. But I reminded myself to be patient, and in my calmest voice ever, asked her to explain what she knew about the gun.

"Ethel was showing off. She bragged that there used to be a gun hidden beneath the pool table. She was quite proud she knew about it, until Doreen interrupted and insisted everyone knew."

"Do they think this was the gun that killed those people?"

"Oh dear." Mother now had Puddles on her lap, too. "I didn't ask. I suppose I just assumed."

"Okay," I said and tried to think of the questions Wilson would want answered. "Doreen told you everyone knew about the gun. Who's everyone?"

"I'm afraid I didn't ask that either."

"Who told Ethel and Doreen about it?"

"Oh dear," Mother said in despair. "I'm afraid I didn't ask that either, Jessie."

I stifled a sigh and thought about Fritz Lupo and his stupid gun while my mother described the Wade On Inn to Snowflake and Puddles. The cat seemed only mildly intrigued, but mention of the waterfalls put a certain gleam in Puddles' eye.

"Oh well," I said as I hopped up to find the dog's leash. "Even if it was Fritz's gun, this wasn't about him. It was about Angela and some ill-fated love affair."

I listed the regulars as I got the leash onto the puppy and stepped into a pair of shoes. "Angela, Bobby, Melissa, Spencer, Henry, Elsa, Fritz. Except for Avis, they all had something going with someone, or at least wish they did."

Mother stopped petting Snowflake. "Who was Fritz involved with?"

"Maybe Melissa, maybe Angela. Maybe even Elsa."

"No, I don't think so."

"I agree all three women would have been too young for him. Especially Angela," I said. I hustled Puddles toward the door and asked him to hold it for just one more minute.

"But, Jessie, honey," Mother called out as I opened the door. "Fritz Lupo was gay."

Puddles lifted his leg and piddled on my penny loafers.

Chapter 21

And Ian popped out of the elevator. He stopped short and looked at my foot. "My sentiments exactly," he told the puppy.

"So sue me, I'm a little early," he responded to my glare. "The old guy downstairs let me in. He says to tell you he's home, and you can send him down now." Ian pointed to Puddles.

"Oh, good heavens. Is that Ian Crawcheck's voice I hear?" Mother rounded the corner of the bedroom and frowned at the three of us, who were more or less frozen in our spots at the doorway.

Ian took one look at my mother, barefoot and in her nightie, and popped back to the elevator.

"Tomorrow," he said and pushed the button.

I blinked at Puddles. "One problem solved."

Mother erased whatever that look was on her face and found the paper towels.

"Umm," I said as we wiped things up. "That was Ian."

She gave me another indecipherable look and informed me it was time for her morning bath.

***

I'm not sure how Snowflake spent the time, but while Mother bathed, Puddles and I made a belated trip outside and then to Peter Harrison's.

"Was he a good boy?" Peter asked as he welcomed the puppy into his home.

I handed off the various supplies. "Candy claims he's practically potty-trained," I said. "But that hasn't been my experience."

Mr. Harrison laughed. "Mine neither. But he's keeping us all busy, isn't he?"

We watched Puddles tear around Mr. Harrison's piano four or five times, and I thanked him for babysitting so late every night.

"You girls certainly are going out a lot these days?" He tilted his head, looking a bit curious, and I promised I would explain someday soon.

Still looking curious, and maybe even a bit nosy, Peter asked after Ian. "He told me he's your ex-husband. I do hope it's okay I let him in?"

"Ian's harmless," I said and then reconsidered. "He's not dangerous," I clarified. "But probably you should have him buzz me before sending him up next time."

Peter patted my hand. "I think I understand," he said and hastened to his piano, where Puddles had just discovered the keyboard.

***

"Ian?" Mother asked. She and Snowflake were sitting on the couch waiting for me when I got back upstairs.

I grimaced. "I guess I have some explaining to do."

"Only if you want to, Jessie. It's none of my business."

"No," I said. "I really need your advice." I sat down and related the latest Ian Crawcheck saga.

"Should I be doing this?" I asked her as I concluded my tale of woe. "Whatever our former issues, he needs a place to shower, right?"

"Yes, Jessie." Mother spoke with certainty. "You know how I feel about that ex-husband of yours, but you're just being kind. And that's always the right thing." She let out a sigh. "Even in Ian's case."

"Wilson doesn't understand."

"He'll come around. Just like you'll come around about Tiffany."

I curled my lip only briefly and got back to the questions Puddles and I had pondered out at the fire hydrant. "What's this about Fritz Lupo being gay?" I asked. "How do you know this? Did Daddy tell you? And why haven't you said something sooner, for Lord's sake?"

"Well now, the subject didn't come up, did it? And yes, your father may have mentioned it years ago. Not that he needed to, mind you. It was fairly apparent. At least to me."

"Why didn't I know this?" I asked indignantly.

"I don't believe Leon and I ever discussed the love lives of our friends with our children."

"Oh."

She patted my knee. "We wouldn't have dwelled on it, would we? Back then people weren't so open about these things. I'm quite sure the Fox wanted to keep his private life private."

"It's not exactly something he'd announce in a pool hall," I agreed.

Mother shook her head. "Not back in the seventies."

"I wonder who knew at the Wade On Inn?"

"Oh, I should guess almost everyone. Nowadays people are far more honest, aren't they?

She stood up. "Now, if you'll excuse me, Honeybunch. It's time I should get going."

Thoughts of Tessie getting going reminded me of something else we needed to discuss. I asked her to sit for one more minute.

I took a deep breath. "It's your driving," I said and waited for the onslaught.

Sure enough, Mother started sputtering, and tut-tutting, and informing me in no uncertain terms that she drives just as well as she ever has.

Unfortunately, I couldn't argue there. Nor could I dispute the fact that she has never had an accident and has never even gotten a speeding ticket. Although I did mumble something about miracles happening every day.

"What did you say, Jessie?"

I sat up. "I said, but at night, Mother. Won't you at least agree to stop driving after dark?"

She reminded me she has almost perfect vision. "My hearing may not be what it once was. But my eyesight? Leon was always jealous of how I've kept my eyesight."

"Daddy wouldn't want you to drive at night." Okay, that was low. But it worked. With a bit more coaxing and cajoling on my part, Mother finally relented and promised to stop driving after dark.

I still wasn't satisfied. "And you'll try extra hard to observe speed limits from now on?"

She sighed and nodded.

"And obey them?"

More nodding.

"And you promise to stop at red lights? All red lights?"

"Yes, Jessie." She yawned. "All red lights. Mm-hmm."

"And stop signs?"

Mother tilted her head. "Don't press your luck, Honeybunch."

***

"Fritz Lupo was gay, it was his gun, and he kept it under the pool table," I offered as a greeting the minute Wilson answered his phone.

"What!?"

I repeated myself.

"Don't tell me. Tessie."

"Now aren't you happy she got involved?"

He may have groaned. But he failed to answer otherwise, and I was able to notice the background noise on his end. He was driving somewhere.

"Where are you?" I asked.

"Fritz Lupo was gay," he said to someone in the car.

"What!?" That was Tiffany, but of course.

I closed my eyes and prayed for strength, and when I spoke again my voice was exceedingly calm. No, really. "Do not tell me you're in my Porsche with Tiffany Sass."

"Okay, I won't."

"Where are you?"

"Can't tell you that, either. What about the gun?"

"You let her drive my car, and I will never speak to you again, Wilson Rye."

"I'm driving. Tell me about the gun."

I did so, and despite himself, Wilson had to be duly impressed by my mother's extraordinary sleuthing skills.

"Apparently everyone out there knew where Fritz kept it. It's embarrassing she found out about it before I did," I admitted.

"Yeah, and look at me." Wilson said. "Tessie Hewitt discovers in one short night what I've been trying to learn for a week?"

"She isn't a threat to anyone. People are always telling her things."

He chuckled. "And no one tells us poor homicide detectives anything."

"At least not at the Wade On Inn," I heard Tiffany chime in.

"Lupo was gay?" Wilson asked again before I could make any snide comments about Miss La-Dee-Doo-Da. "How did Tessie figure that one out?"

"Once upon a time, my father told her."

"Excuse me?"

"Mother doubts many people knew about it way back when. But apparently Daddy knew, and he mentioned it to her somewhere along the line."

"What is it with you Hewitts? All you guys ever think about is everyone's sex life."

"Do you, or do you not, want to hear this?

He apologized, and in a sarcasm-free voice, asked what my mother knew about Fritz Lupo's love life.

I reiterated what little she had told me. "She assumes everyone at the Wade On Inn must have known, but this was the first I've heard about it."

A thought occurred to me. "Is Andre Stogner gay, Wilson?"

I could almost hear him roll his eyes. "I have no idea. But that shooting thirteen years ago was definitely about money. A bet gone bad."

"Oh," I mumbled.

"Do I need to show you the court transcripts?"

I cleared my throat and said that wouldn't be necessary.

"Henry Jack," Wilson said suddenly.

"No." I shook my head. "I really don't think Henry's gay."

Again I could hear the eye-roll. "I'm thinking about Pastor Muckenfuss, Jessie. Remember him?"

"Oh, my Lord." I stood up to pace. "Pastor Muckenfuss is a homophobe, correct?"

"Yep."

I tried wrapping my brain around what that fact might imply, but Wilson was speaking again. "Tonight's your last night at the Wade On Inn, by the way. You'll inform Candy and Karen?"

"But things are just starting to get interesting," I insisted. "And we haven't found the killer yet. We need more time."

"No, Jessie. After that stunt with your mother? Someone's bound to figure out what you're up to. You'd be in danger."

I tried to interrupt, but he continued, "This gun under the pool table information confuses things even further. If Kim Leary checks for it, it could blow your cover, and will certainly blow hers. If she doesn't check—" Wilson left that hanging.

"It might still be there," I said. "I mean, if it wasn't actually the murder weapon."

"Like I said. It's getting too dangerous."

"Let me get this straight." I lowered my voice. "You're on a road trip with Tiffany La-De-Doo-Da Sass in a car that says 'Adelé' on its license plate, and you claim I'm the one who's living dangerously?"

"I didn't chose your pen name, darlin.'"

Chapter 22

I am sure Wilson would have preferred I stay home and work on *An Everlasting Encounter* that afternoon, and certainly Trey Barineau was anxious to save his lady from her unbearable plight. But Sarina Blyss was going to have to endure her unpleasant confinement a bit longer while I attended to some other urgent matters.

My mother the wise woman had mentioned three Wade On Inn regulars who troubled her. Since I had visited Melissa the day before, I decided to give her a break, and since I had no idea where Spencer might spend his daylight hours, he was off the hook, too. I did, however, know where to find Kevin Cooper.

I walked to the university library and made a bee-line for the second floor. This time I didn't hide. I went right up to Kevin and pulled the earphone thingies out of his ears.

"Who are you?" I demanded.

I leaned over, and he stared up at me with what looked like mortal fear. Good. Maybe if I scared the guy enough, I would get some straight answers.

"Who are you?" I repeated and sat down in a huff. "And why are you spying on people at the Wade On Inn?"

Kevin made quite a production of turning off his equipment and stalling for time.

"Maybe I should ask you the same thing?" he said when he finally looked up. "Who are you, lady?"He raised an eyebrow, and the terrified look, which had seemed so promising just a moment earlier, vanished.

"I asked you first," I said brilliantly.

We assessed each other, both pretending to be tougher than we really were, until we finally gave up and giggled in unison.

"If I tell you the truth," Kevin said eventually, "do you promise to keep it to yourself?"

"As long as you didn't kill anyone."

"Kill anyone!" He caught himself and looked around. "Kill anyone?" he repeated in a whisper. "Who do you think I am? Maybe we should start there?"

"Until this morning I thought you were a cop." I pointed to his tape recorder. "I thought you were recording things for Wilson."

"Wilson?"

"He's my beau," I said. "But I still don't know who you are, Kevin. You're not a librarian." I waved a hand at the stacks. "And you're not a cop. So what are you?"

"A graduate student."

"Excuse me?"

He tapped his computer. "I'm just starting my dissertation."

I scowled at the laptop. "You expect me to believe you're writing your dissertation about the Wade On Inn?"

"No one's ever done anything like it!" The frown on his face had suddenly transformed into a smile—a downright beaming, glowing smile. "My working title is *Social Interactivity and Gambling Protocol Among Early Twenty-First Century Billiards Players: An Urban Study.*" He actually said it all in one breath. "What do you think, Tessie?"

Needless to say, I was speechless. I blinked twice, or maybe it was three times, while Kevin repeated his working title.

"Umm," I finally managed. "You're a sociologist?"

"Anthropologist," he corrected. He filled me in on the basics of his PhD research plan and sat back, waiting for my response.

"Well, the title certainly is catchy." I tried sounding enthused. "But you should call it what it is—nine ball."

"I like the sound of billiards better."

"No," I insisted, "I'm a writer. It's best to be as accurate as possible. Don't leave people guessing as to your meaning."

"You're a writer?"

I nodded. "I take it no one at the Wade On Inn knows about this research?"

"You won't tell them?" He seemed anxious. "It would really compromise my research if you did."

I promised I wouldn't. "The murders must have compromised your work, though?"

"I hope not." He was back to frowning. "I wasn't expecting to have to answer to the police. I had to tell the guy in charge what I'm doing. But after he checked me out, he promised not to blow my cover."

"The librarian thing?"

"Pretty decent of Capt—"

Then it dawned on him. "Of Captain Rye." He squinted at me. "Your boyfriend is Wilson Rye? The cop?"

I shrugged, but Kevin reminded me fair is fair. After he vowed to keep my secrets, too, I explained my own true identity, both as Jessica Hewitt and as Adelé Nightingale.

"Wilson has me working undercover to try to catch the killer," I said. "But I'm a complete amateur. I haven't figured anything out."

"You're not an amateur pool player."

Perhaps he expected further explanation about that, but I moved on and asked him about the murders. Surely he had noticed something with all his spying? An anthropologist would possess great powers of observation, no?

Kevin claimed otherwise. "I got started just a couple of weeks before Angie was killed. My research is only in the preliminary stages," he explained and began cleaning his glasses. "I don't know anything."

I refused to accept that and insisted he share his opinion of each of the regulars.

As we discussed all the suspects, we agreed to dismiss Mackenzie and Avis. Upon further reflection, we also decided Ethel and Doreen weren't killers.

"I have no idea who the other old lady was last night," Kevin said. "But let's dismiss her, too."

I agreed that would be a good idea.

But my conversation with Mother was still fresh in my memory. "I'm thinking it was Spencer, or maybe Melissa," I said.

"No way. Melissa can't even aim a cue stick, much less a gun."

"Okay, so what about Spencer?" I recalled my mother's assessment. "I don't trust him."

"Spencer Erring is slime in a suit." Kevin stared straight at me, as if challenging me to argue.

I didn't. "I understand he had an affair with Angela."

"The guy sleeps with anything on two feet, and that might be narrowing it down a little too much."

"Who else has he been with?" I asked.

"Who hasn't he been with would be an easier question." Kevin returned to cleaning his glasses.

"Melissa?"

"Okay, I stand corrected. Melissa's probably the only woman out there he hasn't shown interest in."

"What about Fritz?" I asked.

"No." Kevin sounded sure of himself. "Fritz was teaching Angie to play pool, but that's all."

"No," I clarified. "Did Spencer have something going on with Fritz?"

"Huh?"

"Kevin." I was a bit exasperated. "You just told me Spencer sleeps with everyone. And I know for a fact that Fritz Lupo was gay. So?"

He thought a moment. "No," he said and shook his head. "I'm pretty sure, no."

I asked Kevin if he knew Fritz was gay, and he said he had his suspicions, but he doubted it was public knowledge.

I thought of all the other sundry possibilities. "What about Bobby and Angela?"

"You're awfully interested in everyone's love life."

"I'm fairly certain that's what this was all about."

"Is that what your boyfriend thinks?"

I slumped. "No," I admitted. "But trust me, this isn't the first time Captain Rye and I have disagreed." I sat back up. "Now then, what about Bobby and Angela? I'm getting mixed reports on that."

"Nothing there."

I studied Kevin. "You seem pretty sure about that."

"It's my job, Tes—Jessie. I need to be observant."

"So did you observe anyone else with Angela?" I asked. "We think she was involved with someone new."

"Who else is there?"

Okay, good point.

I got up to leave, but thought of one other question. "Did you know about the gun, Kevin?"

"Fritz kept it under the pool table," he said without hesitation.

"Who told you that?"

"Spencer." Kevin squinted into the stacks. "Or maybe it was one of the old ladies?" Again, the cleaning his glasses thing.

***

Sarina Blyss had all but given up hope by the time I returned to my desk.

She and Trey had tried ever so hard to think of how they might prove her identity. But without the help of yours truly, the hapless couple was reduced to gazing longingly into each other's eyes and fretting over how much time they had left before the loathsome Constable Klodfelder drove Trey away.

Finally, Sarina could bear it no more. She burst into tears and sobbed uncontrollably, her trembling bosom once again distracting the Duke from any semblance of clear thought. He was reaching out to console her when Sarina jumped.

***

Or maybe it was me who jumped. The downstairs buzzer was making one heck of a racket. I stood up and hastened to the intercom.

"Who's down there?" I demanded.

"Amanda Crawcheck. As if you didn't know."

"What the hell?"

My ex-husband's altogether despicable new wife had the audacity to demand entry, but I am not an idiot. I told her to go away and started walking back to my desk. But again she laid on the buzzer.

Poor Snowflake looked to me to make it stop, and I assured her I would. I slipped on my loafers and went to deal with the situation, whatever it was. And yes, the buzzer kept buzzing my entire way down the stairs.

Amanda seemed to think she would walk right in when I opened the lobby door. But I pointed one profoundly perturbed index finger in her direction, backed her up, and stepped outside.

"You have one minute to tell me why you're here," I informed her. I closed the door behind us and glared.

Not such a good idea, since I was glaring at Amanda. She may be twenty years younger than I, but I honestly do not understand the woman's appeal. Frizzy hair, chapped skin, and a perpetual smirk on her perpetually chapped lips are her most charming physical attributes.

Amanda stamped her foot. "I have every right to be here," she said, smirk included. "And I have every right to know what you think you've been doing with my husband." She drummed her own index finger at her chest and then pointed it at me. "Miss Borderline Pornography," she hissed for good measure.

Mindful of Peter Harrison's window right behind us, I walked her down to the sidewalk and put a few buildings between her and my home.

"I know what you're up to," she informed me when I stopped.

I raised an eyebrow. "Oh, really?" I asked. "Because right now I'm about to call my beau and have you removed for disturbing the peace."

"Don't you dare threaten me. I found out all about your little showering arrangement with Ian." She lifted her hands and put arrangement in air quotes.

"And? What's your point?"

She stamped her foot again. "He's my husband, and I will not tolerate it."

"Well then, invite him back home."

She turned red and snorted a few times, and I had hopes she might self-destruct right there on Sullivan Street. Unfortunately, she recovered.

"You've been feeding him, too!" she exclaimed. "BLT's!"

Okay, so I laughed. I mean, a really hearty laugh. Downright cathartic. Heck, I was almost tempted to give Amanda the lowdown on the specialty bacon I had used. But entertaining as that might have been, I had no desire to prolong the encounter.

"Oh, Lord," I said as I came up for air. "Are we done yet?"

She narrowed her eyes. "I am so sick of you embarrassing me in front of my friends," she snapped. "Don't you want to know how I found out about your little arrangement with my husband?"

Not really. But somehow I assumed I was about to be enlightened anyway.

"He was at the club yesterday afternoon, bragging about it, that's how! During his Sunday afternoon golf game!"

Dare I say, this actually was interesting news? First of all, I didn't deem my BLT's worthy of much bragging. But more importantly, I had thought Ian was altogether out of friends. And altogether out of money. A round of golf at the Clarence Country Club couldn't be cheap. And surely this stupid club had a men's locker room? Replete with a working shower?

Not that I knew the details, mind you. The country club thing was one of the many changes Amanda had made in my ex-husband's lifestyle. I doubt Ian had ever played a round of golf until she entered his life, hell-bent on raising her social status.

Oh, but the wannabe socialite was still hissing. "Thank God Lydia Horchild had the decency to call me. She heard Ian talking with Dickie Rumsfield at the bar. He told Dickie he's thinking of going back to you!" she shrieked.

"What!?" I shrieked back.

I was concluding that my ex had taken his last shower in my condo when Amanda informed me I would not succeed in stealing him away from her.

"I'm taking him back," she said. She tossed her head and waited for me to protest.

I took a deep and highly-relieved breath—and there's a first time for everything—offered her my sincerest thanks. Then I pointed her short yet sturdy person in the direction of 209 Vine Street.

***

Now where was I? Oh yes, Sarina Blyss had jumped, and her bosom had trembled magnificently. "Father Conforti!" the lady exclaimed, her eyes aglow with renewed vim. "He knows me!"

Trey was ever so excited to hear about the good Father. For not only did the priest know Sarina, he had been at her dear mother's bedside the night she died, and had witnessed the final request of Gabriella Blyss—that her daughter be given her golden necklace. Why, Father Conforti had even watched as Sarina's father removed the necklace from his beloved wife's neck and placed it into his young daughter's hands.

Trey admired Sarina's delicate hands and asked if Father Conforti might recognize her nowadays.

Oh, yes! Sarina was sure he would. Father Conforti had also attended her father's final hours, and had even ventured out from his parish in Priesters to the Blyss household several times since then. The priest had been concerned about her well-being, but he had no way to help Sarina escape her sister-in-law, other than to suggest she become a nun.

Sarina blushed and whispered that she did not believe she wanted to become a nun.

Trey agreed wholeheartedly. And vowing to journey to Priesters and locate Father Conforti that very day, he sprang to his feet. He bid farewell to his lady, but before departing the jailhouse, he stopped to issue a stern warning to Constable Klodfelder. He threatened to bring the full power behind his title down upon the Constable's head if any harm befell the good lady before his return.

Klodfelder reminded the Duke he was about to lose that title. Everyone knew, the Constable bellowed loudly enough for Sarina to hear, that the Duke of Luxley had to get himself married before the week was over, or cease being a Duke at all.

Trey assured the Constable he already had a lady in mind and would be married forthwith. And Sarina clasped the bars of her cell in an effort to keep from swooning.

Chapter 23

Miss Blyss was indulging in a shockingly vivid fantasy of her wedding night when I shut off my computer. I stood and stretched, and asked Snowflake to help me choose an outfit worthy of my final excursion to the Wade On Inn.

The cat seemed skeptical, and as I perused my wardrobe, I understood why. I had run out of bizarre ensembles. But fortunately, I was supposed to be on vacation. I clad myself in the exact same outfit I had worn for my first night of sleuthing and hoped the folks at the Wade On Inn would understand my limited options.

Karen and Candy didn't seem to mind. In fact, Karen claimed the dog collar necklace was starting to grow on her. I argued that, no, it was starting to grow on me, and we headed to the bar.

On the drive over I broke the news that this would be our last night at the Wade On Inn. "It's so unfair," I lamented. "We were doing so well."

"But gosh, Jessie," Candy argued. "What about last night with your mother and all?"

"I'm surprised Wilson didn't kill you," Karen added.

"Maybe," I said. "But my mother did a fantastic job yesterday." I reported what she had learned about the gun. "She also told me Fritz was gay. Surely that's worth knowing?"

Candy asked why, and I admitted I had no idea. We were pondering the implications, whatever they might be, when Karen asked what specifically we should work on that evening.

"The gun," I said. "Supposedly everyone knew about it, but let's try to verify that. And maybe find out what kind of gun it was."

I thought back on the cop shows I had seen on TV. Not many, since I rarely watch TV. "If we know the make of the gun, and Wilson has the bullets the killer used, maybe he can figure out the connection."

"Hey, girlfriend," Karen said. "I don't know anything about guns."

"Neither do I. But if anyone mentions a brand name or whatever, just try to remember it."

"Caliber," Candy said. "I think there's something about calibers, isn't there?"

The three of us shrugged in unison, blissfully, or naively, ignorant.

I gently elbowed Candy. "And we need to know more details on Angela's love life, Sweetie. Get Mackenzie to tell you who Angela dated after she broke up with Spencer."

"Angela's new boyfriend." Candy sounded determined. "Got it."

"What about me?" Karen asked.

"Work on Bobby Decker and make sure the new boyfriend wasn't him after all." I hesitated, wondering how to make my next request remotely palatable. "And maybe you can work on Henry Jack and find out his opinion on gays."

"Say what?"

"Pastor Muckenfuss doesn't approve of gays," I explained as the truck hit a pothole. "And he has a history of inciting his parishioners to violence."

"Let me get this straight." Karen swerved to avoid another pothole. "You want me to keep dancing with a guy who might be a homicidal homophobe?"

My lack of response clued her in that this was exactly what I hoped she would do.

"Oh boy," she mumbled with little enthusiasm.

"Gosh." Candy start chewing her knuckle. "Maybe Wilson's right. This is getting kind of dangerous."

My mind wandered to Kevin Cooper. Since he wasn't a cop, that meant the only person Wilson had out there protecting us was Goldilocks?

***

We arrived at the Wade On Inn to the not so sweet sounds of Chester Straney, and Karen informed me she loves his stuff. "But he can be kind of sad," she added.

I tilted my head to listen more carefully, and sure enough, Chester was singing a melancholy ballad about his hunting hounds. The woeful tune was clearly having an effect on Mr. Leather and Chains. Much like the lone Drunken Dancer, he was out on the dance floor swaying to the beat. One thing I could say for the Drunken Dancer—at least she was quiet about it.

Karen watched for only a moment before going out to rescue, or at least dance with, the poor guy.

Candy also got right to work. She wished me luck and found the barstool next to Mackenzie.

Inspired by my friends' enthusiasm for their own tasks, I headed for the pool table. I was determined to learn about Fritz Lupo and his gun, even if I had no plan as to how I might go about accomplishing this goal.

If I were more clever, or my mother, I could have delved right on in with the regulars and my interrogation would seem perfectly natural. Heck, the real Tessie likely could have convinced Bobby Decker to crawl under the pool table and look for the stupid thing.

The fake Tessie made do with shooting a few games of nine ball. I played against several people I hadn't met before, hoping the opportunity for sleuthing might somehow present itself.

After the strangers had lost enough money, they wandered off toward the bar. Melissa was clamoring for a game, but the railbirds insisted I play a match with Avis. We agreed on the first to three and lagged for the break. While Avis racked, I assessed the crowd.

Bobby Decker was missing.

I checked again. I glanced over at the bar and scanned the dance floor. Karen was dancing with one of the guys who had just lost a small fortune to me. But no Bobby.

I turned back to the pool table. "Where's Bobby?" I asked casually.

"That's the million dollar question," Spencer answered as he pulled three fifties from his wallet.

The others murmured that they had not seen Bobby either, but everyone was too distracted placing their wagers to give it much thought.

I sunk the one ball on the break and pretended to have some trouble figuring out my strategy for the two. "That's funny," I said to the pool table. "I got the impression Bobby's always here."

"It's not like him," Avis agreed.

"We should always be this lucky," Melissa chimed in, and suggested that since Bobby was absent, I should play her next.

"Better yet, Tessie can play Spencer." Ethel winked at Spencer. "I'll hold your hat, big guy."

Kevin glanced over from cleaning his glasses and mentioned Spencer does not wear a hat.

"Well then, we'll hold onto anything else he cares to offer," Doreen bellowed and poked Spencer with her cane.

Spencer didn't even notice, since he was too busy watching Candy from across the room.

"So," I said in a voice that rivaled Doreen's in volume. "How about that Fritz guy?"

Everyone stared at me as if I had taken leave of my senses, which of course, I had. But I pretended my question was perfectly reasonable and turned to Ethel.

"I mean, would you hold onto anything Fritz offered?" I winked at who knows what. "I hear he was good looking, too."

"Where'd you get that idea?" Melissa asked.

I tilted my head. Maybe from her?

Spencer tore his eyes away from Candy and suggested I concentrate on my game.

I missed the three ball and gave Avis a turn. Somehow he managed to keep his mind on Fritz Lupo even as he sunk the three, four, and five. "Fritz wasn't interested in the ladies," he mumbled as he pocketed the six.

"Why's that?" I asked.

The seven ball disappeared and Mr. Sage stepped back from the table. He beckoned me to bend down so he could whisper something to me. "The Fox wasn't interested in the ladies," he repeated, emphasizing the word ladies.

"Did everyone know?" I whispered back.

Avis pointed to himself. "Just the old man and Melissa. Fritz was real private about it."

A couple of railbirds called over and asked if we intended to talk all night or play pool. Avis finished the game, and I racked while copious amounts of cash exchanged hands.

But Avis broke badly, and soon it was my turn again. The railbirds be damned, I took my time and prowled around the table until I once more stood next to Avis.

"Why did Fritz tell you guys?" I asked. Avis looked puzzled. "You know, sir, about not liking women?"

It felt wrong to be so curious about a gay guy's love life. But, as Wilson was so quick to remind me, we Hewitts are hung up on everyone's love life. And politically incorrect or not, I needed some answers.

Avis again lowered his voice. "Melissa needed to be told, if you know what I mean." I raised an eyebrow, and he frowned. "It was a long time ago, Tessie."

Everyone yelled at me to play, and I hopped up to the table and sank a few. But I reminded myself time was of the essence, purposely missed the five ball, and stepped back.

"This Fritz guy sounds like quite a character." I raised my voice and spoke to no one in particular.

"We miss him," Melissa agreed.

"But things must be safer now," I ventured. I had everyone's attention, but concentrated on Melissa. "Didn't you tell me someone tried to kill Fritz years ago? And now he really did get killed?" I shook my head. "Sounds to me like the guy was trouble."

Everyone was still staring at me, so I did some more bad acting. "What?" My eyes darted from one regular to another. "Things are safer now, aren't they?"

Avis gestured for me to rack the balls. I did so, but also continued on my merry, suicidal way. "I shouldn't be scared playing here, should I?" Again I surveyed the regulars for a reaction.

Spencer Erring was not the only one frowning at me, but he was the first to answer. "You've been hanging out here all week, and no one's killed you yet," he said.

"Yet," Kevin Cooper mumbled as he handed five dollars to Doreen.

"Life's too short to worry about danger," she announced with a firm rap of her cane.

Melissa patted my shoulder and pointed me back to the table. Mr. Sage had missed the three ball and was waiting for me.

"We are safe here, Avis?" I asked as I took aim.

"No need to be scared, Tessie," Avis told me once I made the shot. "The gun's gone now."

Ahhh. The gun.

"Oh?" I ever so calmly kept my eyes on the table. "What about the gun?" I missed the four and looked up.

Avis was shaking his head. "I always knew it would cause trouble."

I actually stopped him from shooting. "Okay, now you're really scaring me. What about the gun?"

Avis leaned on his cue and spoke to everyone. "I guess it's okay for everyone to know now. Fritz kept a gun hidden under the pool table. For emergencies, he said."

"What!?" I acted shocked. "You mean to tell me there's a gun under here?" I held onto the table and pretended to need support, while Avis tried to resume play.

"Oh, for Pete's sake, Tessie." That was Ethel. "It's gone now. The police must have it."

My eyes got wide, Candy-Poppe style. "You mean," I gasped for good measure, "that was the gun? Like, the murder weapon?"

"Well, yeah." Doreen puffed herself up. "Didn't you know that?"

"What kind of gun was this?" I asked.

"A gun, gun," Doreen said impatiently. "You know? The kind with bullets?"

Avis missed the five ball, but I continued to act too startled to resume the game.

"Who knew about this gun, Avis? Everyone?" I waved a hand about, all agitated.

"Just me and Mel and Fritz." Avis frowned at the old ladies. "It was our little secret, if you know what I mean."

Melissa chuckled. "I have news for you, old man. Everyone and his brother knew about that gun." She pointed to Ethel and Doreen. "Even those two."

"I didn't know." Spencer was staring at the pool table like it might explode at any moment.

"Yes you did," Melissa argued.

"Leave poor Spencer alone," Ethel scolded. "If he didn't know, he didn't know."

I turned and blinked at Kevin. But he was busy cleaning his stupid glasses and refused to catch my eye.

"The game?" someone called out.

I stepped forward and ran the table.

Chapter 24

"Don't tell Wilson, but I may be happy this was our last night at the Wade On Inn," I told my friends once we were safely back in the truck. "I'm exhausted and confused." I closed my eyes. "And exhausted," I repeated.

My phone rang from inside the glove compartment. I kept my eyes closed and tried ignoring it, but Candy answered anyway.

"It's Wilson," she said as she handed it to me.

I told him we were on our way, and he suggested we meet at my place again.

"Perfect," I agreed. "I'm ready to climb into my jammies and sleep for about a week."

"I hear you," Karen mumbled.

I closed my eyes and indulged in a brief but splendid fantasy of my pajamas.

"Wake up, Jessie." Wilson must have heard me yawn. "I need the three of you alert for a while longer. Densmore and Sass are joining us, too."

I opened one eye. "Sass?"

"I've called a meeting."

I groaned. "Don't even tell me you've invited Tiffany Sass to my condo."

"Okay, I won't."

I hung up and informed my friends of the plan. "Apparently we are not exhausted enough."

Karen groaned also.

"Come on, you two," Candy said. "It'll be fun."

I may have whimpered.

"No, really," she insisted. "I'll pour some champagne the minute we get to your place, okay? That will make us feel better."

Karen said something about not liking champagne, and I argued that the thought of having Tiffany La-Dee-Doo-Da Sass in my home did not exactly inspire me to celebrate.

Candy would hear none of it. When she again insisted we would have fun, I closed my eyes. I might have prayed for strength, but fell asleep instead.

***

But, bless his hyperactive heart, Puddles has an uncanny knack for energizing people. We gathered him from Mr. Harrison, made a trip to the fire hydrant, and took the elevator up to my place.

Wilson was preparing tea when we arrived, and Snowflake was sitting on the kitchen counter, watching him with an adoring feline countenance. She blinked briefly at Puddles, meowed a greeting to me, and resumed watching my beau.

"We were thinking more along the lines of champagne than tea," I told Wilson and gestured for Candy and Karen to take the easy chairs. I plopped myself down on the couch, and the three of us worked on removing our shoes. Puddles was deciding which of the six choices to destroy, when someone buzzed downstairs.

"Densmore and Sass," Wilson said and buzzed them in.

I glanced at my friends. "Help me."

Actually, everyone could have used some help when Tiffany made her entrance. The word spectacle comes to mind. The girl—and I do mean girl—was clad in an outfit that made Candy Poppe look like an old-fashioned schoolmarm. Her skirt, fire-engine red, was shorter than Candy's by a good inch or two, and her silver high heels were higher.

I forced my eyes to move upward, and ascertained she was also wearing one of those push-up bras Candy is always extolling. The contraption was clearly straining in a heroic effort to uphold all Tiffany had to offer on that front.

Even Puddles, who was used to Candy's less than modest fashion sense, was astounded. He refrained from destroying my left shoe in order to stare at Miss La-Dee-Doo-Da.

"Oh boy," Karen said.

Candy popped out of her seat. "I promised you some champagne, didn't I, Jessie?"

I agreed that would be nice and shifted my focus to Russell Densmore. Hard to imagine, but the Lieutenant's outfit almost rivaled Tiffany's.

I pointed to his purple—and I do mean purple—suit. "I thought Halloween was next month."

"You're one to talk." He gestured to my hair. "Eddie."

"Sit down, Russell." I patted the cushion next to me.

Candy looked up from her task to compliment Russell's yellow bow tie, and Karen admired his purple fedora. It was indeed impressive how well his hat coordinated with his suit, right down its lemon yellow feather accent.

This, of course, is what captured Snowflake's attention. She found a spot on the couch back behind Russell and settled down to do some serious tapping.

Trying to ignore the cat on his hat, Russell explained how he and Tiffany had spent the evening in the lobby of the Wade On Inn's hotel.

"We went undercover as a prostitute and her pimp," she elaborated.

"Yes, Tiffany," I said. "I see that."

Wilson had been taking an inordinate interest in the tea preparations, but must have noticed my tone. He looked up and started, as if seeing her for the first time. "For God's sake, Sass," he said when he came to his senses. He took off his suit jacket and tossed it over.

"Gosh, what did you do?" Candy asked as Tiffany donned the jacket. "You know? When someone asked—you know?"

"We stayed in the lobby and pretended to argue the whole evening," Russell answered. "At one point the desk clerk even threatened to call the police on us."

"That's because you were so good at scolding me." Tiffany shook her finger at Russell and then looked at me. "The Lieutenant—my pimp—kept insisting I'm way too picky."

If only.

I sighed dramatically and gestured for Tiffany to join Russell and me on the couch. But instead she pulled over a barstool and perched on that. Her pose afforded those of us in lower seats an excellent view of her ridiculously long legs.

"I love your place, Jessie," she said. "It's so sleek and modern-looking. This is way nicer than your house, Captain."

Than your house, Captain?

I blinked twice and shifted my gaze to Wilson. But my soon-to-be ex-beau was pretending to help Candy with the champagne cork.

I turned to Karen and mouthed another "Help me," but she also avoided me. She sprang from her seat, asked if she could get anyone else a beer, and scurried away to the kitchen.

I tried Lieutenant Densmore. "I suppose you, too, have some pressing business in my kitchen?"

Bless his courageous heart, Russell remained seated and even had the decency to look me in the eye. "The Captain has the whole department out to his place every year, Jessie. For his Fourth of July party."

"It's a great party," Tiffany added. "You should come next time, Jessie."

You can imagine how thrilled I was by her gracious invitation? I resumed glaring at my beau, who finally summoned up the testosterone necessary to look at me.

"Jessie will definitely be there," he said and reminded the group we hadn't even known each other the previous July. He nudged Candy and waved to Karen, who seemed to be trying to hide behind the refrigerator. "I hope you'll both come, too?"

My friends murmured polite acceptances, and proof positive that there is a God in heaven, Candy finally, finally, poured some champagne.

She made sure to serve me first and sat down with a glass for herself. Karen must have decided there's safety in numbers. Corona in hand, she found her seat also.

Meanwhile Wilson served tea to his colleagues, maneuvered himself around the Sass legs, and found a place on the couch between Russell and me. Even Puddles and Snowflake settled down and decided to share the space under the coffee table.

It was all so civilized, let me tell you.

***

"You first, Densmore," Wilson said. The goal, he explained to us non-cops, was to share our theories about the murders. "If you had to name the murderer right now, who would it be and why? Convince me."

"The Captain always calls a meeting like this when an investigation gets complicated," Tiffany elaborated. "He says it's a good way to review what we have."

"You learn anything at the hotel tonight?" Wilson asked Lieutenant Densmore.

"Nothing," Russell answered. "Plenty of stuff was happening, but it had nothing to do with Lupo. The murders weren't about the hotel, sir. The bar's the key."

"Your theory?"

"Henry Jack." Russell reminded us that Henry believed Fritz Lupo should have died thirteen years ago, and that he's overprotective of the Quinns. "And don't forget Pastor Muckenfuss," he added. "The guy hates gays."

"Yeah, but Henry doesn't." That was Karen.

"Talk to me," Wilson said.

She winced. "It wasn't the easiest subject to bring up, but I forced myself."

"And?" Russell asked.

"And I made some incredibly rude comment that some of the guys hanging out at the pool table looked gay to me, and Henry Jack asked who. I had to think fast, so I said Kevin."

I may have gagged on my champagne.

"So we stopped dancing," Karen continued. "And watched the pool table, thinking about gays, I guess. But Henry was totally bored with the subject. When the Feeters started singing, we got back to dancing."

Candy and I shrugged at each other, and don't ask me how, but I remembered the details. "Rupert and Bunny," I said.

"They're married," Karen enlightened us.

"Excuse me?" That was Wilson.

"Rupert and Bunny Feeters."

He took a deep breath. "Henry Jack," he reminded her. "What's he think about gays?"

"That's what I'm telling you guys. Henry doesn't care about anyone's love life. He tries to mind his own business."

"Come on, Karen," I had to argue. "Henry Jack is always thumping his Bible at someone or other. He's very judgmental."

Puddles had again found my left shoe. I reached down to take it away from him. "You know, though," I said as I sat back up. "He didn't make an appearance at the pool table tonight. I got through an entire evening without a warning that I'm headed straight to Hell for shooting nine ball."

"I can't believe Henry killed those people just because they play pool," Karen insisted.

"What about immigrants then?" Russell asked. "Muckenfuss hates immigrants."

"First of all, Angela wasn't an immigrant. And Henry isn't Muckenfuss." She shrugged at Russell. "Sorry, but before you go condemning Henry, you should know he's left the Zion Tabernacle."

"Since when?" several of us asked.

"Since Elsa refuses to go to church in an old warehouse. Henry's determined to find a place she's willing to attend."

"How'd this come up?" Wilson asked.

"That was kind of weird, actually. He brought it up without me even asking."

Wilson turned to Russell. "So the bouncer's suddenly distancing himself from Muckenfuss?"

Russell nodded. "And why would he do that?"

"I hear you," Wilson answered. "He know about the gun under the pool table?"

Candy chimed in, "Yes, he did. Henry's the one who told Mackenzie about it."

"Mackenzie!?" several of us reacted.

I took a large sip of champagne. Wilson reached for my glass and did the same, and Candy got up to retrieve the bottle.

"Mackenzie says she remembers seeing the gun," Candy continued as she refilled her glass. She handed the bottle off to Tiffany before sitting back down.

I watched Tiffany pour and marveled at the surrealistic quality of the moment. Tiffany Sass was sitting in my condo in a red sequined miniskirt, sipping champagne out of a tea cup.

Meanwhile Candy was explaining how Mackenzie Quinn came to know about the stupid gun. "She used to play under the pool table when she was real little. Until Henry pulled her out and scolded her never, ever, to play there again."

"So Henry must have known the gun was there?" Karen grimaced. "He told me he doesn't allow guns in the bar. Not after what happened to Lester Quinn."

"He lies," Russell concluded. The champagne bottle had made its way from Tiffany, to me, and to Wilson. Russell took it next and poured some into his empty tea cup.

Karen went to fetch herself another beer.

"What's your theory?" Wilson asked Candy. "Not Mackenzie, I take it."

"Gosh, no. And I don't think it's Spencer or his wife anymore either. Not after what Mackenzie told me tonight."

"Which was?" Wilson asked.

Candy blinked. "I need to ask something first—is that guy Kevin a cop, or isn't he?"

Kevin? I sat up straight as Wilson assured Candy that Kevin Cooper was not a cop. "Why the sudden interest?"

"Because I think he's the guy, okay?"

I ignored my beating heart. "Umm, Sweetie?" I said oh so calmly. "Why do you think the librarian did it?"

"Because Kevin was Angela's new boyfriend."

"What!?" I screeched, and everyone jumped.

Wilson turned to study me with that extremely intense cop-like stare of his. Karen, Tiffany, and Russell sat forward to stare also.

Luckily I had woken up the pets. Snowflake simply hopped into Wilson's lap, but Puddles decided to take a few frenzied laps around the condo. That puppy was doing his level best to distract my beau from noticing the stricken look on my face, but somehow I doubted his tactics were working.

"Remember how you asked me to find out about Angela's new boyfriend, Jessie?" Candy stood up and began tossing one of Snowflake's balls to amuse her dog. "Kevin and Angela started dating right before she got killed. That can't be a coincidence, can it?"

Oh, dear Lord, please let it be a coincidence.

"I've never trusted guys who wear sandals," Karen mused philosophically. "Jess hates them, too."

I may have whimpered.

"You have an opinion on Kevin Cooper?" Wilson was still frowning at me.

"I don't like his taste in shoes."

"Me neither," Tiffany chimed in as she got up to find a second ball. Puddles was having a grand time, indeed. "But we live in the wrong town to be hating guys in sandals."

I do believe Russell was about to offer his opinion of men's footwear, but Wilson stopped him. "Kevin Cooper?" he reminded us.

"Mackenzie kept saying I'd never guess in a million years about Angela's new boyfriend," Candy continued. "So I made it kind of a game and asked her about almost every guy at the Wade On Inn.

"We started at the bar, and then moved on to the dance floor, and then to the pool table people. Mackenzie said no to Avis Sage, which I kind of knew, anyway." Puddles barked and Candy remembered to toss. "And we'd already talked about Spencer and Bobby." Candy threw up her hands. "So who all was left?"

"Kevin Cooper," everyone but me answered.

I closed my eyes and prayed for strength.

"Mackenzie says they were madly in love," Candy assured us.

"But they kept this relationship secret?" Wilson's tone implied all kinds of insidious possibilities.

"Supposedly Kevin would lose his job if people knew they were dating."

"But, why?" That was Karen.

"Exactly!" Candy tossed the ball with extra gusto. "Why would it matter who some librarian guy was with? It wouldn't, unless he planned on killing her."

"Sorry, but I still don't get it," Karen said. "Why would Kevin kill Angela? You just said he loved her."

"Good point." I nodded vigorously. "Very good point."

"I bet he's one of those crazy guys you always hear about," Candy answered confidently. "The quiet ones in glasses always end up killing people."

"Did he know about the gun?" Wilson asked.

"Yes," I whispered.

"What about Fritz?" Wilson asked Candy. "What's your theory there?"

She pursed her lips in concentration. "I haven't thought about him. I guess I've been more interested in Angela."

She grabbed Puddles' leash from the counter and bent down toward her dog, who had given up on fetch and found one of Karen's work boots instead.

Karen noticed also and asked if our party was going to end anytime soon. "I'm exhausted. And if Puddles eats any more of my shoes, I'll have to go shopping tomorrow."

Wilson asked everyone to hold on for a few more minutes, but Candy excused herself anyway. "We'll be right back," she promised. "But Puddles can't hold on for a few more minutes."

I turned to Wilson. "Trust her on this one."

Chapter 25

Wilson and Snowflake watched in unison as the door closed behind Puddles. Eventually he turned to Karen. "Your theory?"

"I still think it's Bobby," she said, and Tiffany gasped.

"Remember his dude ranch dream?" Karen asked. "He's dying to buy the Wade On Inn, but with Angela helping Elsa with the bookkeeping, he didn't have a chance."

She glanced at Russell. "Which is another reason Henry looks innocent to me. Angela was helping Elsa sort through her finances. Henry wouldn't hurt anyone helping Elsa."

"Why would Decker kill Fritz Lupo?" Wilson asked her.

"Well, that's not so clear," she admitted. "But Fritz won lots of money the night he died, right? And you guys never found it?"

The three cops nodded.

"Bobby needed that money," Karen concluded.

"Exactly!" Tiffany slapped her very bare thighs and we all jumped. "I've been trying to convince the Captain about Bobby all week," she said. "That's where we were when you called today, Jessie."

"Excuse me?"

"We took a road trip to visit Bobby's mother." Tiffany bounced a bit. "I love your car! It's way nicer than the Captain's truck."

I thanked her for noticing as Wilson informed us they had driven to Charlotte.

"It's just like you're saying." Tiffany beamed at Karen. "Clyde Decker—he's Bobby's brother—is really successful, and his mother Annie couldn't be more proud. But when we asked about Bobby? Both of them seemed," she looked at Wilson, "how would you put it, Captain? Disappointed?"

Karen sat forward. "Do they know about the dude ranch plan?"

"They sure do." Tiffany bobbed her head. "Annie Decker told us Bobby's been talking about it for ages.

And," she paused for affect, "he called her last week and told her the Wade On Inn is about to fold so he can buy it."

"No!" Karen exclaimed.

"Yes!" Tiffany exclaimed back.

The two of them were smiling at each other in mutual admiration when Candy and Puddles returned.

Amazingly, Puddles settled himself for a nap on her lap, as Candy figured out what she had missed. She looked back and forth between Karen and Tiffany. "Do you guys have the same theory?" Candy Poppe may not be the coldest champagne in the fridge, but she does read people pretty well.

"Decker," Wilson told her and then resumed questioning the Bobby Decker contingent. "Did he know about the gun?"

"Bobby's been a regular at that bar, like, forever," Tiffany answered. "Don't you think he knew?" She waved at me. "Even Jessie's mother knew about the gun."

Despite myself, I felt compelled to agree. "It defies logic that my mother would know, and Bobby wouldn't."

"Your mother often defies logic," Wilson mumbled. "But what about Lupo?" he asked Tiffany. "Do you agree with Karen? That he killed him for his gambling winnings?"

"No," she answered. "I agree with Jessie there."

"Me!?" I cried.

"The Captain told me your theory, Jessie—that this was all about Angela? I'm almost positive Bobby killed Angela, and then Fritz figured it out, so Bobby had to kill him, too."

She waved a few fingers at Karen. "You're probably right also. Once Fritz was dead, why not clean out his wallet?"

"Exactly!" Karen exclaimed. "And Bobby was AWOL from the Wade On Inn tonight. What's up with that?"

Tiffany's face dropped. As did Wilson's. And Russell's. And before I could even fathom why, Russell was springing from his seat, rushing to the door, and pulling a cell phone from of his purple pocket.

"Send someone he won't recognize." Wilson began issuing orders. "If they can ID him without actually presenting themselves, even better." Russell made it out to the hallway. "And I want a report, pronto!"

Lieutenant Densmore shut the door behind him, and my friends and I blinked at each other as it dawned on us what was happening.

Candy started chewing her knuckle, and Karen settled her Corona onto the coffee table with an unsteady hand. "I think I'm gonna be sick," she said.

"Wilson!" I pleaded, my poor menopausal heart beating double-time. "Don't tell us Bobby's dead, too!"

He looked at Karen. "I don't know," he said firmly and repeated himself when she finally looked up. "But we need to find him. The sooner the better."

Tiffany tried to relieve the tension. "He probably just stayed at home to watch TV tonight." She, too, insisted on catching Karen's eye. "Or he could be hiding out, because he's the killer, just like you were saying."

Karen took a deep breath. "Or he could be dead."

***

Wilson cleared his throat and ordered us, or at least tried to convince us, not to worry until we knew more. "Let's move on, shall we?" Karen nodded agreement to her beer, and he turned to me. "What's your theory?"

Russell came back, so luckily I didn't have to answer right away. "Richardson's on it," he told Wilson. "He'll call as soon as he finds him."

If he finds him, I thought.

I shuddered and got back to my theory, such as it was. "This was all about Angela," I said. "And Fritz got killed because he figured out who killed her."

"Who was it, Jessie?" Wilson asked as if I might actually know.

I leaned back to ponder the possibilities, and my mother popped into my head. "It was either Melissa, Spencer, or Kevin," I said, even if I did cringe at Kevin's name.

"Why those three?"

"Because they're the people Mother pinpointed."

Wilson was incredulous. "For God's sake. She was only there for one night."

I reminded him Tessie defies logic, and he groaned accordingly.

"Why did your mother narrow it down to those three?" Russell asked.

"She didn't give exact reasons," I admitted. "But maybe it was jealousy. One of them, Kevin, Melissa or Spencer, was jealous." I squinted up at the skylight. "Of something or other."

"What did your mother say about Kevin?" Candy asked.

"He doesn't belong at the Wade On Inn."

"That's it?"

I shrugged.

"And Melissa?" Wilson was curious despite himself.

"She says Melissa likes her little fantasies. Melissa liked Fritz a lot, by the way."

"But Fritz Lupo was gay," Russell reminded me.

"Well, yeah. But once upon a time Melissa had a crush on him. Avis told me that. And Fritz was giving Angela lessons at pool. Melissa would have been jealous of that. Trust me."

"So Melissa Purcell killed one of her oldest friends because he gave pool lessons to the wrong woman?" Wilson was skeptical.

I shrugged.

"She was also looking for a job there, right, Jess?" That was Karen.

"And Angela worked for Elsa Quinn." Lord help me, now Tiffany was arguing my cause. "Maybe Melissa was jealous of that."

"There, you see?" I sat up and looked at my beau. "Melissa had all kinds of motives. And she definitely knew about the gun."

"Mm-hmm." Wilson remained unconvinced. "Your mother mentioned Spencer Erring? What's his motive?"

I gave it some thought. "His would be fear. He was afraid his wife would find out about his affair with Angela."

"That's what I thought until tonight." That was Candy. "Until I decided it was Kevin."

"And Spencer Erring was probably the one who lost the most money to Lupo," Russell added. "Which gives him another motive."

"There now, you see?" I appealed to Wilson. "All three of Mother's ideas have merit."

"Mm-hmm." Wilson refused to be even remotely intrigued.

"Well then, what about you, Captain Rye?" I asked. "What's your brilliant theory?"

"Hey, that's right," Karen said. "Who do you think did it, Wilson?"

"He won't tell you that," Russell informed us.

"Why not?" Candy asked.

"He never lets us know his own theory until we're closer to solving the case."

"Makes people work harder. And it looks like we have a lot of work." Wilson looked at Tiffany. "Let's you and I pay another visit to Kevin Cooper tomorrow and find out why he failed to mention his relationship with Ms. Hernandez."

"And Densmore." He turned to Russell. "You call on Henry Jack. Find out why the sudden change of heart on Pastor Muckenfuss."

He checked his watch. "And apparently Sergeant Richardson didn't find Bobby Decker asleep in front of his TV. Let's hope locating Decker doesn't end up on our to-do list."

Wilson moved Snowflake to my lap and stood up. "Good work, ladies, but we'll take it from here."

"No way." I, too, stood up. "You can't fire us at this critical juncture." I appealed to Candy and Karen. "Can he?"

"Gosh, it does seem kind of unfair," Candy agreed. "Mackenzie will wonder what happened to me."

"And the guys on the dance floor will wonder about me." Karen frowned. "And I'll be wondering about Bobby. Whether he's the killer, the killee, or what."

Wilson stood his ground. "It's getting too dangerous," he insisted. "I don't have the manpower to protect you three amateurs if this thing blows up."

"Amateurs?" I said indignantly, but Wilson only repeated the insult.

"Kim's out there," Russell suggested. "Nothing will happen to them under her watch, Captain. She's the best you have."

Wilson blinked, and I knew what he was thinking. Lieutenant Russell Densmore was the best he had, not Kim Whoever-She-Was Goldilocks.

Tiffany spoke up. "I can be right upstairs, like I was tonight. If Kim calls for backup, I'll be down there in a flash."

I glanced at Tiffany's stiletto heels and somehow doubted her optimism, but Russell spoke again. "Tiff is great backup," he said. "And I can be out there, too, if you want."

Wilson pointed to the purple ensemble. "You have another suit like that?"

Russell grinned. "Hot pink."

"I'll wear a matching skirt." Tiffany actually winked at me.

And I actually smiled back. What can I say? I was really, really tired.

Wilson finally accepted defeat. "But tomorrow night is definitely it," he said sternly.

Candy clapped her hands in glee. "What should we work on our last night there?" she asked him.

"Staying alive would be nice."

***

Tiffany Sass was the last to leave my condo. As she sashayed her bright red bottom through the door, I collapsed back onto the couch and closed my eyes. Eventually I opened one eye and caught Wilson staring at me.

"What's up with you and Kevin Cooper?" he asked.

"Probably a lot less than what's up with you and Tiffany." I sat up and resigned myself to staying awake.

"Come on, Jessie." He leaned against the door. "I saw your reaction when Candy mentioned him. What have you done?"

I cringed. "I may have visited him at the library once or twice."

"Twice!?"

I tapped my lap and Snowflake joined me. "At least Melissa Purcell works where she claims she does. Which is more than I can say for Kevin." I petted the cat from head to tail. "He was at the library, technically speaking. But working on his dissertation is a bit different than helping freshmen find their way around the reference section, no?"

"Please tell me Cooper doesn't know who you really are."

When I didn't answer Wilson let out a four-letter word.

"Will you relax?" I said. "Melissa has no idea who I really am. And Kevin—"

"And Kevin?"

"Knows who I really am."

Again the four-letter word. "For God's sake, Jessie. What possessed you to confide in the guy?"

I tried to remember what possessed me to confide in the guy. "I was so sure he was a cop."

Wilson was practicing some deep breathing.

"But I found out the truth this afternoon. Kevin told me all about his research at with the Wade On Inn." I frowned. "Except for the fling with Angela Hernandez thing."

Wilson continued the deep breathing while I continued rationalizing my screw-up. "Even if he is the killer," I concluded, "I doubt he would want to blow my cover. We're safe." I looked down at Snowflake. "I think," I mouthed.

"You're a little scary. You know that?"

"What about Tiffany?"

"What about her?"

"Did she wear that stupid outfit on your road trip?"

"No, thank God."

Okay, so I may have smiled.

"She's a good cop, Jessie. Sergeant Sass does whatever I ask her, and she does it well."

"That," I said to Snowflake, "is exactly what I was afraid of."

"How much did you win tonight, Miss Cue-It?"

"I did quite well, thank you."

"May I stay a while?" Wilson asked me.

I hesitated, but Snowflake rushed over and wound herself around his ankles.

"Mother insists you're a faithful guy," I told the coffee table.

"She thinks I'm darling."

"She says I should trust you."

"Do you?"

"Yes," I said quietly. "I do."

Chapter 26

A woman of stout constitution, Winnie Dickerson was not accustomed to fretting. But the day's events had been most unsettling, even for someone of Winnie's resolute nature.

First, Constable Klodfelder had barged into her shop and arrested Sarina Blyss, or Daisy O'Dell, or whoever she was. And then the Duke of Luxley had appeared, only to admonish Winnie for allowing the damsel to be treated with such disrespect. Indeed, the Duke insisted Sarina was not at all the common criminal that Constable Klodfelder maintained.

Upon reflection, Mrs. Dickerson had to agree with Trey Barineau. Not only was Sarina Blyss a fine seamstress, she was punctual, pleasant, and poised. Why, until the Constable accused her of all manner of wicked deeds, Winnie had found no reason whatsoever to doubt the young lady's integrity.

Giving herself a stern scolding, Winnie put down her sewing and stood up to pace. But a commotion outside the shop interrupted her thoughts. She rushed out to the curb just as Trey Barineau's horse galloped past.

"Make way!" he shouted, and people jumped aside willy-nilly to clear a path. "I'm in a hurry!"

Winnie knew not where the Duke was headed, but his haste inspired her to action also. She donned her shawl and set a course for the outskirts of town. That innocent girl would not be spending the night in Klodfelder's jail. Not while Winifred Dickerson lived and breathed!

***

Mrs. Dickerson's change of heart might have gotten the completely exhausted Adelé Nightingale a bit choked up, but Snowflake wasn't nearly so impressed. She stood up and stretched, yawned dramatically, and hopped down from her windowsill. It was snack time she told me in no uncertain terms, and headed to the kitchen.

I, too, stood up and stretched. I fed Snowflake her treat, yawned for good measure, and made the morning's second pot of coffee. Maybe the extra caffeine would help me decide what Winnie was going to do once she arrived at the jail.

I poured myself another cup and glanced down at Snowflake. "Of course she'll get Sarina out," I said. "Klodfelder is no match whatsoever. But then what?"

Snowflake meowed.

"Maybe the two women will hire a carriage and venture out to the Blyss estate?" I suggested. "You know, to confront the altogether evil Agnes?"

The cat tilted her head, and we were pondering the possibility when my mother called.

"Have you and Wilson kissed and made up?" she asked.

"Repeatedly."

She giggled. "I'd be scandalized if he weren't so darling. And the murders? Have you two figured that out?"

"No." I sighed. "And if possible, it's actually getting worse. Now Bobby Decker's missing and, God forbid, might be dead. Or, of course, he could be the murderer."

"Oh my," Mother agreed. "That does sound worse, doesn't it? Poor Wilson must be fit to be tied. But what about you, Jessie? You don't think Bobby did it?"

"No," I said. "I assume it's one of the people you suspected."

"I suspected?" Mother's voice rose. "But I don't have any idea who killed those poor people."

"Yes, you do," I argued. "Just yesterday morning you told me you suspected three people—Spencer, Melissa and Kevin. Don't you remember?"

"No, Jessie. I told you there was something fishy about those three. But fishy's a lot different than what you're suggesting."

"Daddy always trusted your intuition, Mother. Why can't I?"

"Oh, Honeybunch, you can. But your father never asked me to pinpoint a murderer, did he? I'm not sure I'm up to that."

"Maybe," I conceded. "But right now all three of them are looking pretty darn," I hesitated, "fishy. For instance,

Melissa could have been jealous of Angela for any number of reasons. Or Spencer might have killed her to stop her from talking to his rich wife. And you were definitely right to wonder about Kevin."

I explained that Kevin Cooper was not a librarian at all, but a graduate student. "Let me see if I can remember his dissertation title—*Social Interactivity and Gambling Protocol Among Early Twenty-First Century Billiard Players* or something like that. It's quite a mouthful, no?"

"College students studying pool players?" Mother chuckled at the idea. "Is there a need for that sort of thing?"

"Who knows? But Kevin lied about something else, too. He had started seeing Angela right before she got killed, but never mentioned it to anyone." I stopped and waited for my mother's reaction.

Nothing.

"So Kevin is Candy's number one suspect now," I continued. "She insists it can't be a coincidence that they had just started dating before Angela got killed."

"I see."

"You do?"

"No," she admitted.

"Good! Since I truly hope it wasn't Kevin."

"Although he does wear sandals, doesn't he?"

***

As I predicted, the Dickerson-Klodfelder confrontation was quite straightforward. The triumphant Winnie Dickerson was escorting a most grateful Sarina Blyss past the duly chagrined Constable and out of the St. Celeste jail when my intercom buzzer went berserk.

"Let me in, Jessie," Ian demanded and laid on the buzzer for about the tenth time.

Clearly the man had taken lessons from his wife, and I was beginning to rue the day Wilson had talked Karen into installing the stupid thing. I might be safer with the intercom system in place, but life had actually been more peaceful when obnoxious visitors could simply come on up and bang on my door.

While Ian continued his frenzied bell-buzzing, I fortified myself with another gulp of coffee, slipped on my shoes, and braced myself for the day's Hewitt-Crawcheck confrontation. I promised Snowflake I would be right back. "Alone," I added before closing the door.

It took some effort to push my ex off the stoop and out to the sidewalk. But when there's a will, there's a way. I poked, and prodded, and persevered, and finally got him a few yards away from my building.

Meanwhile Ian was pointing to his watch and tapping vigorously. "It's 11:20, Jessie, just like we agreed. What the hell's your problem?"

Where to begin? But here was a task I was definitely up to, so I delved on in. "You lied to me, Ian," I began. "You are not altogether broke, you still have the money to play golf, and you still have friends. If this Dickie-person's so willing to play eighteen holes with you, you can shower at his place from now on. Or at that stupid country club you and Amanda are so proud of."

"I risked my life at the Wade On Inn the other day," he snapped. "You owe me."

"Yeah, right," I snapped back. "And why are you even here, anyway? The last time I saw Amanda she was huffing, and puffing, and stamping off in the direction of your office. Did she not invite you back home?"

"My marriage is none of your business."

"No kidding! But you and your stupid wife both seem bent on making it my business."

Ian backed off, at least for a moment, and conceded that Amanda had begged him to come back home.

"Proof positive that there is no accounting for taste," I said.

"But then I told her about us."

I blinked twice. "Us?" I finally managed. "You mean, like, in you and me—us?"

The look on my ex's face told me that was exactly what he meant. "Come on, Jessie. Just the other day you were telling me all about your new book." The man actually winked. "We both know what that means."

I closed my eyes and prayed for strength.

Then I did some deep breathing exercises while I wondered, not for the first time, why I had ever married this fool.

All I can figure is that some people get smarter as they age, and some people get stupider. I'll place myself in that first group, and Ian Crawcheck definitely falls into the second category. So, if you do the math...

But that's ancient history. Or at least I wished it was. I waited until my ex wiped the stupid smile off his face.

"Go to Dickie's house," I said firmly. "Or better yet, go home." I began walking away. "Do not be buzzing my bell ever again, or else."

"Or else, what? You'll have me arrested?" he called after me. "He's too young for you, Jessie. What is it, like ten years' difference?"

I remembered my theory that I'm getting smarter every day and kept on going. I did not turn around, and I did not correct my ex's misconception. But it was only five years' difference. And my relationship with Wilson was perfect, thank you very much.

I stopped short and almost fell over. My relationship with Wilson was perfect.

Lord help me.

Chapter 27

The Duke of Luxley steered a course for Priesters and reached his destination at dusk. The humble chapel was just as Sarina had described it. And Father Conforti was just as she described him—a sensitive soul who noticed at once the highly distressed countenance of his visitor.

Indeed, the two men had barely introduced themselves before the good Father saw fit to inquire as to the Duke's well-being. Trey confessed that he was not at all well. He explained how he had come to know Sarina Blyss, and the harrowing circumstances in which the poor lady now found herself.

As he reported the dire situation, Trey became more and more agitated, and Father Conforti confessed that he, too, was sorely vexed. He assured Trey he would happily identify Sarina Blyss, the true owner of the golden necklace. Indeed, he insisted on making the journey to St. Celeste that very evening.

Trey's relief was short-lived, however, when Father Conforti led him to the stable behind the church and introduced him to his trusty steed, Barnaby. The priest smiled fondly at the beast, but Trey only frowned. A donkey? And a very old donkey at that? It would take the man until midnight to get to his destination on that bedraggled creature.

Alas, Father Conforti would entertain no other alternatives. Barnaby accompanied him on all his pastoral visits, and dear Sarina had always been so fond of Barnaby. Why, the Father recollected one occasion when Sarina was but ten years old, and Barnaby had been much younger himself, when—

The Duke of Luxley held up a hand in surrender. He ceased arguing and arranged to meet the devoted priest and his devoted beast in St. Celeste as soon as possible.

With that, Trey jumped back on his horse. Next stop? The Blyss Estate, to confront Agnes and Norwood Blyss about their horrid mistreatment of their own flesh and blood!

Thoughts of Sarina's flesh left Trey momentarily woozy, but he quickly recovered and dashed away.

***

Inspired by the Trey Barineau's quest for justice, I stopped writing and stared at Snowflake. "Kevin Cooper," I said.

The cat opened one eye.

"He may not be as altogether evil as Agnes, but he has been lying. And he must be confronted." I stood up with a determined nod, and Snowflake promptly resumed her nap.

So much for encouragement. Wilson would likely disapprove also, but I ignored them both and hastened over to the University of Clarence library.

I was climbing the stairs to the second floor when the thought occurred to me that Kevin could be dangerous. I stopped. What would I do if he really were the killer? Or more importantly, what would he do?

But surely I was safe in a library? I kept climbing and found him in his usual spot, doing the transcribing thing. He pretended not to see me, but I hovered over him until he was forced to look up.

He sighed dramatically and switched off all his machinery. "You and your boyfriend have something against me getting any work done?" He made a point of frowning as he pulled out the ear bobs, but I pretended not to notice and sat down anyway.

"So Wilson's already been here?" I asked.

"Earlier this afternoon. He and Sergeant Sass. She's gorgeous, but she's as nosy as you are."

"That's because you lied to us, Kevin."

"Nooo. I just chose not to tell you about Angie and me. It's none of your business."

"It is if you killed her." I raised an eyebrow. "Did you kill her?"

"Does your boyfriend know you're here?"

"No. And you better not tell him."

Kevin actually grinned.

"Now then," I said. "Please tell me you didn't kill Angela."

"What do you think?"

"I think my mother and Candy are both wrong."

"Huh?"

"My mother was the old lady with Doreen and Ethel the other night. She thinks you're fishy."

"Your mother?" Kevin seemed rather puzzled, so I took a moment to explain why my mother had been at the Wade On Inn while he stared at me, aghast.

"It wasn't the most brilliant plan," I conceded.

"Wow. You're a little scary. You know that?"

I decided to move on. "My friend Candy thinks you're a little scary. She says it can't be a coincidence that just when you started dating Angela, she ended up dead."

Kevin took off his glasses and began the cleaning routine. My patience shot, I grabbed them from his startled hands and placed them on the table, just out of his reach.

"Come on, Kevin. I need some answers here." I began counting off questions on my fingers. "Why didn't you tell me or anyone else about your relationship with Angela? Why was it such a big secret? And why are you still hanging out at the Wade On Inn, now that she's gone?"

He waited to be sure I was done and then tapped his computer. "This answers that last question. I still have tons of data to compile." He shook his head. "If Tessie Hess visits that bar next year on her vacation she's apt to run into me again. Research takes time."

"And Angela?"

"And Angie and I were only together twice before she got killed."

He leaned over and stretched to get his glasses, glanced up to ascertain that I was not going to stop him, and placed them back on the bridge of his nose. His hands were shaking through the whole drawn-out procedure.

"Twice was enough," he said quietly.

I studied him as he stared off into the stacks. "You loved her," I whispered.

He took a deep breath. "Which of course, makes me looks guilty as hell. Women tend to get killed by the men in their lives. Unfortunately, I know this kind of stuff."

"Sociology?" I asked.

"And anthropology. Like I told Captain Rye this morning, it probably does look weird that I'm still spending time at the bar. But I have my research. And being in a place she liked so much makes me feel better somehow." Kevin searched my eyes. "Do you believe me?"

I did. "But why did the two of you keep this relationship such a deep dark secret?"

"It only lasted about a week before she got killed. We weren't being all that cagey."

"Maybe," I agreed.

"I still don't understand how everyone found out about it. The only people who knew about Angie and me, were Angie and me."

"Mackenzie Quinn," I said, and he muttered a four-letter word. "You do know Angela confided in her?"

"That girl knows way too much."

"Angela trusted her."

"Angie trusted everyone." Kevin checked his voice and returned to a whisper. "She trusted that little blabbermouth, she trusted Fritz Lupo, she trusted Elsa. She worked for her for practically free, you know?"

"Oh?"

"Oh yeah! You know what the deal was? Angie did hours and hours of bookkeeping and paperwork for her, and Elsa let her drink for free. But Angie drank maybe one glass of beer a night." He threw up his hands. "She earned about a penny an hour at that stupid job."

"She was friends with the Quinns," I argued. "Maybe she was doing them a favor?"

"Maybe that favor got her killed."

A vision of Bobby Decker in his Stetson hat flashed through my head. "Do you think the murders had something to do with Angela's bookkeeping?"

He slumped. "No. Not really."

"Do you have any idea why Bobby Decker was missing last night?"

"You realize I just answered these exact same questions for your boyfriend?"

I might have felt the teensiest bit guilty for being so annoying, but I still waited for an answer.

"I think Bobby's scared," he said. "Just like me. He's paranoid he'll be blamed, so he's hiding."

"Who do you blame?" I asked.

"Earth to Tessie." Kevin waved a hand in front of me. "I mean Jessie. Didn't you hear Spencer Erring's blatant lie last night?"

"About the gun?"

"Well, yeah! He lied when he claimed not to know about it."

"Or else you're lying."

"What? To divert suspicion away from me?" Kevin snorted. "I haven't done very well at that, have I?"

"Have you?"

"Look, I'm not lying, okay? Erring's definitely the guy who told me about the gun."

"When?"

"Hell, I don't know. I talked a lot those first few nights when I was starting my research. I was nervous, so I asked everyone all kinds of stupid questions—just to get something on my tape recorder." He tapped his machinery. "Erring must have mentioned it then."

I knew the answer, but asked anyway, "So why would Spencer feign ignorance about the gun?"

Kevin knocked his head. "Earth to Jessie."

***

I stood up before he hit me over the head with his laptop, made my way over to the library's computers, and Googled Spencer Erring.

Nothing. Or almost nothing. The guy had no Facebook page, no Twitter account, and apparently no job. About the only information I could find on him—and I admit I stink at this sort of thing—was in relation to his wife and his in-laws.

"Weird," I whispered to myself, and moved on to Dixie Wellington-Erring and the Wellington family in general. Why not?

Now here was some data. But, as always happens when I start down the slippery slope of Internet-searching, it took an inordinate amount of time to sort through all the info on the Wellingtons. And I easily got sidetracked for no good reason. Also the norm.

At some point, I got a grip and gave up on mom and dad, Ricky Senior and Maria Wellington. I mean, did I really need to know Ricky had gotten his start in the grocery business by slicing deli meats at a corner store in Atlanta when he was fifteen?

I redirected my efforts to the Clarence contingent of the family, namely Dixie and Ricky Junior.

I do believe Dixie Wellington-Erring was living the life Amanda Crawcheck aspired to. The woman belonged to every club known to mankind, or at least to Clarence—the Country Club, the Garden Club, the Bridge Club, the Ladies' Benevolent Society, et cetera, et cetera, et cetera.

In fact, it occurred to me that Amanda probably knew Dixie. She, too, was a member of the Country Club and Garden Club. And I was quite certain she was working on joining all the et ceteras. For a brief and totally irrational moment, I almost considered calling Amanda to ask about Dixie, but sanity prevailed. I may be scary, but I'm not that scary.

I gave up on Dixie's social calendar and moved on to Ricky, Jr. And lo and behold, things finally got interesting. Unlike his sister and brother-in-law, this guy actually worked. Ricky Wellington, Jr. was a professor, right there at the University of Clarence. Two years earlier he had been promoted to full professor. In the Anthropology Department.

I cringed at the computer screen and cursed myself. Of all the regulars at the Wade On Inn, why oh why had I chosen to confide in the guy in sandals?

***

Coincidences happen. Heck, they happen all the time in Adelé Nightingale's stories. I reminded myself of this over and over again on the walk home. So what if Spencer Erring's brother-in-law happened to be Kevin Cooper's dissertation advisor?

"Why would this be even remotely significant?" I asked Snowflake the moment I stepped through the door.

"Why would what be significant?"

I jumped ten feet in the air and landed to find Wilson at work in my kitchen.

"What the hell are you doing here?" I asked.

"Gee, it's nice to see you, too. Don't you remember I promised you an early dinner tonight?" He held up the package of tagliatelle I had purchased at Wellington Market. "We're having a vodka cream sauce. I was going to put it over plain old rigatoni, until I found this in your fridge."

He tapped the label and tilted the package back and forth. "I take it you've been to Wellington Market recently?"

"It was just a trip to the grocery store, for Lord's sake. And you'll be happy to know I learned absolutely nothing useful. Except how to spend tons of money on unnecessary non-essentials."

I walked over to the drawer where I had hidden the cat toys and dug them out. "These are for Wally and Bernice." I put two of the organic catnip chewies on the counter. "And this one's for you, madam." I nodded to Snowflake and tossed her the third.

She looked extremely pleased and hopped down to inspect further. But, entertaining as she was, rolling around in ecstasy with her new toy, Wilson hadn't forgotten his original question.

"So what's not remotely significant?" he asked.

I hesitated but could think of no reason not to divulge my latest discovery. So I did.

"You Googled Ricky Junior?" Wilson shook his incredulous head at me. "Why?"

"Why not?" I asked. "Did you know about this, Wilson? Do you think it's significant?"

"Yes, I knew. And no, I doubt it means anything. Clarence is a small city, Jessie. Coincidences happen."

"There, you see?" I asked Snowflake, but the cat was still busy with her new toy.

Like the cat, Wilson was also in performance mode. He fired up the sauté pan, literally. Not only is this particular sauce delicious, it's also entertaining. He actually ignites the vodka for a few seconds during the prep.

"Have you found Bobby Decker?" I asked once the flames had subsided.

"Yep. He's home now."

"Thank God. I'm sure Karen will be relieved."

Wilson raised an eyebrow. "Unless of course she's right, and he's the killer."

"Where was he?"

"Everywhere. Officer Richardson never did locate him last night, but his car was spotted late this morning at Hastie's Diner, and then he did errands all over town. Laundry, the post office—"

"Hastie's?" I interrupted. "Is that significant?"

"I don't know. I had a couple of officers following him, but I told them not to stop him for questioning. After all, he didn't break any laws by not showing up at the bar last night, or by eating at Melissa's place of employment today."

I thought about it. "Does Bobby have a place of employment?"

"Construction off and on. He's actually worked for A and B. Nothing steady, though."

"Oh?" I asked in a meaningful tone, but Wilson shook his head.

"Coincidences, Jessie. They happen."

"Well, I am glad he's okay," I said. "And if he shows up at the Wade On Inn tonight, I intend to find out why he wasn't there yesterday."

"Jessie." Wilson used his most ominous cop-voice. "There's a reason we didn't question Decker today. We don't want to make the guy paranoid, right?"

"Yes, sir, Captain Rye."

He waited until I stopped smirking. "Don't do anything stupid tonight. Stay safe. You get it?"

I rolled my eyes. "Yes, sir, Captain Rye."

He stopped stirring the pasta and studied me. "You haven't been doing anything stupid today, have you? No more casual visits to potential murderers?"

I tossed my head indignantly and denied getting into any mischief whatsoever. "In fact, I did something rather smart today," I said. "I told Ian he is no longer welcome here. He'll have to shower elsewhere."

"Excellent." Wilson's smile was genuine. "Why the change of heart?"

I thought about why, and decided my beau didn't need to concern himself with the silly details. "Let's just say, Ian's a jerk."

Wilson smiled some more. "Yeah, Jessie. Let's just say that."

Chapter 28

Poor Karen was looking a little the worse for wear when she showed up at my door later that evening.

"Are you okay?" I asked as she stumbled inside.

"These late nights are killing me, Jess." She collapsed onto my couch. "Did Wilson ever find Bobby? I can't believe I'm actually worried about the guy. And worried he might be the killer. How sick is that?"

I assured her Bobby was safe. "Although the jury's still out on whether or not he's our guy. Hopefully he'll be there tonight, and you can find out."

"Oh boy," she said and sank further into the cushions. "Don't hate me, but I'm kind of relieved tonight is it."

I had to agree, and we were comparing the dark circles under our eyes when Candy arrived. It had been her day off, so she, of course, was well-rested and raring to go. Indeed, she was so optimistic as to inform us that Puddles was now completely housebroken.

"One hundred and ten percent!" she said and proudly reported that Puddles hadn't piddled inside in over ten hours. "Ten hours!" The woman was positively gleeful until she took a long, hard look at the two of us slumped on the couch.

"Gosh," she said, trying to maintain her smile. "An extra layer of mascara will do you both good." She pulled Karen up—no easy feat—and steered her toward my dressing table.

"With an extra layer of mascara, we could probably tackle world peace," Karen mumbled as Candy eased her forward.

"Or at least solve the energy crisis," I suggested as I followed behind.

Testimony on tired she was, Karen actually sat still and silent, and allowed Candy to perform her magic. And of course she perked right up when it came time to select my jewelry for the evening. She and Candy decided to adorn me in scads of sterling silver and turquoise for my final night at the Wade On Inn.

"I've never been crazy about the southwestern look," I said to no avail as Candy slipped the fourth or fifth bracelet onto my wrist. "And these big bracelets might mess up my game."

"Nothing messes up your game, Jessie." Candy concentrated on securing a difficult clasp.

Karen was also unsympathetic. She fished out three gigantic turquoise rings from Candy's jewelry box and was clearly pleased when they fit a few of my fingers.

"Wake me up when we're ready," she said. She lay back on my bed and promptly commenced snoring.

"She's going to ruin her mascara doing that," Candy told me and began examining my own face. I tried not to notice the frown. "Maybe a little extra concealer under your eyes tonight?" she suggested.

I told her to have at it. And while she applied considerable time, effort, and concealer to my face, I thought about my most recent conversation with Kevin Cooper.

"So," I broached the subject. "I've been thinking about the murders."

"Me, too." Candy brushed some blush onto Eddie Munster's cheekbones.

"And I think your original theory has a lot of merit, Sweetie."

She stood back and assessed her work thus far. "You mean about Spencer?"

I nodded. "I think he's our most likely candidate."

"No." Candy came at me with the mascara wand. "I'm just sure it was Kevin." I cringed, and she scolded me to hold still. "I've been thinking about it all day, okay?"

I used the logic Kevin had earlier, and argued that Spencer had known about the murder weapon, but was feigning ignorance. "Why would he lie?" I blinked before Candy got to that second coat. "Unless he was trying to look innocent?"

"But, Jessie," she asked. "Why are you so sure he did know about the gun?"

"Umm." I blinked again. "I think Kevin Cooper may have mentioned it."

Candy tut-tutted in disapproval. "That would be just like him, wouldn't it? I bet he's trying to pin this on Spencer. Those smart, quiet guys can be so tricky." She caught my eye in the mirror, waiting for verification.

"Kevin might be a bit, umm, fishy?"

"Exactly!" She offered an satisfied nod at my reflection, and as she finished my face, I was left wondering about Kevin Cooper. Again.

Had the guy ever point blank told me he didn't kill Angela? Or had he just cleaned his stupid glasses every time I asked about it? And why did I have to keep learning these interesting little tidbits about him, piece, by slow, painful piece. He was fishy, darn it.

Candy misunderstood when I groaned out loud. "Don't worry, Jessie. I'm done." She screwed the top onto the mascara and announced me "Ready."

Karen caught the word and sat up. "You look nice, Jess," she said through a yawn.

I waited until she was fully coherent.

"Okay, so you look ready," she corrected herself.

***

Much to my chagrin, Candy continued discussing Kevin Cooper's guilt on the drive out. Hoping to distract her, I pulled out a bundle of cash and laid it on her lap.

"Oh my gosh!" she said. "Where did this come from?"

I explained she was looking at about a quarter of our winnings from the week. "I left the rest at home, but we've been doing quite well."

Karen stopped at a red light and glanced down at the wad of bills. "Holy moly, girlfriend. I had no idea you were winning that kind of money."

I shrugged. "After we pay back the original five hundred to the Clarence Police Department, we'll split the rest in thirdsies."

"Split it?" she protested. "No way, Jess. You're the pool shark. Not Kiddo and me."

"We didn't earn this, Jessie." Candy handed me back the stack of bills. "It's all yours."

I argued that they, too, had done their fair share of the work at the Wade On Inn, but still couldn't persuade them to split our winnings evenly.

"Okay, so how about this?" I said as Karen turned onto Belcher Drive. "I'll take half and you two get a quarter each. Fair enough?"

It took some coaxing, but they finally agreed, and we were planning one heck of a shopping spree at Tate's when Karen steered the truck into the rutted parking lot of the Wade On Inn.

I glimpsed Henry Jack guarding the doorway. "We need to stop pussy-footing around and find the murderer, ladies."

"Tonight." Candy reached over and squeezed my hand.

"What have we got to lose?" Karen agreed as we climbed out of the truck. "Even if we blow our cover, it's now or never, right?"

I decided not to mention that I had already blown my cover to Candy's prime suspect, hoisted my cue case over my shoulder, and smiled stalwartly at Henry.

***

By that point we had the routine down pat. Karen didn't even need to tell me we were listening to the Wicket Brothers, or how much she loved their stuff. She simply grabbed the bouncer's willing hand, and onto the dance floor they went.

Candy wished me luck at the pool table and tottered away to find her spot between Mackenzie Quinn and the Red-Headed Ogler.

I waved to Elsa, who smiled back, winked at Goldilocks, who frowned, and tried to move along to my own appointed station. I was dodging a particularly inspired pirouette by the lone Drunken Dancer when Mr. Leather and Chains jumped in front of me. Apparently he was also a creature of habit. We went through our usual rigmarole, and eventually I reached the pool table.

Discussing my jewelry became the first order of business. Ethel and Doreen were impressed. I mean, who wouldn't be?

"They have turquoise in Hawaii?" Doreen asked. "I thought that was Texas."

"More of my friend's things," I said, and fondled my necklace in a Sarina Blyss-like manner. "It's too bad," I lied, "but I won't be able to borrow Candy's jewelry after tonight."

"Don't tell me you're going home already?" Melissa looked disappointed, especially when I made up a time that I needed to be at the airport the next morning.

"The old man will miss you, Tessie." Bless his heart, Avis Sage seemed truly sad.

Even Ethel agreed. "I've won a tidy sum betting on you, my girl."

"Look on the bright side," Doreen argued. "With Tessie gone we'll have one less woman to compete with." She poked her cane into Spencer's adorable behind, but of course his attention was focused across the room at Candy.

"What about your friend?" he asked me without moving his eyes. "Will she be back?"

"I doubt it."

"She doesn't like it here?" Melissa was clearly perplexed at the notion.

I considered Candy, who was giggling conspiratorially with Mackenzie. "She likes the Quinns, but she's not all that interested in the workings of the pool game."

I waved in Karen's direction. "And Karen loves the music. But it's a long drive from downtown just to hear the Wicket Brothers."

"The old man will miss you," Avis repeated, and we started the evening off with our usual warm up match to three. While we lagged for the break he suggested that someday he might visit Honolulu. "We'll play on your turf, Tessie. Wouldn't that be something?"

I agreed that playing Avis Sage in Honolulu would indeed be something, and fell into a funk thinking that the old man's days of shooting pool anywhere were likely numbered. While I was busy feeling forlorn, Avis won our match. He then took on a semi-regular, and I stepped back from the table to console Melissa, who was also in a funk.

"How will I ever get better if you leave?" she asked. I didn't have an answer, but I did agree to play her before I left.

"Well then, get it over with," Ethel said. "I'm sick of hearing her whine."

A bit harsh, but others murmured agreement, and I was soon racking the balls. I let Melissa break. Mistake number one—Melissa Purcell, breaking.

The one ball may have rolled half an inch, but nothing else happened. Despite a lot of complaining from the railbirds, I racked them again and demonstrated the proper technique without actually hitting the cue ball.

"You have to put your whole body into it," I explained. "Use your hips."

"Melissa would like to use her hips for something," Doreen snickered and again prodded Spencer with her cane.

Melissa ignored her, and her second attempt at breaking was far more successful than her first. I also managed to teach her a couple of other tricks, but still found it impossible to lose. She begged for a re-match, but the crowd wouldn't tolerate it, and Spencer stepped forward.

It was time to start gambling—and not only on my pool game.

I chalked up and boldly announced my intensions. "I plan on making my last night at the Wade On Inn really count."

"She's gonna beat the socks off us," someone said and several people chuckled.

"Maybe." I blew on the tip of my stick. "But more importantly, I want to find out who killed those people last week. I can't go home without knowing the outcome of the story."

I glanced around. "It seems to me y'all would want to know who killed your friends."

"And it seems to me you're awfully interested in people you never met." Spencer laid a hundred-dollar bill on top of the light.

"I'm nosy," I agreed and slapped my own bill up there. I spotted him the seven-ball and let him win the lag.

Meanwhile Bobby Decker arrived. Between a shucks here, and a golly gee willikers there, he agreed that it was high time the truth came out. He smiled broadly, and I once again noticed the chipped tooth.

"Well then, let's start with you," I challenged him, and he lost the smile. "Everyone tells me you never miss a night. So where were you last night?"

"I decided to try out the Squeaky Cricket."

I tilted my head and squinted. Where had I heard about the Squeaky Cricket recently?

Melissa glanced at Avis. "You will never guess in a million years who he met there."

"Andre?" Avis asked, and I snapped to attention. The Squeaky Cricket was Andre Stogner's new bar of choice. But coincidences do happen, I reminded myself.

"Jeepers, Avis, how'd you know?" Bobby was saying. "I went to Hastie's today to tell Mel about meeting him, but she didn't even know he was out yet."

Mr. Sage shook his bald head. "I heard he's been seen over there. How is Andre?"

"How do you think he is?" Melissa asked. "He just got out."

"Got out of what," Doreen bellowed. "Is anyone going to tell us who this Andre fellow is?"

"Or why we should care?" Spencer added and pointed me to the table.

But I stood my ground, determined to listen to Avis. He leaned on his cue stick and explained the significance of Andre Stogner, the man who had killed Lester Quinn thirteen years ago. For once the railbirds listened attentively and didn't yammer at me to keep playing.

"I heard tell he was paroled," Avis concluded. "I've been wondering if we'd see him in here again." He looked at me. "Andre used to be a fine player."

"Andre won't be coming back to the Wade On Inn," Bobby said. "He told me this place scares him."

"Just like it scared you last night," Melissa said.

He shrugged. "Shucks, maybe I was a little nervous," he admitted.

Doreen reiterated her mantra that life's too short to ever be scared.

"Yeah, but Bobby's scared he's the next one to go jail," Melissa said. "The cops are onto him."

Bobby frowned at her and explained to the rest of us what he and Melissa had discussed at Hastie's earlier that day. Apparently he had learned about Wilson's visit to his family, and the news had left Bobby a bit paranoid.

"That Captain Rye guy went clear down to Charlotte to talk to my mother," Bobby said. "I couldn't believe it."

"She tell him what a fool you are?" Spencer asked. Miracles do happen—he was actually sinking a few balls.

"They asked her all kinds of personal questions." Bobby pointed to himself and winced. "About me."

"They think he's the murderer," Melissa announced.

Bobby again frowned at her. "That's the last time I tell you a secret." He appealed to the rest of us. "It made me nervous. Jeepers, wouldn't you be nervous if your own mother thought you were a murderer?"

A few people, including myself, murmured in sympathy.

"But I decided I didn't do nothing wrong, so here I am." He gave his hands one swift clap and resumed that goofy smile. "And I'm with you, Tessie. Let's find us the killer."

Spencer looked up from the five ball and wished me luck. "You'll need it if Decker's helping you."

Chapter 29

"Okay, Bobby," I plunged ahead, ready to ruffle some feathers. "Since you're so interested in the truth, tell us once and for all about this fling you had with Angela." His face dropped. "Did you or didn't you?"

"Didn't!" He backed up and stepped on Ethel's foot. "I already told you guys, lots of times. I was just bragging is all. There wasn't nothing going on between us."

Melissa shook her head. "That's not what you said this afternoon."

"What!?" Bobby shouted, and even the people on the dance floor glanced over. "What are you talking about, Mel?"

Spencer missed the six ball and stood up. "Whatever these two fools are arguing, Angela was never with Bobby." He paused for effect. "She was with me."

Doreen and Ethel exchanged a few hoots, hollers, and high-fives, as everyone else gasped in amazement, either at the news, or at the idea of Spencer Erring being so honest.

"And me," Kevin said.

Heads snapped.

"And you what?" Doreen's voice did tend to carry.

"Angela was with me." Kevin spoke up. "After she broke it off with Erring."

"What!?" Bobby and Melissa exclaimed in unison, and everyone gasped again.

"You mean to tell me that girl gave up you." Ethel pointed at Spencer. "For you?" She looked back at Kevin.

He gazed at her over the top of his glasses. "Being single does have its advantages," he said.

Doreen said she wasn't so sure about that, and the old ladies high-fived again.

I myself was marveling at my good luck. Who would have imagined Bobby Decker, Spencer Erring, and Kevin Cooper all telling the truth? All at the same time?

Avis coughed. Oh yeah, my pool game. I cleared the table and began to collect my winnings.

"Does your wife know about your affair?" I asked Spencer as we shook hands.

He gripped my hand a bit too tightly. "You have a lot of nerve, you know that?"

"I told everyone about the cops and my mother." Bobby came to my defense. "It's your turn to fess up."

"Answer Tessie's question, Spencer." That was Melissa. "Did Dixie know?"

"If you didn't kill Angie, you have nothing to hide." Kevin took off his glasses and tried to look threatening. Indeed, even Ethel and Doreen seemed to expect a straight answer.

"Okay, okay." Spencer recovered his false charm and flashed a few dimples here and there for good measure. "Dixie doesn't know about Angela. And I'd like to keep it that way."

"Oh?" I asked, my tone implying who knows what.

Spencer lost the dimples. "I didn't kill Angela to keep my wife in the dark, if that's what you're getting at. And I will remind everyone, Dixie's thrown me out anyway."

"But only after Angela died," Melissa said, and I wondered if she had forgotten her fantasy that she herself was the cause of his marital problems.

I was shaking my head in confusion and dismay when Bobby invited me to play a match. He twisted his cowboy hat and grinned. "Shooting a few games will help us think better, Tessie."

I mumbled that it certainly couldn't hurt, and waited patiently while wagers were negotiated. Then Bobby and I did the lagging and the breaking thing, and I didn't get back to dear Spencer until Bobby had our second game well underway.

"What are you still doing here?" I asked him. "Now that Angela's gone?"

"Yeah, Spencer, what's keeping you at the Wade On Inn?" Melissa demanded, and I almost felt sorry for the guy. If Melissa Purcell was giving him a hard time, maybe Spencer really was in trouble.

He appealed to me. "I hoped to get her back."

"She was dead," I reminded him.

"But none of us knew that for days, Tessie. And then what was I supposed to do? Just stop showing up? Like that wouldn't have looked suspicious?"

"I hear you," Kevin mumbled.

I kept my eyes on Spencer. "Why did you lie about the gun?"

"Huh?"

"The gun, Erring," Kevin helped me out. "You knew about it all along."

Darn it! Bobby missed the five ball. I stifled a groan and returned to the pool table to drop the five, six and seven. This pause might have given Spencer time to come up with a good lie about the gun, but apparently he couldn't think of anything.

"Maybe Angela mentioned the gun," he said quietly.

"Maybe?" Doreen and Ethel asked each other, their usual merriment all but gone.

"I'm not a complete idiot," he snapped and looked back and forth at all of the women staring at him. "Between my affair with Angela and knowing about the gun? You don't think that looks bad?"

"I hear you," Kevin said again, and Spencer spun around.

"Are you, or are you not, accusing me of murder, Cooper?"

Kevin cleaned his glasses, and after an extremely pregnant pause, looked up. "Not," he said.

Not!?

Demonstrating heroic self-control, I resisted the urge to pummel Kevin over the head with my cue stick. Wasn't this just a fine time for him to be changing his tune? I must have groaned out loud because Spencer swung back around to challenge me.

"What about you, Tessie? Do you think I did it?"

I glanced at Kevin who refused to catch my eye. "I don't know," I said. I looked up and frowned at Spencer. "Frankly, I have no idea who killed anyone."

I pushed him aside and waited while Bobby finished our second game. I racked for the third, determined to lose the stupid match and be free of a pesky pool game for at least a few minutes. My time at the Wade On Inn was running out. And I still had no idea.

***

"You know what doesn't make any sense at all?" Avis asked as Bobby dived into game three.

I took a deep breath and endeavored to regain my patience. "What's that, sir?" I asked.

He shook his head in bewilderment. "The Fox's gun was a secret, Tessie. Only the three of us knew about it—Fritz, and Melissa, and me."

"Oh, for God's sake, old man!" Evidently Melissa wasn't too worried about the patience thing. "Like I told you last night—everyone and his brother knew about that stupid gun. It's been here since Lester got killed, for God's sake." She threw her hands into the air, announced that she needed a drink, and left us for the bar.

"She's right." Kevin watched her skirt around Mr. Leather and Chains.

"We all found out about the gun at some point or other," Bobby agreed, as did the old ladies. And Spencer.

Utterly exasperated, I stepped up to the table. All of these people knew about the stupid gun. I shot in the five and six. All of them. The seven fell. I scanned the rest of the room. Henry knew, too, as did Elsa, and her daughter.

Oh, for Lord's sake, the Drunken Dancer probably knew about it. And she had probably informed Mr. Leather and Chains!

I pocketed the eight and nine balls with far more gusto than necessary and reached up to collect the cash on top of the overhead light.

Avis led the applause as several large bills changed hands. A few of those bills were being placed into my hand when Henry wandered over from the dance floor.

I braced myself for a stern lecture on the evils of gambling to make my irksome evening complete, but Henry didn't seem all that concerned.

He told Bobby that Karen was looking for a new dance partner, and dear Mr. Decker forgot all about helping yours truly catch the killer. Instead he grabbed his hat from Ethel and bounded out to join Karen, almost knocking Spencer Erring over in the process.

But Spencer was distracted by something across the room. In fact, I doubt he even noticed the game had finished or that the music had changed, since he was so busy staring off in Candy's direction.

What was it with this guy and younger women? The railbirds were lining up to collect their winnings from him, and I joined the queue.

I pretended not to notice his interest in Candy. "I do believe this is Heidi Perkins and the Pink Flamingos," I told him. "Karen loves their stuff."

As if to prove my point, she and Bobby were attempting to get a line dance underway. But they had to work around the lone Drunken Dancer, who was stumbling about in the middle of the floor.

Spencer continued staring at the bar, uninterested in the dancers. I checked again and realized he was not focused on Candy after all. He was watching Melissa.

"The Pink Flamingos," I repeated.

He heard me that time. "Is this really necessary?" he asked.

"Apparently. The crowd here really likes country and western music."

"You know what I mean, Tessie," he scolded. "All these questions about Angela?"

I patted his well-shaped forearm and promised I would pick on someone else for a change of pace, as one of the semi-regulars asked me for a match.

"One game," I insisted. "Then it's someone else's turn."

While she racked, I looked around the table. It was someone else's turn. But who to pick on next?

Wilson popped into my head. Hadn't he insisted days ago that I should stop worrying about everyone's love life and instead concentrate on what actually happened on the nights of the murders?

I decided it was worth a try and appealed to the group. "Maybe if we all—you all—think about what exactly happened in here last week we can get somewhere. Did anything unusual happen around the time of the murders?"

"Two people got killed," someone called out and got a few chuckles.

I ignored the sarcasm and ran some balls.

Avis Sage spoke up. "The Fox was real drunk the night he died, Tessie. That was unusual." He frowned. "But we already talked about that."

"Everyone knew Angela had been killed by then, correct?"

"That's right," Henry agreed. "The cops had just been in here, questioning us all."

He held up his Bible, but somehow the gesture seemed a lot less threatening than on previous occasions. "Those who love their life lose it," he told me.

The quote was probably a bit out of context, but I was pretty sure it was accurate, especially when Avis mentioned that the Gospel of St. John was one of his dear mother's favorites.

"Fritz played real well that last night." Doreen tried to get us back on track. "I remember because I was betting on him."

"Nothing unusual there," Kevin mumbled.

"I lost a ton of money to him." Spencer had finally stopped studying the bar.

"Nothing unusual there," Kevin repeated.

I turned to Mr. Sage. "I am surprised Fritz was playing so well if he was drunk. I can't sink anything if I've had too much."

"Me neither, Tessie. The old man hadn't seen the Fox that drunk since way back."

"Not since he got Lester Quinn killed," Henry added. He again held up his Bible, and said something about a two-edged sword.

"It was a gun," someone mumbled.

I shook my head and returned to topic. "Why was Fritz drinking like that?" I asked no one in particular.

"Silly." That was Ethel. "He was upset about Angela. He kept muttering her name every time he made a good shot."

"Everyone was upset that night," Kevin added. He took off his glasses, but forgot all about cleaning them.

Doreen patted his knee. "Must be Fritz was drowning his sorrows. Angela was a real loss, wasn't she?"

"He got so wasted he ended up under the pool table." Henry was much less sympathetic. "He rolled around like an idiot until Melissa finally dragged him out."

"No one else was helping him," Melissa said. She had finally rejoined us.

"And he kept on playing?" I was incredulous. "Even after he almost passed out?"

"No," Avis corrected me. "He took a break then, and gave the old man the table."

"What did Fritz do?"

Spencer pointed to the huge window overlooking the waterfalls. "He propped himself over there and let Avis play."

"But he wasn't paying any attention." Doreen elbowed her friend. "Remember, Ethel? He wasn't even betting anymore. He just stood there like a zombie once Melissa got him back on his feet."

"No one else would help him," Melissa repeated.

Since I had wisely spotted her the six, my opponent won the game, and I finally got a break from playing. Mr. Sage started a match with her, and I stepped back to the window. Perhaps if I stood in the exact spot Fritz had the night he died, the identity of the killer would come to me in a fit of inspiration.

Speak to me, Fritz.

***

But the ghost of Fritz Lupo failed me. Unless Karen and Candy were having a lot more luck than I, we would be forced to admit defeat to Wilson. The prospect was altogether disheartening and worthy of some serious pouting.

I lost track of time, and my mind actually wandered to the pressing issues facing Trey Barineau, Sarina Blyss, and even Winnie Dickerson. Was everyone really going to converge at the Blyss household? I smiled at the thought of the altogether evil Agnes finally getting her just due.

"Play one last game with me before you go, Miss Tessie?" The voice of Avis Sage harkened me back to reality. He winked at me. "For old times' sake."

Excuse me?

I studied the Wiseman, but Avis offered his usual benevolent smile. Clearly, he was only referring to the past week. I yawned and stretched, and revived myself for my final game at the Wade On Inn.

Sometime during Avis's first turn it occurred to me to ask what Fritz had been drinking the night he was killed, since almost everyone at the Wade On Inn drank beer only.

"It would take a lot of beer to get that drunk," I observed.

"Well then," Melissa deduced, "he must have had a lot of beer."

"Nothing harder?" I persisted and waited for Avis to shoot.

But Mr. Sage had frozen in position aiming for the three. I waited patiently and let him take his sweet time. Lord knows the old man must have been as tired as I.

Eventually he called me over. "Look at this odd angle, Tessie," he said and actually yanked me down to where he was bent over the table. "Fritz didn't drink anything," he whispered in my ear. "It's tricky, isn't it?" he spoke up for the rest of the crowd to hear.

We exchanged a meaningful look and bent our heads over the table again. "But, Avis," I, too, spoke softly. "Everyone's been insisting he was drunk as a skunk. Even you."

Avis stared at me. "He wasn't drinking anything that night." He was still whispering, but I heard him loud and clear.

I leaned closer. "Then he wasn't drunk?"

"No, Jessie. I don't think he was." The poor guy looked like he might start crying, but instead he stalwartly made an effort at the three ball.

Jessie?

I closed my eyes and prayed for strength. But the stupid railbirds were demanding a faster game. I opened my eyes, bent over, and made a haphazard shot at the stupid three. I missed magnificently, and Mr. Sage took over the table and ever so slowly started pocketing the balls. Slowly. Very, very slowly.

I decided to worry about the Jessie comment some other time, and concentrated on the more pressing issue. Fritz Lupo had been sober the night he was killed. He was only pretending to be drunk. But why?

So he would have an excuse to crawl around under the table in search of his gun, of course. And, of course, he didn't find it.

I blinked at the six ball Avis was aiming for. By the time Melissa had dragged him to his feet, Fritz Lupo knew it was his gun that had killed Angela.

When Avis pocketed the six, the crowd got excited, and the railbirds insisted on a short break to up the various antes. While the spectators were speculating, I placed another fifty on top of the light.

"For old times' sake, Mr. Sage?"

He winked and put his own bill up there. "For Leon," he said, and I let out a sob before I could stop myself.

Chapter 30

Avis missed the seven, and with his blatant mention of my father, I am sure I missed a few heartbeats. But I stepped up to the table and pushed my intuition into high gear. That's what the Wiseman was trying to jolt me into doing.

That night, when Fritz Lupo was acting the fool and rolling around on the floor, he had figured out who murdered Angela. Avis had faith that I could figure it out, too.

Speak to me, Fritz, I again pleaded to his ghost.

What a shocker, I missed the seven. While Avis tried again, I searched the crowd. Who, Fritz? Who hated Angela enough to kill her?

I sighed out loud. We had already established that lots of people had some sort of motive. When Avis missed the eight ball, I sighed even more and went back to the game.

But then something else occurred to me. Fritz must have trusted this person enough to confront him, or her, with the truth. I know pool hustlers, and they have a healthy sense of self-preservation. Fritz did not expect whoever he accused of murder to kill him also. He judged that wrong.

The railbirds were their usual impatient selves, but I ignored them and considered each of the regulars. Certainly he had not suspected Avis. And certainly not Doreen or Ethel. I focused on the bar. Neither of the Quinns made sense either. Elsa or her daughter may have held some sort of vague grudge against Fritz about Lester's death, but neither had any reason to kill Angela. And as I had been insisting for days, this was all about Angela.

The music changed, and some shifts on the dance floor captured my attention. Henry wished Avis luck in beating me and stepped out to dance with Karen as Bobby returned to the table.

Bobby Decker. In his warped mind Angela's bookkeeping was thwarting his dude ranch dreams. Bobby had found the bodies, and he knew about the gun. But would Fritz feel safe accusing Bobby of murder? Bobby was a big guy. When he grinned at me for no good reason, I saw that chipped tooth.

"The game, Tessie!" That was Ethel.

I bent over and sunk the eight ball, took cursory aim at the nine and missed. Avis stepped forward amid much commotion as even more last minute bets were negotiated.

I held up a hand when a few people asked me to up my own wagers, and paid attention elsewhere. Out on the dance floor Henry Jack was helping the Drunken Dancer to her feet.

I considered Henry for a split second before dismissing him. He might have disapproved of Angela, but he loved Elsa Quinn far more than he admired Pastor Muckenfuss, or his warped prejudices. Angela was helping Elsa get out of a financial hole. Henry would not have killed her.

"It's Isabelle Eakes." I jumped ten feet in the air and turned to see Spencer Erring and his dimples. "If you ask me, the Cornhuskers are even worse than the Pink Flamingos."

"Eakes?" I squeaked.

"Yeah, you know, Tessie? And the Cornhuskers?"

"Oh. Oh yeah." I shared a chuckle with Spencer and pondered him as a possibility.

Maybe he had worried that Angela would tell his wife about their affair. Or maybe he was angry she had dumped him and moved on with her life.

Doreen poked him with her cane and he good-naturedly agreed to up their wager by a hundred dollars. I relaxed my shoulders and dismissed Spencer. Whatever Kevin Cooper had been implying, Spencer was too careless to be the killer. And murder must take at least a little bit of planning, no?

The crowd gasped, and I looked over to see that Avis had missed the nine. I whimpered slightly, stepped around Spencer, and assessed my chances for the nine ball.

I bent down and made a serious attempt at aiming. But let's face it—I was a bit preoccupied. I took my time to chalk up again. And what about Kevin Cooper? I turned and blew on my stick and studied the would-be librarian, who was busy making another five dollar bet on me. This time with Bobby.

Why had I chosen to confide in Kevin all week long? Because I trusted him, one writer to another. Angela had trusted him, too, even if my mother found him fishy.

I glanced down at the sandals and stifled a groan. Clearly, wimpy Kevin would not have seemed threatening to Fritz, a shark who knew his way around the roughest pool halls in the country. Fritz would have confronted Kevin without a second thought.

Lord help me, was it Kevin Cooper?

But why would Kevin kill Angela?

I had stalled so long even Avis got wary. "You should play," he told me, and Doreen helped me along by prodding me with her cane.

I bent down and banked the nine ball off the bottom rail and into the side pocket. And the crowd went wild.

Amid the ensuing chaos, Spencer picked me up and twirled me around and around. "I needed that win, Tessie," he kept shouting in my ear. My eyes landed on Melissa Purcell with each passing spin. She must have hated the attention he was giving me, but to her credit, she kept smiling.

Spencer finally put me down, and scads of other people swarmed around to shake my right hand or put money in my left. Doreen poked me with her cane yet again. I twirled around and she slapped several fifties into my palm. Out of the corner of my eye I noticed Kevin gleefully collecting a tidy sum of five-dollar bills.

With apologies to my mother and her stellar intuition, and to Candy with her own impressive insight into human nature, I simply could not picture Kevin Cooper, smiling down at his twenty-dollar take, as a deranged homicidal maniac.

So who else or what else was I missing? A couple of the more boisterous spectators were jostling me about and asking how I had managed that last bank shot when it occurred to me. Avis had thought only three people knew about the gun—himself, Fritz, and Melissa.

Oh, my Lord. What if Fritz had been under the same impression?

I elbowed my way out of the throng and desperately tried to locate teeny-tiny Avis Sage. There he was, standing across the pool table from me, paying close attention.

"Melissa," I mouthed at him and his face dropped.

***

I spun around in search of Melissa. She was close by also, but luckily she was too busy admiring Spencer to notice me, or the horror-stricken look on my face.

Did Melissa Purcell have cause to kill Angela? Jealousy popped into my head. Wilson considered it too trite a motive, but whether my beau approved or not, Melissa was jealous of Angela. Of her job with Elsa, of her love life, of her pool playing.

Fritz was even about to take Angela out on the road with him—a fact which Melissa had adamantly denied, since she hated the idea so very much.

My mother's voice came back to me. "Melissa likes her little fantasies," she had said.

Melissa likely had some visions of Fritz taking her out on the road. Not only had Angela gotten Spencer, she had gotten Fritz, too. Melissa Purcell was mad. Mad enough to murder.

I experienced a disconcerting sense of déjà vu. Just like the last time I had identified a killer, I was standing at a pool table, and the murderer was within a few feet of me. Like last time, I really, really wished Wilson were there to take charge of the situation. And like last time, he wasn't.

But surely I had learned something since last time, when I had almost gotten myself and my poor cat killed by running away? This time I would stand my ground. And more importantly, stay with the crowd.

The crowd had calmed down, by the way. I took a deep breath and forced myself to do the same. Okay, so I wasn't exactly the epitome of Zen, but at least I managed to unscrew my cue stick and put it back in its case while I thought about my options.

I needed some help, but my cell phone was locked in Wilson's truck. I looked down at Kevin and willed him to read my mind. But he was still admiring that twenty dollars he had won and paid no attention to me. And Avis Sage, all hundred and ten pounds of him, wasn't exactly built to manhandle Melissa into submission.

I turned toward the bar. Of course Candy and Karen would help me. But even better would be those undercover cops Wilson had promised me.

Thank God for Goldilocks! Goldilocks, or Kim, or whatever the heck her name was, would help me.

That was the ticket. I would nonchalantly mosey over to Goldilocks, identify the killer, and let her take it from there. Very handy.

But just as I was about to begin my journey, Melissa popped up at my side. This time I really did jump ten feet in the air.

"Thanks, Tessie," she said.

"Excuse me?" I squeaked.

"I just won ninety dollars on you." She offered a friendly nudge and pointed to the pool game that was about to begin. "Who you betting on this time?" she asked.

I hoped she couldn't see my heart beating, but with my push-up bra in place, I imagine my bosom was trembling almost as much as Sarina Blyss's did whenever she thought of Trey Barineau.

"Umm," I managed.

"Bobby or Ross?" she persisted, and again pointed to the table where Ross, a semi-regular, was racking.

I took a step backward and landed on Kevin's toe. He yelped loudly and I jumped again. Smooth, let me tell you. I mumbled an apology and forced myself to speak to Melissa.

"I think I'm done for the night," I said. "I, umm, have that early flight tomorrow. You know, back to Hawaii?"

I turned and walked away, and hoped those weren't Melissa's eyes I felt on my back as I wended my way across the dance floor. My own eyes were firmly planted on Goldilocks, which is probably why I bumped into the Drunken Dancer. We both went down.

Karen must have noticed. She hopped over and grabbed me before I stumbled again.

"You know, Jess?" she asked as we locked eyes.

I blinked, and Karen nodded. "Yep, you know," she said. She picked up my cue case, got a firm grip on my arm and practically carried me off the dance floor.

"Who?" she asked as I regained my footing.

"Goldilocks," I whispered.

"Huh?"

"She's a cop." I jerked my head toward the blond at the bar. "We need Goldilocks."

Karen still looked confused, but she helped me along anyway, and we finally reached our destination.

"It's Melissa," I whispered.

Goldilocks looked up from her beer. "Huh?"

I whispered a bit louder. "It's Melissa Purcell. You know, the tall woman with frizzy hair at the pool table? What do we do now?"

"Do about what? Who's Melissa?"

I closed my eyes and prayed for strength.

Even if Wilson hadn't instructed me on how to confront a killer, surely this cop had gotten some training? I opened my eyes and silently appealed to Karen.

She patted my shoulder and repeated my claim. "It's Melissa," she told Goldilocks. "Trust me, girlfriend. Jess is never wrong about these things."

"What things?" Goldilocks the Einstein asked.

At least Candy had caught on. She spotted us from across the bar and came over to add her support.

"Who is it?" she whispered.

"Melissa," Karen whispered back and tilted her head toward Goldilocks. "And she's a cop."

Candy looked at me for verification. When I nodded, she put her hands on her hips and whispered orders to Goldilocks. "Well then, go arrest Melissa," she demanded. "What are you waiting for?"

"Huh?"

"It's Melissa, you idiot!" I was about to pounce and start shaking some brains into her extremely thick skull, but Candy distracted me.

"Umm, Jessie?" she said.

I twirled around. "What?"

She and Karen slowly rolled their heads toward the other end of the bar, and I froze in stunned horror as Melissa took the barstool Candy had just vacated.

The one next to Mackenzie.

Melissa whispered something in her ear, and Mackenzie jumped. A couple of seconds passed, and then the girl slowly and methodically closed her books. She stood up at the same time as Melissa, and the two of them started backing up together.

What the hell was going on?

Elsa noticed, too. "What is this?" she asked. "Where do you two think you're going?"

"She's got a gun, Mama."

Chapter 31

Elsa let out a scream that drowned out Isabelle Eakes.

That got everyone's attention. Someone had the decency to stop the music, and all eyes watched as Melissa and Mackenzie took two more steps backward into the corner. Then Melissa revealed the gun she was hiding behind Mackenzie's back by pointing it at her beautiful young head.

The Drunken Dancer fainted. As did Goldilocks. She toppled off her barstool and landed at my feet.

Other people sprang into action, however. The Redheaded Ogler knocked over the two empty barstools next to him and pulled out a gun of his own. Bless his heart, the Ogler was a cop! And Mr. Leather and Chains hopped up on one of the tables at the edge of the dance floor. He, too, had a gun pointed at Melissa.

"Don't shoot!" Elsa shrieked.

She flapped her arms, and her head darted back and forth between the three guns. "Oh, please God! Don't anyone shoot."

She dropped her arms and started sobbing, and Henry startled us all when he literally leaped over the bar from halfway across the room to stand with her.

Melissa was shrieking by then also. She shouted for everyone to shut up. "Let me think," she screamed. "Everyone just back off!"

Everyone backed up a step except for Mr. Leather up on the table. Mackenzie was starting to unravel, as was her mother. Henry held Elsa up. And unfortunately, Melissa held Mackenzie up. I believe it's called a human shield.

"Talk to her." Karen kept her eyes on Melissa, but nudged me.

"Good idea." Oh, good Lord, Candy had actually started walking toward the action-packed end of the bar. And she actually made it half way there before Melissa told her to stop.

"Shut up and stay away!" she warned.

Candy did stop. But she did not shut up. In fact, it appeared she wasn't paying any attention to Melissa at all.

She spoke to her friend. "It's gonna be okay, Mackenzie." Candy's voice was remarkably steady. "I know these people," she lied, and pointed to the cops who had their guns at the ready. "I know Captain Rye, too. You've talked to Captain Rye, right?"

Mackenzie let out a tiny squeak.

"They won't let anything bad happen to you," Candy promised, and I swear the girl did stand up a bit straighter, even as Melissa tapped her temple with the gun.

"Help her, Jess," Karen insisted, and I took a small step forward.

Melissa noticed. "Stay away from me, Tessie. You stay way back."

She aimed her gun at me, and all hell broke loose.

The Redheaded Ogler started shooting, as did Mr. Leather and Chains. As did Melissa.

Once the gunfire ceased everyone stood up on wobbly knees to assess the damage. Make that, almost everyone. Goldilocks was still huddled beneath her barstool and the Drunken Dancer was still passed out on the dance floor.

Mr. Leather and Chains had joined her. He hadn't passed out, but was instead writhing around. He was holding onto his leg, which if you haven't guessed, was bleeding. The Redheaded Ogler was also bleeding. But he held onto his arm.

So much for the cops.

***

At least Mackenzie wasn't bleeding. But then again, neither was Melissa.

"They must have worried about hitting the wrong person," Karen whispered.

Meanwhile Melissa was issuing orders about how she and Mackenzie were going to leave the bar together.

"Y'all back up and give us some room to get up those stairs." She jerked her head towards the entrance. "And no one else gets shot. Get it?"

I guess we didn't, since no one made a move to back up.

"Now!" she barked, and everyone jumped.

I bumped into Karen as we all took one baby step backwards. "Talk to her, Jess," she hissed at me.

Why me?

I didn't know, but clearly someone had to do something.

"Where did that gun come from, Melissa?" I spoke as if I were enquiring as to where she had bought that lovely green blouse she was wearing. "It's not from Fritz?"

"Stuart Hastie keeps a gun hidden. I stole it." Melissa snickered. "He hasn't even noticed it's missing."

What was it with these damn hidden guns?

"Oh?" I continued. "So, it's from Hastie's Diner, then?"

"I'm a good shot," Melissa mentioned in case anyone hadn't noticed. "I might suck at pool, but I took Angela out from across the parking lot," she bragged.

"And Fritz?" I'm sure I sounded even stupider than Goldilocks, but Melissa and Mackenzie had yet to start moving. "Did you shoot Fritz, too?" I asked.

"You're just like him."

"Oh?"

"Nosy as hell and play pool like a fiend."

That reminded me. I glanced over at my pool table buddies.

Even from across the room, they weren't missing a thing. Poor Avis Sage looked like he might collapse, but Bobby was standing with him, as was Spencer. Thank God, Ethel and Doreen were already sitting down. I caught Kevin's eye, and he sent some positive vibes in my direction.

I turned back to Melissa. "Fritz figured out you killed Angela, and so you killed him, too? Is that right?"

"He was nosy." She shoved Mackenzie forward and they started moving.

"How could you do it, Mel?" Avis broke free from Bobby and Spencer, and stumbled out to the dance floor. "How could you kill the Fox? He was your friend."

Melissa stopped. "Yeah, right," she snapped. "If Fritz was such a good friend why'd he decide to teach Angela to play instead of me? I've been begging him for years.

Years!" she screamed, and Mackenzie flinched. "And he was about to take her away!" She appealed to the rest of us. "It should have been me!" she shrieked, and we all nodded in agreement.

She jerked herself and Mackenzie around to face the bar again. "Fritz was supposed to die all those years ago, anyway. Right, Henry?"

"No one was supposed to die all those years ago," Elsa whined. "Please, let's stop this."

"Screw you, Elsa." Melissa's contempt was palpable. "Why'd you have to give her a job? I've been here, like, forever. But noooo. It's Aaangela you hire."

Karen nudged me again, and I remembered to keep talking. "Umm." I spoke up. "Spencer was at fault, too. Wasn't he, Melissa?"

"Oh great!" That was Spencer. He threw up his hands and shook his head at me. "Thanks so much for reminding her, Tessie! Next thing you know, she'll be shooting at me."

"No, Spencer," Melissa assured him. "I'd never hurt you." She turned to me. "But you?" She shoved Mackenzie out of the way and took aim.

I ducked. Karen must have joined me. And we both landed on top of Goldilocks. I heard a bullet or two ricochet off the stone wall behind us while Goldilocks screamed at me to get off of her.

I rolled sideways in time to see the Drunken Dancer rise up from the dance floor. She had a gun.

And she shot Melissa Purcell between the eyes.

Chapter 32

By the time I remembered to breathe again, the Drunken Dancer was kicking Mr. Leather and Chains in his good leg. "Call Rye, you stupid idiot," she demanded. "Call 911!"

He rolled back and forth to avoid her foot. "Hold your horses, Kim. I'm on it."

Kim?

"It's already done, Kim." Still sitting on our duffs, Karen and I twirled around to watch Tiffany Sass leap over the stairway railing and nail a perfect landing on the stiletto points of her silver high heels.

"Impressive," Karen mumbled.

"Darned impressive," I agreed.

"Thanks." Tiffany offered a brief curtsey before stepping over us and making her way to Melissa's gun. The woman was indeed steady on her stilettos. She kicked that gun, and it skidded clear across the dance floor and landed underneath the pool table.

I let out a loud groan, but no one was paying the slightest attention to me. How could they, when Tiffany Sass, resplendent in her hot pink mini-skirt, was bending over to help Mackenzie to her feet? After making sure the girl was all right, she knelt over Melissa and announced the perp dead.

Russell Densmore had also arrived somewhere in there. He checked that Karen and I weren't hurt, waited until our eyes adjusted to his hot pink suit, and went to help Tiffany.

Amidst commotion that was rowdy even by Wade On Inn standards, Goldilocks, Karen, and I pulled each other to our feet. By the time we were standing, Elsa, Mackenzie, Henry, and Candy had one heck of a group hug going. Karen went to join them, as did Bobby Decker.

I watched the Drunken Dancer, a.k.a. Kim, put away her gun and kneel down to help her wounded partner. Surrealistically weird.

Speaking of weird, Goldilocks had a compact out and was reapplying her lipstick.

"You're not a cop?" I asked her.

She torn herself away from her task. "Do I look like a cop?"

I shrugged and explained why I had been so sure of it. I told her who I was, and what I was doing at the Wade On Inn.

"But if you aren't a cop, then who are you?" I asked. "I recognize you from somewhere."

"Charlotte's Webb," she said and closed her compact.

Oh, for Lord's sake. Of course! Goldilocks was the woman getting blond highlights the day Sally Caperton had made me a brunette. Goldilocks was the woman in foils.

She dropped her lipstick into her purse. "I figured out who you reminded me of after I got home that day."

"Eddie Munster," we said in unison.

I took my leave and approached Kim.

She and the Redheaded Ogler were sitting cross-legged in the middle of the dance floor with the Leather and Chains cop. He was still lying down.

I joined the group on the floor. "Is everyone okay?" I asked stupidly and cringed at Mr. Leather.

"Just a flesh wound," the Ogler assured me with a brave smile. "Jeff Fogle," he said and reached his out right hand.

I shook it while he mumbled something about how lucky it was that his left arm took the bullet, and not his right.

I cringed again, and Kim pointed to Leather and Chains. "Simmons is a little more serious," she said. "But he'll be up and around and annoying me in no time."

Poor Mr. Leather and Chains managed to chuckle. "Gabe Simmons," he informed me. "You should have danced with me when you had the chance, Jessie." He tried to sit up, but Kim made him lay back down.

She invited me to stand up, but kept a firm foot on Mr. Simmons' chest so he couldn't move. She also told Jeff Fogle she'd shoot his other arm if he tried to get up before the ambulance arrived.

I caught Kim's eye. "Thank you for saving the day." I held out my hand and introduced myself unnecessarily.

"Wilson's been telling me how great you are. Now I see why."

She shrugged and shook my hand. "Kim Leary," she said. "You really didn't know who I was?"

"Heck no. You could have knocked me over with a feather when you stood up and started shooting."

"You were already knocked over," she reminded me.

Tiffany joined us. I turned and gave her a hug, but she brushed off my thank you also. "You and your friends have been heroic all week," she insisted. "That's why Captain Rye added these two to the watch." She pointed a hot pink fingernail at her colleagues on the floor, and I shook my head as it finally dawned on me.

The Ogler and Mr. Leather had not even been at the Wade On Inn our first night out. Wilson must have added them to the mix once he understood Karen and Candy would be joining me each night.

"We should be thanking you, Jessie," Tiffany was saying. But when we heard sirens out in the parking lot, she and Kim quickly excused themselves to start getting statements from the crowd.

"The Captain will kill us if he comes in and sees us dilly-dallying with you." Tiffany winked, and the hot pink Sass ass skedaddled away.

Karen and Candy were still surrounded by the Quinns and company, so I walked over to the pool table to see how everyone was holding up.

Ethel and Doreen looked a bit shell-shocked, but the old ladies insisted that all they needed was a good night's rest, and they'd be raring to go once again.

"Kevin's been telling us all about you, Jessie." Doreen emphasized the J. "Are you really Adelé Nightingale? I love her stuff!"

I thanked her for her enthusiasm, and Ethel asked if I'd be willing to do a book signing at The Cotswald Estates. Of course, I said I would be delighted.

I told Kevin he hadn't gotten rid of me either. "I'll be seeing you at the library." I whispered that I planned on offering him my editorial and proofreading services when he was further along with *Social Interactivity and Gambling*

Protocol Among Early Twenty-First Century Billiard Players.

"*An Urban Study,*" he added. He tilted his head toward the other end of the pool table, where Spencer Erring was trying to get Avis Sage to sit down. "I think someone over there wants to say goodbye to you."

***

I stepped away and approached Spencer. "Sorry if I put you in danger back there." I waved to where Melissa had been brandishing her gun.

"It wasn't your fault, Tes—I mean, Jessie." Spencer looked up from Avis. "The Wiseman's been talking about you. And he's convinced me the pool table isn't where I'm meant to be. So I think I'll go home and try flirting with my wife for a change." He shrugged. "Who knows?" he said. "Maybe Dixie will take me back."

I hugged him and wished him luck.

"Bring some of those hugs over this way, Spencer honey," Doreen called out. Spencer flashed me one last dimple and walked off.

Ever the gentleman, Avis Sage stood up when I turned to him. He was looking very, very sad. I imagine I was, too.

"Are you okay, Mr. Sage?"

He reached for my hand and kissed it. Then he looked up and smiled. "I'd bet my Balabushka cue stick you're Leon Hewitt's daughter. Is the old man right?"

I gave him a hug. "How've you been all these years, sir?"

"I can't complain, Miss Jessie."

"But how did you figure it out?"

"The old man had his suspicions the first night you came in here." He pointed to the pool table. "You remember that triple bank shot for the seven you made in our second game?"

"Kind of brilliant?" I asked.

"Oooo-eeee, little girl. That shot had Cue-It Hewitt written all over it."

He stopped smiling. "I was real sorry to hear about your Daddy, by the way. He was one of the greats."

I nodded and the tears started flowing.

There was a whole lot of commotion behind us, as the paramedics arrived. I heard Wilson and Russell calling out orders behind me. But I figured they knew what they were doing, and indulged in a good cry with the Wiseman.

Eventually we got a grip, and I explained what I had been doing with myself the past few decades, how I ended up playing pool at the Wade On Inn, and what the heck I was doing with masquerading as a brunette.

"And your Mama?" Mr. Sage asked. "You be sure to apologize for my rude behavior the other night. I didn't suppose she wanted me to recognize her, either."

"But you did?"

"Oh, little girl, I'm not likely to forget Tessie Hewitt. You know about your Mama?"

"What about her?"

"She invited me into her home and to her supper table, didn't she? A white woman in South Carolina? This was back in the early seventies, remember."

I stared at Mr. Sage as it dawned on me what he was saying.

"Not only was Tessie Hewitt beautiful, she was gracious beyond all get out. Inviting a black hustler like me to Easter dinner with her family?" Mr. Sage was shaking his head. "Old man will never forget that."

"Mother was sorry she couldn't acknowledge you the other night," I said and explained why I had gotten her involved in things.

Avis asked after her health, but it was him I was concerned about. "No offense, sir, but you're getting too old for this." I waved at the pool table.

He disagreed and insisted he was even planning to go back on the road. "In honor of the Fox." He chuckled and assured me he'd probably be dead within a month. "I'm ready, though. When it happens I'll join your Daddy and Fritz at that big pool table in the sky."

I was threatening to cry again when Wilson tapped me on the shoulder. I turned around to accept a huge hug and an even bigger scolding. He didn't let go of me, but he did offer a significant lecture about putting myself in danger. Yadda, yadda, yadda.

Eventually we remembered Mr. Sage, and Wilson freed one arm to shake his hand.

"This is Captain Rye." I turned around to Avis. "I believe you've already met?"

"He your beau, Miss Jessie?"

I nodded. "Yes, Mr. Sage. I suppose he is."

Avis looked up at Wilson, who was at least twice his size. "Me and your lady friend are thinking of taking us a road trip." He winked at me. "The two of us could hustle the pants off every shark from here to San Francisco. What do you say, Miss Jessie?"

I raised an eyebrow at Wilson. "That does sound tempting."

"Take some advice from the old man." Avis spoke to Wilson. "Hold on tight to this lady friend of yours, before someone younger than me comes along and steals her away."

"Don't worry about that, sir." Wilson pulled me back against him and spoke into my left ear. "I love this lady friend of mine way too much to let anyone steal her away."

I blinked at Mr. Sage.

Wilson Rye loves me? Way too much?

And here I thought I had just escaped grave danger.

Epilogue

"Today we'll work on the happy ending," I told Snowflake.

The confrontation between Trey Barineau, Sarina Blyss, and Winnie Dickerson versus the altogether evil Agnes promised to be a doozey indeed. But Adelé Nightingale was far too exhausted to think about it that morning.

Especially since I had not yet decided how Norwood would react during the showdown at the Blyss family home. Like his wife, was he evil also? Or would he take the side against Agnes, and in support of his lovely sister Sarina?

"We'll worry about poor Norwood's dilemma tomorrow," I said, and instead concentrated on Father Conforti and Barnaby. I worked on moving them along to St. Celeste at a nice, slow, steady pace befitting of Adelé Nightingale's mood.

As promised, Father Conforti finally did meet with Constable Klodfelder, and he formally identified Sarina Blyss. All charges against her were officially dropped. And as soon as the Constable made known her innocence, all of St. Celeste was atwitter in eager anticipation of the Duke of Luxley's impending nuptials.

Thus, on the day before Trey Barineau's twenty-eighth birthday, Father Conforti united him and his lady love in holy matrimony. The bride looked more radiant than ever in her golden necklace and the glorious wedding gown Mrs. Dickerson had created for the occasion.

Trey's white carriage awaited the newlyweds as they emerged from the church. As the Duke lifted the new Duchess into the passenger seat he mentioned how anxious he was to show her Luxley Manor.

Sarina blushed and said her new home would have to wait. "I would much rather visit the lavender field right now, dearest," she said.

Happy to oblige his bride's every desire, Trey drove them away.

***

I was still writing the climactic—and I do mean climactic—love scene in the lavender field when Wilson arrived. He let himself in and read over my shoulder as my fingers flew across the keyboard. Adelé Nightingale was in a groove.

Wilson waited.

Finally, I had the lovers resting in a bed of lavender, panting gently in each other's arms.

I sat back. "What do you think?" I asked, my eyes still on the computer screen.

He reached over and pointed to the passage that had left even Trey Barineau sapped of energy.

"Let's give that a try," he suggested.

I twirled around and reminded him of his age. And mine. "I'm not nearly as lithe and limber as Sarina Blyss-Barineau," I warned.

He grinned. "Well," he sang, "let's give it a try anyway. What do you say?"

I said I admired his optimism.

We were recovering a while later when Wilson broached the all-important subject. "So, Jessie?" He put his arms behind his head and stared at my ceiling. "How much money did you end up winning this week?"

"Enough."

"Enough to take an overworked and underpaid civil servant out for a few fancy dinners?" he asked hopefully.

I reached over and pulled a seriously impressive stack of fifties and hundreds from my nightstand.

"In Hawaii," I said and dropped the cash onto his chest.

The End

If you enjoyed Jessie's adventures in *Double Shot* and want to read more, check out the other books in Cindy Blackburn's Cue Ball Mysteries series:

Book One: Playing With Poison

Pool shark Jessie Hewitt usually knows where the balls will fall and how the game will end. But when a body lands on her couch, and the cute cop in her kitchen accuses her of murder, even Jessie isn't sure what will happen next. *Playing With Poison* is a cozy mystery with a lot of humor, a little romance, and far too much champagne.

Three Odd Balls

Did you miss seeing Jessie's rabidly hyperactive agent Geez Louise in *Double Shot*? Are you hankerin' to see more of Jessie's delightfully spry mother Tessie? Do you lay awake at night wondering when Jessie will ever get a chance to meet Wilson's surfer-dude son Christopher? Fear no more! Jessie and Wilson's plans for a romantic vacation sink into the farthest pocket when these three oddest of odd balls decide to tag along. A vacation for five wasn't exactly wasn't what Jessie and Wilson had in mind when they planned their trip to the tropics. They didn't plan on solving a murder either. But guess what?

Three Odd Balls

Chapter 1

"I'm loving it, Babe!" Louise shouted into the phone. "Love, love, loving it!!"

I held the receiver a foot away from my ear and wondered why my literary agent even bothered using a telephone. Geez Louise Urko speaks so loudly, and with so many exclamation points, I would have heard her if she had simply opened her office window and bellowed out. Never mind that she works in Manhattan. And I live in North Carolina.

The reason for her excitement? *My South Pacific Paramour*, my alter ego Adelé Nightingale's next novel. Adelé was venturing into new and untried territory with this one. Instead of placing her energetic and altogether over-sexed lovers somewhere in Europe, sometime in the sixteenth century, Adelé had Delta Touchette and Skylar Staggs seeking adventure and discovering romance in a tropical paradise.

"In the nineteenth century no less!" Louise was shouting. "It's, like, practically a contemporary, Jessica!"

I shook my head at Louise's math. "Maybe by Adelé Nightingale standards," I said. "But the sixteenth century was starting to bore me."

"Oh, absolutely! All those lords and dukes and earls, with their castles and turrets and dungeons? They were getting downright dreary."

"And this new setting makes sense." I winked at my cat Snowflake. "What with Wilson and I heading to Hawaii tomorrow for seven days of sun and fun."

"You'll be inspired, Jessica! A vacation is just the ticket!"

Speaking of which, I remembered the task at hand and returned to packing. "Heck," I said as I dropped a tube of sunscreen into the suitcase on my bed. "I may even be able to write off part of this vacation as a research expense. The IRS doesn't need to know I never bother with anything so tedious as actual research, do they?" I rummaged around in the closet for the ridiculous pair of daisy-adorned flip flops I had purchased for the trip. "But no." I stood up, flip flops in hand. "I'm far too law-abid—"

"Oh my God!" Louise interrupted. "I just had a fantastical idea, Jessica! I mean, beyond fantastical!"

"Oh?" I tossed the new shoes onto the bed, where Snowflake took immediate interest in the fake daisies.

"I'm coming!" she shouted.

My face dropped. "Excuse me?"

"To Hawaii! With you! And Wilson! What an utterly fantastical idea! I'll meet you there!"

My face dropped a little further with each new exclamation point, and I struggled to find my voice as Geez Louise continued on her merry and insane way.

"I need a vacation," she shouted. "And I've never been to Hawaii! And I've never met that hunky heartthrob of yours! The man who inspired Adelé Nightingale to new heights of sexual fantasy? I am dying, dying, dying to meet Wilson Rye the mystery man for myself. I must meet your paramour, Jessica! Must, must, must!"

"But now?" I squeaked. "During my vacation?"

"Yes, now! Of course, now! I can help you with him."

"Help?" I took the sandals away from Snowflake and hid them in the suitcase.

"Yes, help! I'll help you uncover the mystery man's deep dark secrets! You know how you've been wondering about his past, Jessica? Well, just leave it to Louise! By the end of this vacation, all will be revealed. Every single, scintillating detail. The man will be an open book, I tell you. Oh! And that gives me another idea, Jessica!"

"I think I need to sit down," I said.

"The plot for *My South Pacific Paramour*! I'll help you with that, too! No more plot plight for Adelé Nightingale. We'll lounge by the pool, sip silly drinks—you know, the kind with little umbrellas in them—and brainstorm together. I can't wait! Can't, can't, can't!"

I sat motionless and blinked at the cat.

Louise cleared her throat. "Now then," she said, all business-like. "Tell me your exact travel plans."

I was so stunned I actually did so.

Snowflake was still staring at me as I hung up the phone . "Wilson is going to kill me," I told her.

The cat did not argue.

***

"Oh now, Honeybunch, you and Wilson just go on and have a grand time," Mother said. "I don't want you to worry about me even for one minute, do you hear?"

My mother might not have the lungs of Louise Urko, and she definitely needed the aid of the telephone, but I heard her loud and clear. I again cringed at the cat and wondered why I had ever chosen to answer my phone that day.

"No, Mother," I argued as I arranged a stack of shorts into suitcase number two. "I cannot go off and have this grand time you're insisting on, knowing you'll be alone for Christmas. Why aren't you going to Danny's? Wasn't that the plan?"

The fact is, I had never, in all my fifty-two years, spent a Christmas away from my mother. So when Wilson and I planned our Hawaiian vacation, I took pains to be sure she could visit my brother Danny and his family for the holiday. But, as Mother was now informing me, Danny's wife Capers had decided otherwise.

"Capers says she needs a vacation, too," Mother explained. "They're taking the twins to Saint Martin for the holiday."

"And they just informed you of this today?" I gave up on packing and plopped down on the bed.

"Oh, Jessie, please don't be mad at me."

I hastened to tell my mother that I most certainly was not angry with her, but with my hapless brother and his inconsiderate wife, who lives to make my life difficult. Of course, Capers wouldn't tolerate me, Jessica Hewitt, enjoying a fun-filled tropical vacation if she couldn't do so herself. So of course, she made these last minute plans. And of course, she thought nothing of leaving my eighty-two-year-old mother in the lurch.

"The Live Oaks is planning a very nice Christmas party for us residents," Mother was saying. "I'm sure it will be lovely."

She was putting up a brave front, but I knew she wasn't looking forward to spending Christmas without any family, even if she did have lots of friends at The Live Oaks Center for Retirement Living.

I pursed my lips and made an executive decision. "You'll come with us," I said. I ignored Snowflake's shocked expression and headed toward my desk.

Mother started protesting, but I was already getting online to see about her plane tickets on such short notice. While she repeated over and over that she wouldn't dream of interfering in my vacation, I played with the internet and made her reservations. The Hawaiian gods were smiling on me—there was even space available at the resort where Wilson and I were staying.

Interrupting a rather involved description of the elaborate Christmas Eve dinner The Live Oaks was promising, I gave my mother her flight information. I had gotten her on the early morning flight from her home in Columbia, South Carolina to Atlanta.

"Wilson and I will meet you at the Atlanta airport," I said. "And from there, the three of us can fly together." I tapped on the keyboard some more. "Believe it or not, they even had a last minute cancellation at the place we're staying. Soooo," I hit the enter key, "I've just booked you a bungalow at The Wakilulani Garden Resort. Wilson keeps calling it the Wacky Gardens. Doesn't that sound fun?"

"Jessica Hewitt!" she scolded. "You are not listening to me. I will not be ruining your vacation with that darling beau of yours. I will not be a third wheel, so you just cancel those reservations this minute!"

"Non-refundable," I argued. "And besides, you won't be a third wheel, but a fourth. Louise Urko is meeting us there, too."

Mother skipped a beat. "Geez Louise is coming?" she asked, her tone considerably brighter. "Well then, I'd better start packing, hadn't I? What should I bring, Jessie?"

I told her to remember a bathing suit and hung up.

Snowflake was watching me. "Wilson is going to kill me," I said quietly.

Once again, the cat did not argue.

***

"You're gonna kill me," Wilson informed me the second he made it through the door of my condo. He's a big guy, but even he was struggling with everything he was lugging. He turned around and gestured to the bottle of champagne he had tucked under one elbow, and I grabbed it before it fell.

"Hopefully that will keep you in a good mood, despite my news," he said as he set down his luggage and the huge cat carrier he was holding. He bent over to open the door and glanced up. "Ready?"

"Of course we're ready." I offered an encouraging nod to my cat. "We're looking forward to seeing our new friends, aren't we, Snowflake?"

She yowled and jumped to the top of the refrigerator.

Okay, so maybe not. But Wally was banging his skinny black body into the door of the cage, and Wilson did the honors anyway. Out Wally popped, and right behind him came Wilson's other cat, an enormous calico named Bernice.

She took a moment to glower at Snowflake, yawned dramatically, and found a corner of my couch for her next nap. Meanwhile, Wally had located a jingle-bell ball under the coffee table and started flicking it across the floor and going for the chase.

Wilson sat down with Bernice. "You still think this will work, right?"

I sure did hope so. I poured the champagne and reviewed our cat-care plans. My downstairs neighbor and good friend Candy Poppe had volunteered to look after our pets while we were away. So far, so good. But her offer rested on all three cats staying at my place for the week. And what if Wally and Bernice didn't like my place? Or what if Snowflake wasn't the most gracious hostess?

With the what-ifs in mind, we'd been practicing for days, and Wilson had been bringing his cats over for play dates. Thus far, no one had actually played together. But then again, no one had started fighting either. I decided to take that as a positive sign.

"Our cats are not going to kill each other," I reassured everyone. I took a seat beside Wilson and handed him a glass. "But you may kill me."

"Why's that?"

"Well, umm, Louise called this afternoon," I began in the breeziest voice I could muster. "She's very excited about my new book."

"Isn't Geez Louise always excited?" He clicked my glass. "To Hawaii."

"In fact," I continued, undeterred, "she became so enthused with the tropical paradise theme Adele Nightingale is planning, that you'll never guess what she's decided to do." I tilted my head and waited for him to guess.

His face dropped. "You're kidding, right?"

I grimaced. "She's meeting us in Hawaii! Please don't kill me." I grimaced again and kept going. "Louise has no family at all, Wilson. She considers me her family. And it is Christmas. And she wants to help me with my book. And—" I stopped and tried to think of more excuses. "And, umm—" Nothing more was coming to me, but when I hazarded a glance sideways, Wilson was actually grinning. Indeed, he seemed altogether disinclined to kill me.

"Are you feeling well?" I asked and then repeated that Geez Louise Urko would be joining us on our vacation. "She pulled a few strings and booked herself a last minute bungalow at the Wakilulani Gardens and everything."

He kept grinning.

I eyed him suspiciously. "What exactly is the bad news you have for me?"

***

Whatever it was, Wilson's news would have to wait— Bernice was on the move. She hopped down from the couch, yawned expansively, and in typical Bernice-fashion, sauntered past several cat toys, ignored Wally's invitation to play, and found the food dish. Snowflake's food dish. Wilson and Snowflake were on it in a flash.

While Snowflake scolded her guest, Wilson spoke to me. "This will be the issue while we're gone." He pointed to Bernice, who was involved in an intense stare-down with my cat. "It's the reason she's so fat. She steals food. She eats Wally's all the time."

I shifted my gaze to Wally. But he had discovered one of Snowflake's catnip mice and was completely unconcerned about the food-dish showdown. I shrugged and reminded everyone Candy had been apprised of Bernice's dietary regimen. "She promises to make sure everyone eats only the food allotted to them."

"Good luck, Candy," Wilson mumbled. He picked up Bernice—no easy feat—and returned to the couch.

"Your bad news?" I asked.

He cleared his throat. "You know Chris?"

I blinked twice. "No," I said. "I do not know Chris. Your son refuses to meet me, remember?"

"Well, he's changed his mind. He's tagging along."

"With us!?" I jumped and would have spilled my champagne if Wilson hadn't caught the glass.

"The ski trip to Vermont with his buddies fell through," he explained and quickly put the glass back in my hand. "His roommate Larry broke his leg."

"Excuse me?" I shook my head in dismay. "That's what happens while one is skiing, not before."

"Maybe. But Larry was cramming on his way to his chemistry final and wasn't watching where he was going. Bumped into a brick wall and fell backwards down a flight of stairs."

I groaned and took a gulp of my beverage.

Perhaps I should mention that Christopher Rye is a junior at the University of North Carolina. And yes, I had never met the guy. This, despite the fact that I had been dating his father for months, and despite the fact that Chapel Hill is quite close to Clarence, where Wilson and I live. Apparently Chris chose to hate me, sight unseen.

"Larry will be fine," Wilson was saying. "But it ruins the ski trip. Chris sounded pretty disappointed."

"So you asked him to join us."

"He's meeting us at the Atlanta airport. I can't stand the idea of him being alone for the holidays, Jessie. The kid's pretty independent, but." He caught my eye. "You okay with this?"

I considered the news. "Maybe. But I thought he hated me?"

"Well," Wilson sang. "Maybe he's changed his mind."

"Maybe? Chris has never even given me a chance."

"So here's your chance. What do you say, Jessie?"

I had to say I was quite curious to meet the Rye offspring. "Who knows?" I said. "Maybe I'll win him over, and he'll tell me all your deep dark secrets." I raised an eyebrow. "Unless, of course, you'd like to do that yourself?"

Wilson kept his gaze steady and said nothing.

I sighed dramatically. "Okay, so Chris is unlikely to tell me anything of any use," I grumbled. "But will he at least be civil to me?"

"Absolutely. But I doubt we'll see much of him. I booked him his own bungalow at the Wacky Gardens. And if I know my son, he'll spend the week surfing and chasing bikinis."

Thinking the matter settled, he leaned back and relaxed. But that would just not do.

"Umm, Wilson?" I said soothingly. "Going back to the idea—your idea—that no one should be alone for the holidays? There's one more teensy reason you may want to kill me."

He blinked at the index finger I was holding up. "What's that?"

"My mother."

"Your mother, what?"

"She's coming with us!" I blurted out and quickly dived into the whole spiel about Danny, and Capers, and the twins, and Saint Martin.

But Wilson stopped me before I had gotten very far. "Tessie Hewitt goes Hawaiian." He offered one of his signature grins. "This, I have got to see."

I reached out and squeezed his hand. "Mother is right about you, you know?"

"She thinks I'm darling."

Testimony to our whimsical and flexible natures, we toasted our impending vacation and vowed to have a fantastic time, despite the three odd balls who were tagging along, and the three odd cats we were leaving behind.

It was only later that night, as I was tossing one last bathing suit into my suitcase, that a thought occurred to me.

I shooed Snowflake away as she tried to join the bathing suit and spoke to Wilson. "I wonder why the Wakilulani Gardens had so many last minute cancellations during the holiday week. I mean, isn't it interesting that everyone got their own private bungalow? On such short notice?"

Wilson looked up from pushing Bernice out of his suitcase. "Interesting," he agreed.

"Downright wacky," I said and closed my suitcase.

About the Author

Cindy Blackburn has a confession to make–she does not play pool. It's that whole eye-hand coordination thing. What Cindy does do well is school. So when she's not writing silly stories she's teaching serious history. European history is her favorite subject, and the ancient stuff is best of all. The deader the better! A native Vermonter who hates cold weather, Cindy divides her time between the south and the north. During the school year you'll find her in South Carolina, but come summer she'll be on the porch of her lakeside shack in Vermont. Cindy has a fat cat named Betty and a cute husband named John. Betty the muse meows constantly while Cindy tries to type. John provides the technical support. Both are extremely lovable.

When Cindy isn't writing, grading papers, or feeding the cat, she likes to take long walks or paddle her kayak around the lake. Her favorite travel destinations are all in Europe, her favorite TV show is NCIS, her favorite movie is Moonstruck, her favorite color is orange, and her favorite authors (if she must choose) are Joan Hess and Spencer Quinn. Cindy dislikes vacuuming, traffic, and lima beans.

www.cueballmysteries.com

www.cueballmysteries.com/blog

Made in the USA
Middletown, DE
01 May 2020